REIGN

A Henchmen MC Novel

--

Cover image credit:
Improvisor/shuttershock.com

Dedication:

To the bad boys- where would
romance novels be without them?

ONE

Summer

I shouldn't have been able to get away.

That was all I could think as I hauled ass through the underbrush inside the front gate. There was no good reason I was able to slip out unseen. I should have still been tied tightly to the bed. The door should have been locked. There should have been men everywhere: outside the door, on the roof, manning the gate. Even though there was a serious hurricane going on. V didn't give a fuck about his men. They could get tossed from the roof and become splattered, twisted versions of their former selves on the driveway and all he would say was he needed the mess cleaned up; human remains didn't exactly help the curb appeal.

I shouldn't have been able to get away.

I checked behind me, the wind too loud for me to hear anything, including men coming at me with guns to drag me back to hell. Then I rushed forward, hit the button, half hidden by a stupid ornamental bush, and watched as the gate slid open.

Open.

I was almost free.

I rushed to the car closest to the gate, my heart wedged so far up my throat I'd swear I was choking on it. I wrenched open the door, praying, not so silently praying that the keys were in it. The keys were always in the cars because no one would ever think of stealing from V. Not if they wanted to live through the night.

"Please God. Please God. Please God..."

Yes.

Keys.

I jumped in, slinging my soaked hair out of my face, turning the key, and flooring it.

I didn't look back.

I couldn't.

I should have taken some measure of pleasure from seeing the fortress that had been my torture camp, my prison for the past three months slipping away. But I couldn't look. If I looked, the fear would come back - terrifying, crippling. I wouldn't have been able to keep going.

So I kept my eyes forward. I focused on keeping the car on the road despite the wind thrashing into it, despite the rain pelting so hard on the windshield that the wipers couldn't even make visibility an option.

I just had to keep going.

I needed to get as far as I could.

Lose the car.

I had to lose the car.

But I had no money. I had no ID.

I couldn't call anyone. I couldn't rent a car. I couldn't even pay a cab.

But I would have to lose the car regardless.

If I stayed in it, I was a target.

Hell, knowing V's paranoia, the fucking car probably had a locater device thingy on it; so he could know where his men were at all times.

Shit.

I could have been tracked anywhere.

The car needed to go.

Soon.

I just had to get back to some sort of civilization. I needed to find some all night diner or store or something. I needed to ditch the car. Then I needed to find someone who would give me a ride or money for a pay phone. God, were there even pay phones anywhere anymore? I never knew what it was like to not have a cell phone so I had never even thought to look for such a thing. But my cell phone was back at V's, along with my dignity, and copious amounts of my blood.

"Think ahead," I murmured to myself, trying to shake the memories from my mind. They wouldn't do me any good. I lived through it, that was all that mattered. I lived through it and I got a chance to get away. And I had to get *away*. Because if they found me, if they dragged me back...

No.

I couldn't go there.

I needed to think ahead.

I could go to the police. I could do that. But what were the chances that they could help? What were the chances that they weren't in V's pockets? V's very deep pockets.

No police.

Where did that leave me?

I switched on the heat, the cold October rain was soaking through my thin white tank top and pink silk pajama shorts. It was the same outfit I had been wearing when V's men took me three months before. I was not given a change of clothes. I was only given the opportunity for a whore's bath in the sink when I was given five minutes to use the bathroom per day.

So while, yes, the rain was cold and I was shivering, it was the cleanest I had been in months. *Months*.

It was another little piece of freedom.

It was amazing how much I had once taken for granted: showers, soap, toothpaste, wrists that didn't constantly ache from being bound, a belly that didn't concave from starvation, a body without scars, a soul without them.

Never again.

Whatever happened to me, wherever I ended up, I would make sure I never took the little freedoms for granted again. I knew how hard it was without them.

I passed through a seedy- looking part of town. And when I say 'seedy,' I mean that if there wasn't a hurricane raging wild, I was pretty sure I would have been carjacked, raped, and buried in some dumpster somewhere.

I didn't stop. I probably should have stopped. I should have lost the car. I should have found somewhere to hide, or tried to make it on foot.

But I couldn't bring myself to pull over.

So I kept going. I turned off into an industrial part of town full of blue collar businesses, some apartment buildings. The lights were all off. Which could only mean a power outage. Great. That was just great. Nothing would be open.

I kept going. I drove past some building with high barbed wire fences and no windows. And then things got rural. Like... *rural* rural.

Shit.

Shit. Shit. Shit.

I should have stopped in that bad area.

"Think ahead," I reminded myself. What was done was done. I had to keep my eyes forward.

Then...

Oh my God.

Shit.

But it was too late.

It was too late to react on a slick road.

There was something in the street.

And I was going to hit it.

I slammed the brakes, trying to turn the wheel.

Then I hit.

It took less than one second for the airbags to deploy, slamming my wrists away from the wheel and burning across my cheek, the sound louder than I could have imagined, making my ears ring painfully. All I could feel was the impact, the jerking of the car backward as it hit. All I could hear were the sounds, sharp, metallic, and crushing over the howls of the wind and the pelting of the rain.

Okay.

I was okay.

My wrists hurt.

My cheek hurt.

But I was okay.

I needed to focus. I needed to...

"Fuck," I said, my eyes going huge, my shock-suppressed heartbeat going into overdrive.

Because there was a light. There was a headlight and it was coming toward me.

Fuck.

I needed to *go.*

And the car was totaled.

I reached over, wrenching the door open. Then I saw what I hit: a downed tree. Great.

But I had to go. The rumble of the bike was getting closer. I had to go.

So I did. I jumped over the tree and I hauled ass, my bare feet slapping against the ground as I went, my wet body somehow getting wetter. But all I could think of was escape.

It was them. It had to be them.

And they were coming for me.

I had to keep going. No matter how tired I was, no matter how weak.

The growl of the bike got closer, like it had somehow managed to skirt the tree and was coming up behind me.

Shit.

I broke my rule, looking over my shoulder.

I got to see the outline of a man on a bike before I felt myself falling.

Then I hit. Hard. I went down on one side, the road burning the skin down my arm and thigh, the impact knocking the wind out of me.

I groaned, trying to scramble because the bike's motor cut off. And that could only mean one thing. He was coming for me.

I had to go. I had to get away.

So I pushed up onto my hands and knees, trying to scramble away.

"Babe, what the fuck you doin'?"

TWO

<u>*Reign*</u>

Weird fuckin' night.

I tore out of the compound. I was sick of the shit. I was sick of the bitches and the constant nagging feeling that Mo wasn't the only rat we had. He was gone. He was taken care of, dead. His body was buried in the woods where no one would find him. He was put there by me and Cash, my brother. Literally. He was my blood brother, not one of my MC brothers. But Cash didn't seem to be carrying around the heavy load. It made sense. He was vice, I was prez. It was my fuckin' job to carry that burden.

And I had a feeling we weren't done with the blood spilling.

And I needed out.

So I went to the bar around the corner, breaking up some bullshit fight the Mallick brothers had gotten themselves into, had a couple rounds, then hit the road.

Only to find some bitch running down the road on skidrow.

I stopped to help her.

I wanted to fuck her.

But I lost her to one of those Mallicks I had stepped between earlier.

I felt the unfulfilled desire stab through me, but I wasn't fighting a friend for some random hot bitch.

Then there was the crash.

Even over the rain and wind and my bike... I could hear it- the metal crunching, the glass breaking.

It was no surprise. Out driving in a hurricane was stupid as fuck.

I drove up just seconds after; the slick silver late model car was hammered into a downed tree in the road.

And then the weirdest fucking thing happened.

The door opened and some chick ran the fuck out like I was the devil and she was trying to save her damn soul.

Why the fuck she would be running from a car accident was completely beyond me, so I followed. I wanted to make sure she was alright, see if she needed to call someone.

I might have been a vicious, often violent fuck, but I wasn't gonna leave some chick in the middle of the road in the middle of the damn night during a hurricane with her mangled, un-driveable car.

I pulled around the tree, closing in on her.

Then she looked over her shoulder at me. And if I wasn't mistaken (and I fuckin' never am) she looked terrified.

Then, as if in slow motion, she fell right down on her side. She hit the ground with a muffled groan.

I cut the engine and she was up on her hands and knees trying to scramble away.

What did I say?

Weird fuckin' night.

"Babe, what the fuck you doin'?" I asked, going up behind her, looking down at her scrambling body. And I mean *body*. The girl was fuckin' blessed with her tiny (but nice and plump) ass, thin waist, and slim legs. She was short though. She was short enough to be mistaken for a kid if I hadn't gotten a glimpse of that ass and those hips.

"I'm not going back," she said, her voice fierce, but it shook. "You'll have to kill me. I'm not going back."

The fuck?

Kill her?

She must have hit her head or something in the crash.

Great. I had a trip to the hospital ahead of me.

All I wanted was dry clothes and my fucking bed.

She finally stopped scrambling, moving to sit her nice ass on the wet ground to look up at me.

Fuck me.

Okay.

I needed to remind myself she had a head injury, otherwise I'd have grabbed her and fucked her right there in the street. Right in the middle of a God damn hurricane.

She had one of those faces, those delicate faces that was all plump cheeks, soft chin, and big eyes. They were big gray eyes to be exact. And her hair was long and red. It was soaked and darkened, but you could make out the red. There was no mistaking it.

She was fuckin' perfect.

And I had to be a damn gentleman because she might have brain damage.

Just my luck.

"I'm not going back," she repeated, her voice close to hysterical this time.

"I not takin' you nowhere but maybe the hospital. I think you knocked your brain loose in that crash, darlin'."

"I don't need a hospital," she said, eying me funny, like she was trying to figure something out. "And I haven't knocked my brain loose."

That last part sounded almost haughty.

"Well I'm not leavin' you out here in the street so you're goin' somewhere."

"With you?"

"Yeah, babe. With me."

"On your bike?"

Jesus Christ. Was she dense or something?

"Yeah. On my bike. See any other vehicles out here?"

"Where will you take me?"

"My place."

Wait. What? What the fuck? I couldn't take her to my place. That was the stupidest fuckin' thing I could...

"Okay," she said, her face looking... relieved? She was relieved to go to my place.

Seriously.

Brain damaged.

THREE

<u>*Summer*</u>

Maybe it was a stupid plan. Okay. It was totally a stupid plan. But I was in the middle of bumfuck nowhere next to a stolen car that belonged to a very dangerous man who would do anything in his power to get me back, to get his leverage back. So I needed to get gone. And Tall, Dark, And Deadly was really my only option.

Tall. Dark. Deadly... and the best looking man I had ever seen in my life.

It was almost wrong for one man to possess so much beauty. He had a strong, chiseled jaw, and stern brows over stunning hazel eyes. And then there was the body. He was tall and lean, but strong. He wore black jeans and a dark wifebeater with a leather cut over it. That was it. In the cold October rain.

Yeah. Everything about him from the boots to the bike suggested he was trouble.

But he was trouble who offered me sanctuary.

"Say again?" he said in that rough, deep voice of his.

"I said okay," I said, wiping my hands down the fronts of my shorts, seeing blood. What was a little more blood?

"You're bleedin'," he observed.

"Yeah," I said, trying to get to my feet without touching my cut palms on the ground.

His hand reached down to me, grabbing my wrist and tugging me onto my feet. "I don't have a helmet." Great. I got freedom only to have my head cracked open on the pavement during my escape. "But I've never crashed either," he added and I found myself nodding. "Ever been on a bike?" he asked, leading me over to it and throwing his leg over.

"No."

"Get on behind me and put your arms around me."

And, with that, he turned the bike over and I climbed on. I paused, not entirely comfortable putting my arms around him.

"Hold on, babe," he said, then the bike lurched and all my reservations about holding on vanished. I was pretty sure I was holding on tight enough to start burrowing into his skin. I shut my eyes which years of carnival rides told me was the worst idea possible, but I couldn't take the scenery flying by at God-knew-what speed when it was raining and dark and there was nothing to prevent me from becoming some cautionary tale people told their kids about motorcycles - getting scraped up off the pavement.

It seemed like we drove forever before the bike idled beside a huge wrought iron gate connected to an enormous penny brick fence. I felt my spine stiffen, too many memories of gates and walls in my recent past. But I had no time to freak out because he plugged in a code, the gates opened, and we pulled through. I turned my head, watching the gate close, praying I hadn't just made the choice to trade one prison for another.

We drove up a long driveway. There were no trees; actually, there was no greenery whatsoever. The entire space was open. It was a huge rolling field surrounded completely by the red brick fence.

The house wasn't as huge as I had been imagining with so much money put into protecting it. It was a one level rustic cabin, all weather-worn wood with a huge porch perfect for sipping coffee on in the morning.

He pulled the bike up next to the house, under an overhang, getting off, then reached for my arm before turning and moving to the front door to unlock it. Then he waited, door open, for me to hustle through.

The inside of the house was, surprisingly, brick. All the walls, the massive fireplace, everything was brick but the floor which was weathered wood that matched the outside. The main house area had an open floor plan. The kitchen melted into the dining room which melted into the living room. The living room had two big, worn, caramel-colored leather couches with a scuffed coffee table around the fireplace. There was a record player in a corner, an milk crate full of vinyls underneath it.

"Babe, where the fuck are your shoes?" Tall, Dark and Dangerous asked to my side.

I looked down at my bare feet, looking for an excuse. "Flip flops. They ah... fell off while I was running."

His brows drew together like he didn't quite buy it. But he didn't know me well enough to know I was lying.

"I'll grab a towel," he said, walking toward the hallway past the fireplace.

I felt myself nod though he was already walking away from me. Curious, I moved further inside the door, glancing over at the kitchen, cut off from the rest of the room by a brick island. The counter tops were butcher block; the appliances were stainless steel. The dining room was a few feet from the island and...

Holy shit.

Holy. Shit.

What the fuck did I get myself into?

I needed to get the fuck away.

Before he came back.

Because there sprawled across the table was an assortment of guns and an enormous sum of money.

Shit.

Normal people didn't keep guns and cash on their dining room tables.

Normal people didn't keep ten foot fences around their entire property.

Shit.

I needed to...

"Keep your mouth shut about it. Don't ask questions. And we won't have any problems."

Shit.

I felt myself jerk.

His arm raised and I flinched away from him. It was knee-jerk. I wasn't even aware I was doing it. But he saw. His hazel eyes darkened, his brows lowered. "Towel," he explained and I looked and saw the white material in his hand.

Shit.

Again.

Way to let your trauma show, Summer.

"Thanks," I mumbled, taking the towel and scrubbing it over my face, then rubbing it through my hair.

"What's your name?" he asked, watching me.

"Summer," I answered automatically. Crap. I shouldn't have said that. I should have come up with some fake name. "You?"

"Reign."

"Rain?" I asked. "Like... precipitation?"

That made him snort. "No, babe. Reign. Like a king."

Well then. Okay.

"I'm gonna get changed. Find you something dry," he said, moving toward the hallway again. "Don't touch the guns unless you know what you're doin'. They're loaded."

Right.

I wasn't planning on touching them. I had never even touched a gun before. Though it seemed like any idiot could handle one, as evidenced by V's ragtag group of morons. Evil, sadistic morons.

I forced my eyes away from the dining table, looking out the back windows into the darkness.

I didn't have to think about them. I was, for the moment, relatively safe. Okay, well, maybe not *safe* safe, judging by the very criminal looking supplies laid up like Thanksgiving dinner on the dining room table, but safer than I had been. And as soon as the storm let up, I could ask Reign to drive me somewhere.

I wanted to go home.

But that wasn't safe.

Not yet.

Not until Daddy got more men in to try to...

"Yo, babe," Reign's voice broke through my thoughts, making me jump.

"Yeah?" I asked, turning to see him walking down the hall, dry except for his hair, dressed in a pair of thick dark gray sweatpants hung low at his hips. And... no shirt. It was in my personal opinion that men with bodies like Reign's should never wear shirts. Because, damn. He was built. He was not bulky, but strong, muscled, tattooed. Hot. Oh, my God he was hot.

"You gonna keep starin' or you want to get changed?" he asked, a smirk playing at his lips. Because he was hot shit and he knew it.

I shook my head, walking toward him, still toweling my hair. Reign turned, walking back down the hall, leaving me to follow behind him. He walked up to a door, opened it, and stood there.

"Christ. You're shiverin'," he said, watching me.

I'd been shivering for hours. "I'm fine."

"Take a hot shower," he said, shoving clothes at me.

Oh my God. Yes. *Thank you. Thank you. Thank you.* "Okay," I said, giving him a weak smile and going into the bathroom.

I shut the door, dropping the dry clothes on the sink in front of the huge dome-shaped mirror. I found a spare toothbrush still in its packaging and added a massive amount of paste, brushing my teeth mercilessly until they felt smooth and clean. Turning to the shower bay, I reached in and turned the water on hot, stripping as fast as my hands would allow, then throwing myself under the hot water.

I shampooed four times. I scrubbed every inch of myself five times. I wished for a razor and half stepped out of the shower to rummage in the linen cabinet until I found a spare disposable one, thanking my lucky stars.

I must have been in there for an hour. But it still didn't feel like enough. I was worried I was never going to feel clean ever again; the kind of clean that never knew the touch of filth. The kind of clean I had been before.

But that was just another cross I had to bear.

I grabbed a fresh towel, drying off, making my way over to the clothes. The black wifebeater would definitely fit so I slipped it on. It hung loose around my breasts and belly but it was warm and clean. I was definitely not complaining. I wasn't taking anything for granted anymore.

I was pulling up the pants which looked hopelessly too large when the door flew open and my heart slammed up into my throat. PTSD-type memories flew through my head until I forced myself to focus and saw Reign standing there. Not V. Not his men. Reign.

But it wasn't a sigh of relief.

Because he wasn't looking at my face.

His gaze was stuck on the outer side of my left ass cheek. It was more like upper hip meets thigh, but far enough back for it to technically be ass.

That's where his eyes were.

And they were angry.

"Looks like we have a fucking problem."

FOUR

Reign

She flinched. Flinched. Like I was gonna fucking hit her. Shit. She was not brain damaged. She was abused.

I had some abused chick in my house. I never brought any chicks to my house. I fucked them in my room at the compound. I never took tail home. And now the first piece of ass I brought back was damaged.

That was just my luck.

I walked away from the bathroom door, going to the kitchen to put a pot of coffee on. Then I cleared the money and guns away, taking them to the safe, locking them up. I didn't need some damaged chick thinking I was some fucking psychopath.

She was lying to me too. About the shoes; she was lying. There had been no flip flops. She had been barefoot when she flew out of that car. Which left another question unanswered. Why the fuck would she be out in a hurricane, driving barefoot, in a ritzy fucking car, in pajamas?

She said she wasn't going back. She said I was going to have to kill her because she wasn't going back. Back to what? Back to some piece of shit who liked to knock her around? Some domestic abuse shit? Did she steal his car and get the hell outta dodge?

I had to respect that.

I made a cup of coffee and drank it. She still hadn't come out of the bathroom. I made another cup and drank that. Still nothing.

I sighed, slamming my mug down, walking down the hall. The shower had been off for a while. I was half-worried she had some kind of injury after all and passed out in there.

Worried.

Me.

What the fuck?

I pushed open the door. And there she was in my wifebeater, pulling my pants up her thin legs. She was so tiny, like a bird, fragile looking. My eyes dropped to her upper thigh/ ass area. And any story I had come up with about her past flew away.

Because there on her ass was a brand.

A fucking burning flesh brand.

And it was V's.

It was a letter V inside of an upright triangle.

It was a brand that meant she was one of V's girls.

And she was in my house.

Fuck.

What the fuck did I get myself into?

I didn't fuck with V.

It was club rules that none of us went near V or his girls. I didn't mind my guys getting their dicks wet with any willing pussy they could find. But they did not, under any circumstances, take someone unwilling. And V's girls were all unwilling. Because V's girls were forced into the mother fucking skin trade.

V was also one sick fuck.

That was another reason to not go anywhere near his operation or his girls.

Fuck.

Mother fucking shit.

"I swear I will be out of your hair tomorrow," she said, yanking the pants up and having to hold them fisted in the front or they'd fall down. Her gray eyes were wide and pleading.

"You want to get outta that shit situation, fine. Good. Fucking good for you. You saw an opportunity and you took it. Smart. But I ain't fucking with V's business."

"I'm not his business," she objected, her eyes flashing. Pride?

"That brand on your ass says otherwise."

"The brand says nothing other than he was trying to scare my father."

Her father? What the fuck?

"Get your skinny little ass out into the kitchen so I can get more coffee. Then you're going to explain your shit. Got it?"

She nodded.

That was all I needed. I turned and walked back to the kitchen.

FIVE

<u>*Summer*</u>

Okay. I believed in telling the truth as a rule, ninety-eight percent of the time. The extra two percent was saved for those times your friends asked if their new dye job looked good and you personally thought it was absurd for someone who routinely baked in the sun to dye their hair red and think it looked natural; or when a relative gave you a gift certificate to a store that you wouldn't be caught dead shopping in. In essence, lying was only acceptable to save you from hurting someone's feelings.

But then again, that was *before*.

Fact of the matter was, I didn't know Reign from Adam. And aside from what I had already stupidly admitted, I needed to keep my wits about me. He could see an opportunity to help himself and whatever criminal underground thing he had going on by dropping me right back in V's arms.

Or to barter me.

V would pay.

I knew that. But I wasn't going to let him know that.

I needed to start playing things smart. My freaking life was on the line. I had to stop blurting stuff out like a teenager caught with a six pack.

I was a good liar. At least I was pretty sure I was. I just really needed to commit to my story. Whatever the hell that story was. Which I was going to have to come up with on the fly seeing as the space between his bathroom and his kitchen wasn't nearly long enough to come up with a cover.

Reign reached up into the cabinet for a second mug, filling it, and handing it to me. Now, I was always a coffee person. Before. I would get up in the morning and take the drive to the coffee shop around the corner and get my fix. Then I would go again in the afternoon. And if it was a rough day, I'd go in the evening too. But I liked my drinks milky and sugary, preferably with some sort of flavor: caramel, mocha, pumpkin.

I had never had black coffee in my life.

But the fact of the matter was, I hadn't had anything but struggled handfuls of water from the bathroom tap for months. So I was going to drink it and I was going to learn to enjoy it.

"Thanks," I said, cradling it between my hands for a second before taking a sip. It wasn't bad. It wasn't good either. But it wasn't bad. And it was strong. It felt like it kicked the whole way down.

"Talk."

Well then.

"What do you want to know?" I hedged.

"I want to know why you got the brand of a fucking skin trader on your hip. I want to know what happened to you. I want to know how the fuck you escaped that fortress."

"I have a brand because he brands all the girls he brings in." That was true. Even though I wasn't one of *those* girls. It felt wrong to say 'thank God,' but *thank God*!

"So you're just one of his chicks?"

"Yes." Nope.

"How'd you get out?"

"Honestly?" I could do this honestly at least. "I don't know. I have no idea what happened. My binds were loose and I slipped out of them. I got up and went to bang on the door to go to the bathroom and... no one answered. Someone always answered if I made a fuss. Even if it was with their fists, they answered." Did he just wince? I was pretty sure he winced. That was good. I could play the beaten woman card. It was really the only one I had anyway. "So I looked out. And... there was no one. I didn't even think about it. I just ran. Which was probably really stupid."

"Yeah," he agreed, nodding.

"But it worked. I got outside and... there was no one there either. I just bolted to the gate, hit the button, hopped into one of the cars and floored it."

"You hot wire it?"

"No," I said, half-laughing. Because if he knew me, he would know how absurd a question that was. I didn't even know where to put wiper fluid in my car back home. "No, they leave the keys in the cars."

"That's careless."

"I guess they never thought anyone would get the chance to run."

He nodded, looking out the window for a second. "Who is your father?"

Shit.

Shit shit.

I never should have said that.

"Just a guy. A normal guy. V wanted to screw with him I guess."

"Babe," he said, his voice very flat. "I know criminals. And I know crime lords. V is a fuckin' crime lord. No way he wanted to fuck with your daddy for shits and giggles. He had a reason. What's the reason?"

"I don't know," I said, putting a little desperation into the words, making them convincing. Because I did know and it was horrible. I was willing to keep going through the torture every day that my father denied V what he wanted because he was doing the right thing. I begged him to do the right thing.

"You come from money? You sound like you come from money."

I sounded like I came from money? That sounded like an insult. But if his mind was running toward extortion, well that was a good direction for him to go. "Yes. I come from money."

"V likes money. Almost as much as he likes stealing girls off the streets and making them suck and fuck until they're too used up to be useful."

I felt myself shiver because it was true. It was so awfully, disgustingly true. That was what he did. I saw them all the time getting dragged in, screaming, crying, trying to claw away. But it never did any good. The men were too strong. They were too immune to it all. And the women would be held down. They would be forced to endure the searing, unbelievable pain of branding. Then they would be thrown into some building with a hundred other girls, waiting to be transported out, waiting to spend their lives being raped and tortured by whoever paid the most money.

And that was what Reign thought had happened to me.

So be it.

"Yeah," I agreed, my voice quiet from disgust.

"You're lucky as fuck to get out. But if he was using you to extort money, babe, he ain't gonna stop lookin' for you."

"I know that." God, I wish I didn't know that.

"You put me in the middle of your mess."

"Technically you put yourself in the middle," I corrected, feeling annoyance rise up. "You could have left me on the side of that road."

"No, I couldn't."

"Yes," I said, firmly, "you could have. You chose not to. I am grateful for that, but don't put it on me. I told you I would be out of your hair once the storm blows over. Drop me anywhere. I'll figure it out from there."

"Ain't dropping you nowhere," he said, looking at me like I was crazy.

"Why not?"

"You got any fuckin' idea how crazy that piece of shit is? He'll have every man, every cop, every lackey out looking for you. Hair like that, babe, they'll find you."

"Then I'll dye it."

"Nah."

I fought the urge to roll my eyes. Like it was any of his damn business what I did with my hair. "Do you have any better suggestions?"

"You'll stay here."

What?

No. Seriously. *What?*

"I'm sorry?"

"You'll stay here. Give it a few days to blow over. No one saw me with you. It was dead as fuck out tonight. Everyone with their power out in town and shit. He'll find the mangled car, figure you got taken to the hospital. He'll spend some time on that. Then he'll hit the streets. You need to stay hidden for a while. No better place than here for that."

Was he seriously offering me sanctuary? Like, actual sanctuary?

"You can't be serious."

"Do I look like I'm fuckin' jokin'?"

"V is dangerous."

"I know."

"If he finds out you helped me, you'll be on his shit list."

"I know."

"Then why would you ever offer..."

"Babe. He ain't gonna find out. It's that simple. You stay here. Inside the house. Couple days. Week. Two at most. I can get you out of here and far away from all this."

"Why would you do that?"

Reign's shoulder shrugged. "Certain criminals give us all a bad name."

I snorted. Then my eyes widened, my hand slapping over my mouth. Shit. I wasn't supposed to snort at the nice criminal who was offering to help me. *Good going, Summer.*

"Sorry," I mumbled, looking down at my coffee.

I got another shrug. "Might not get it, but we all got a code."

"A code?" I prompted.

"Yeah. A code. That's why you see some good old fashioned cell block justice when a baby raper ends up in prison. Fucker doesn't get to live long enough to regret his life choices."

"Have you been to prison?"

Damn it.

I was prying. And he had said not to ask questions. I was royally screwing up my chances of being allowed to stay.

"Yeah, babe. I've been locked up."

"For a long time?" Oh my God. What was wrong with me?

"Sixty seconds behind bars is a long time."

Well, that was true. And, in my own way, I knew exactly what that felt like. I had been in my own prison for months. But without regular eating schedules, without trips to the yard, without anyone to come in and stop the beatings.

"Seems you might know a thing or two 'bout that. How long did he have you?"

"What's the date?"

"What?"

"What is today's date?"

"October fifteenth."

"I was taken on July second." I had done that thing you see in movies, when people get caught, or when they're in jail and they start scratching days into the wall. Four lines. One across. Four lines. One across. I had one-hundred and five days. Three months and two weeks. It felt so much longer. But knowing how long it actually was helped me keep my sanity through all the pain and the hunger.

Reign nodded.

"He hurt you?"

I swallowed. "Repeatedly."

"Fuck."

"I'm fine," I said, shrugging.

"You know that's a lie."

It was a lie, but it was one I was trying really hard to make myself believe.

"Alright. It's late," he said, putting his mug in the sink. "Let's sleep. Talk more tomorrow."

"Okay," I agreed, sucking the rest of my coffee down greedily. It was something in my belly. It was the first thing in there in days. And I wished it had more calories, but at least caffeine suppressed the appetite. I could get by a few more hours.

Then he turned and, at a loss for what to do, I put my mug in the sink and followed him down the hall. We walked past the bathroom and I realized it was a bathroom I wouldn't have to ask to use. I could use it more than once a day, instead of sitting, rocking and praying I didn't pee myself until I got the chance.

Reign disappeared into the room across from the bath and I followed. Then froze. It was the master bedroom. I glanced back into the hallway. There were no other bedrooms. Crap. I hoped he didn't think I was going to sleep with him; that because I was one of V's girls that I was happy to spread my legs for any favor.

"Relax," he said, turning to look at me, his head cocked to the side. "The bed is huge. You won't have to touch me."

"I can..." I started, licking my lips. "I can sleep on the couch. It's fine."

"You're sleepin' here where I can keep an eye on you," he said with finality in his tone.

I wasn't really in a position to fight him. And the bed was huge. I was small. He was right. There would be feet between us.

"Okay."

He turned away from me, grabbed the remote off the nightstand and flicked on a massive flat screen television across from the bed. Oh, my God. TV. I missed TV. And music. I missed any sound other than men taunting me and women screaming. And my own mind driving me half crazy.

"You pick," he said, tossing the remote across the bed as he got in one side.

It took everything I had to not dive at the remote. I made my way around the bed, pulling back the sheets, and climbing in. I settled, picked up the remote, and started flicking through the channels. I finally settled on old black and white reruns that made Reign's head turn toward me, one of his brows quirked up.

"Seriously?"

"You can change it," I said automatically. It was another knee-jerk reaction I had learned over the past few months. I had to try to never disagree with the men when I could help it. I had to always try to appease them. I had to save myself from the beating. Except on the days when they called my dad; those days I disagreed. I took the beatings. I practically asked for them.

"Nah, babe. I said you pick. You picked."

Then he left it at that, lying there, watching the TV.

I cuddled under the blankets, smelling deeply of man. It was something undefinable, but familiar: a trace of cologne, plain old male musk, a non-floral smelling laundry detergent.

And then, to my absolute horror, my stomach growled ferociously, sounding like I had monsters trapped inside.

Reign's head turned to me automatically and I tried to ignore his eyes on me. "You're hungry, you say you're hungry," he said simply, getting up off the bed.

"No. It's okay. I can wait till morning. Trust me."

"Trust you?" he asked, turning back. "They didn't feed you? You're used to bein' hungry?"

I felt my face blush. Which was ridiculous. It wasn't like I had starved myself. "They fed me when they felt like it."

"How often did they feel like it?"

I sucked in air. "Every few days if I was lucky."

"Fuck."

"It's really no big deal. I can wa..."

"How long you been waiting?"

"What?" I asked, pulling my knees to my chest.

"How long since they last fed you?"

Oh. Right.

"Um," I started.

"The fact that you have to fuckin' think about that shit is why you're getting your ass up, coming in the kitchen, and stuffin' your face."

Two days. It had been two days.

But Reign was gone and I was jumping out of bed, holding onto the waistband of my pants, and following behind.

As if sensing my presence, he said, "Do I even want to fucking know what they threw at you when they did feed you?"

No, he didn't. And I didn't have a choice about eating it either.

"No."

"Fuck."

Then there was a lot of movement. He put pots and pans on the stove. He pulled items out of the cabinets and refrigerator.

"It's late. I can just have some cereal or something..." I supplied, watching him move around, his strong back muscles turning and twisting in an altogether too sexy way for three o'clock in the morning.

He simply ignored me, moving around some more. He poured water into a pot. He chopped something right on the counter; because, well, it *was* butcher block.

"Can I help with anything?"

I wasn't really a cook. Okay. I wasn't a cook in any way shape or form. Dad always had servants for that. But being a motherless kid, I had spent a lot of time in the kitchen with Mae, our very heavy, very jovial Italian cook. At her apron tails, I was taught it was always proper to offer to help, even if you didn't know what you were doing.

"You just spent three months in a hellhole having God-knows what done to you and you don't think you've earned the right to relax and have someone take care of you?"

Take care of me?

Was that what he was doing?

It was.

And it was too good.

I just...

Okay. I was a little emotional.

And by 'a little emotional' I meant I was pretty sure I was about to cry in front of him. And not just cry. Ugly snot cry. I turned away, looking off into the living room, deep breathing.

"Can I put music on?"

"As long as it's vinyl, yeah."

I all but flew across the room, making a show of looking through the records, pretending to ignore my shaking hands. I knew I was dealing with some heavy shit, especially heavy considering what a pampered life I had led, but I needed to keep my head on straight. I couldn't go all hysterical woman because someone was taking care of me. That was what you were supposed to do when you find someone in need of help, right? Even when you were a big, bad, criminal biker dude.

I grabbed a record I recognized, lifted the needle, and dropped it. There was a hum for a long second before the sound came flooding out of the speakers. I backed up toward the couch, lowering myself down. I was planning on just keeping my distance for a few minutes. But the couch was one of *those* leather couches, the well-loved ones, the ones that felt buttery to the touch. And as soon as I had myself up on it, comforted with the idea of not being startled awake by someone trying to hurt me, I fell fast asleep.

And I had nightmares.

But they weren't nightmares.

They were memories.

**

"Wakey wakey!" one of them, Deke, I had heard one of the other guys call him, said. No, not said. Screamed. He screamed it right in my ear. I lurched up in bed so fast I forgot all about being tied to it and the ropes seared at the already torn skin on my wrists, the pain so intense I had to choke down the bile in my throat.

"Almost pissed the bed," Martin said, chuckling.

The smell of them was always what got me the most. The cigarette smoke seemed to seep out of their pores. That, mixed with the vodka on their breaths, and the almost overpowering smell of body odor.

You could literally smell them coming down the hall if you were awake.

Being I had been fast asleep, it assaulted me at once, cutting through the fog of sleep like a strong wind.

"She really is a pretty one," Deke said, his fingers reaching out for my face, stroking down the side of my neck. "So ripe," he said, his hand moving over my breast that had no protection of a bra from his prying fingers. "She needs a good fucking, don't you think, Mart?"

"Damn right. From both ends at once, I'd say."

"Yeah," he said, his hand sliding down my belly. "They always like it like that, don't they?"

I bit my lip to keep from screaming or pleading. They weren't supposed to touch me. V made that point clear.

"She gets hurt when I say she gets hurt. How I say she gets hurt. Hands and dicks off otherwise." Those had been his words.

But I knew that meant nothing to them. Not when they came in the middle of the night, half drunk, eyes cloudy with lust. I knew they could lie their way out of it.

"Fucking dead fish," Deke scolded, grabbing my breast so hard tears sprang to my eyes. I looked away. Because I might not have known much about men like them, but I knew they got off on the reaction. They got off on the power they held over girls like me, the fear. If I didn't give them that, they might just go away. They might not be able to get it up; or they might just get annoyed enough to leave me alone and go find someone else.

God. How I hated myself for thinking that: that I hoped they went to someone else, knowing that girl had no rules around her. No one gave a shit if she screamed or died. But I wanted it so badly to not be me, that I hoped they moved on.

And when they eventually did, I rolled halfway onto my stomach, my face buried in the pillow, and I screamed. I never cried. I never let there be traces of weakness in the morning. So instead, I screamed until my throat was raw. Until no more sound would come out. Until I passed out again.

**

I bolted up on the couch, my heart slamming hard.

"Just a dream," Reign's voice reached me, calm, reassuring. Close. My head snapped, my eyes wild, to find Reign sitting on the coffee table, looking very much like he had been there a while. "Take a breath. It was just a dream."

"No," I said, pushing my hair out of my face, "it wasn't."

Reign's eyes flashed with recognition and he nodded. "I didn't know if I should wake you," he said, sounding strained. "You were screaming and screaming but I didn't know if it would be worse to wake up to someone holding you."

I put my feet on the floor, stuffing my shaking hands between my knees and shrugging. "I don't know," I answered honestly. "I've never had nightmares before."

"You want to talk about it? Shit can't stay bottled up. I know it's fresh and it smites, but you can't let it get infected. It'll eat you up."

I don't know why, but I found my mouth opening. I found myself needing to share. I needed to share the burden and the guilt. It was so heavy on my shoulders that I felt like I couldn't lift them.

I was free.

The rest were still there.

Still praying, every night praying, it would be someone else.

Instead of them.

"They used to come in at night," I started, looking down at my feet. "I would be tied to the bed," I said, lifting my wrists as if he needed proof. I knew he really didn't. Maybe I did. "Scare me out of sleep. And then... touch me. And..."

"And," he prompted.

"And I would just lay there praying they would go on to someone else. That they would leave me alone. Lose interest in me and go find another girl. And when they did, I felt so bad. So guilty. So disgusted in myself that I would scream into my pillow until I couldn't scream anymore. Because that was such a horrible thing to think. I shouldn't have..."

"Hey," he said, his big hand landing hard on my knee. "Eyes," he said, and my gaze lifted. "You were scared. They wanted to hurt you. You wanted it to stop. You didn't do anything wrong. Okay?"

Somehow, hearing someone else say it made it feel a little more true. Though I was pretty sure there would never be a time in my life where I didn't feel that guilt, it didn't feel quite so all-consuming when I shared it.

"Okay."

"'Kay," he said, his hand dropping as he stood. "Food is ready. You still want to eat?"

No. I didn't.

But then my stomach twisted and groaned and I knew I was going to eat. It wouldn't do me any good to punish myself because I felt bad for being free when they were still trapped.

So I ate.

I watched reruns.

And then I slept.

SIX

Reign

I'd never heard a woman scream like that. Men, yeah. I had made men scream like that. Men I had needed to teach a lesson to, men who needed to not be of this earth anymore. They were screams of pure, unfiltered fear and pain.

I heard those screams in my head before sleep at night. They were my own personal demons that I could never seem to shake. And hoped I wouldn't. Because if I ever got to a day where I was okay with what I had to do, then I would be a monster.

So I knew those screams.

It was so much worse hearing them from a woman, hearing them from someone who suffered at the hands of some scumbag. To hear them coming from someone who wasn't able to defend herself.

I set the food aside, moving toward the couch, toward her, her hair half-covering her face, her eyes closed, her body taut as a bow as she just... screamed.

I never had to sleep next to someone before so I knew jack shit about waking people up from bad dreams. So I just sat there and listened, waiting for her to wake up so I could remind her that she was okay, that she was away from those things.

And then she told me she felt guilty.

The girl who endured fuck-knew what for months said she felt guilty because there were nights she didn't want to suffer anymore.

Fucking hell.

I wanted to find those sons of bitches, whoever the hell they were, and show them some vigilante justice.

But I needed to watch myself. I needed to think of my men first. Brotherhood came before everything else, most especially bitches. Especially bitches I didn't even know.

So then I fed her.

Then she slept.

I did too for a few short hours before the sun started coming through the windows and I climbed out of bed, going through to the kitchen to put coffee on and call my brother.

"Cash," he answered, sounding as awake as I was. Neither of us had ever been much for sleeping. We could be up all night and still be wide awake in the early morning.

"Got a problem."

Whatever noise that was going on around him stopped and his normally laid-back voice got serious. "What kind of problem?"

"A big clusterfuck of a problem," I admitted, running a hand down my face.

"Can't help if you don't talk to me."

"I have one of V's girls."

There was a long silence. "The fuck?"

"I was driving home from the bar and I heard a crash. Then some bitch hopped out of the car and started running. Thought she was half-whacked. And I fucking took her home."

"To the compound?"

"To my house."

"The fuck?"

I snorted. Cash was the only other person aside from me who had been to my house. Bringing some random car-crash woman over was not only unexpected, but completely out of character. "I dunno. It was late. The storm was bad. I wasn't thinking. She's got V's brand on her ass."

"You fucked her?"

"No, I didn't fuck her," I said, rolling my eyes. "Just caught sight of it. V had her for three months. The storm made his men careless. She got away."

"Shit."

"She has nightmares, man."

"What?"

"Nightmares," I said, shaking my head. "Like... where she screams."

"Fuck."

"Yeah."

"What are you gonna do?"

"I told her she could stay until things blow over and I'll get her on her way."

"Seriously? You're keeping one of V's girls from him?"

"The fuck else am I gonna do? Hand her back? He's a fucking monster, Cash."

Cash let out a low whistle. "What do you need?"

"For you to keep your mouth shut. This doesn't involve the club."

"You know that that isn't..."

"This isn't going to touch the club."

"Alright," he conceded, but I knew he had more to say.

"I need supplies," I decided, shrugging.

"Supplies?"

"Yeah for bitches. She looks sweet in my clothes and all but they're falling off her ass."

"So clothes?"

"Yeah. Small. She's tiny. And I don't know... shampoo and soap and shit. Whatever the fuck bitches like. You'd know better than me." It was no secret my brother was the biggest whore around. He liked women. And they damn sure liked him back.

"Anything else?" he asked and I could hear the humor in his voice.

"Food. Don't know what she likes but I know they've been starving her."

"Fuck."

"Yeah," I agreed.

"Be there in an hour."

"Aight," I said, hanging up and going back into my bedroom to grab clothes.

She was still on the bed, curled up on her side, knees to her belly, her wrists on full display. They were wrists that had barely-healed ligature marks marring them. There were several of them. She'd been tied up for most of the time she had been there.

All I could think about through my shower was her screams.

There was a knock on the door a little over an hour later, loud, like he was kicking instead of actually knocking, making the door shake in the jamb.

I walked over, pulling it open.

And there was Cash.

We were similar in facial features and that was about it. He got our mother's dark blond hair that he kept long on one side, but shaved to a buzzcut up the other. His eyes were a deeper shade of green, and he walked with a fucking swagger. Always had. He was a toddling swaggerer. There was an air about Cash that I didn't have. He had a laid-back, calm, almost jovial demeanor that made women flock to him in droves. That wasn't to say he couldn't handle his shit. He was a capable, deadly fuck when he needed to be. But any other time, he was the guy a man wanted to have a beer with and a woman wanted to roll around the sheets with.

"Gonna let me in? Hands are kinda full here."

And they were. He had a dozen bags in his hands and hanging off his arms. There was the strong smell of eggs and I noticed a brown bag in his hand. The other hand held a tray of coffee.

Well, there were two coffees. And then there was one monstrous frozen drink thing with whipped cream on top.

Cash moved in past me, going toward the kitchen, pausing, and looking down the hallway. "Heya sweetheart," he said, giving her one of his smiles.

"There's two of you," she said timidly, looking at Cash like he might pounce on her at any minute.

"This is my brother, Cash. He brought some stuff for you."

"Starting with," Cash said, putting the tray down and none too gently dropping all the bags on the floor. He grabbed the huge frozen drink and held it out to her, smiling. "This. Trenta mocha frap with a shot of espresso and whipped cream."

And just like that, her face lit up.

Lit. The. Fuck. Up.

Her sad eyes brightened, her smile spread across her face. And, for a moment, she didn't look so haunted.

"I take it you like my choice?" Cash asked, watching as she took it from his hands.

"It's perfect. Thank you." She gave him a smile and took a long swig from the straw, her eyes closing.

Fuck. I'd given her *black coffee*.

"Good," Cash said, nodding, moving back to the counter and pulling open the brown bag. "I also got us all sausage, egg, and cheese on bagels with sides of hashbrowns," he said, pulling foil-wrapped bagels out followed by a huge box stained with grease. "Plates, bro," he said to me, watching me watch Summer drink her frozen coffee with a lifted brow.

"Right," I said, going to grab the plates.

"You hungry?" Cash asked her.

"I could eat."

She was starved for months. Yeah, I bet she could eat.

"Want to put on some clothes that fit first?" he asked, reaching for the bags.

"You brought me clothes?" she asked, her eyes going wide.

Cash's head tilted, looking at her. "As per orders."

"Orders?" she asked, brows drawing together.

"Reign said you needed girl shit. Clothes. Soap. The works."

Her gaze went to me and her eyes glistened. Glistened. Like she was going to cry over clothes and soap and shit. Because she'd been living in such hell that even the smallest gesture was making her all emotional.

"Unfortunately, I didn't get a bra size," Cash went on, easily skirting her obviously tear-filled eyes. "Which is..." he looked at her. "Thirty-four B," he guessed and she blushed. Blushed. Because he was right. "So you'll be going commando on that front, but I got pretty much everything else," he told her, holding out the bags that weren't from the food store. Five of them.

"Thank you," she said, looking between us. "Both of you. That was really considerate. I swear I'll reimburse you when I get back to my..."

"They're clothes, not a sports car," I said, shaking my head. "You ain't payin' me back for shit."

"And by that he means *You're welcome and don't worry about it*," Cash said, smiling. "Go get yourself dressed so we can eat."

And with that, she was off.

"Where the fuck did you get all that shit?" I asked, raising a brow.

"Went into the store, found a pretty little thing that worked there. Great rack. So lush. Wanted to motorboat the fuck out of her right there. Anyway," he said, shaking his head, "told her my sister was coming to visit and lost her luggage and that I needed all the shit bitches need day to day. That's what she came up with." Cash paused at my silence and raised a brow. A smirk was toying at his mouth. "Seriously? You left out that she's the prettiest fucking thing to ever cross your path?"

"She's traumatized. Sorry if I didn't notice she's good looking."

"Oh, fuck off," he laughed, rolling his eyes. "You absolutely noticed. I bet you've thought about ten different ways to fuck her already."

"Hands off, Cash," I said, my voice a warning.

That only accomplished making his smirk stretch out. "'Cause she's yours."

"She's not mine," I growled, plating the food. "No one is touching her. Who knows what the fuck they did to her. She doesn't want any man touching her."

"Admit you want to and I'll let it drop."

If I didn't agree, he literally would never let it drop. He was a stubborn fuck and I was perpetually short on patience. "Fine. I want to. But it ain't happening."

"Sure it isn't," he smiled.

"It's not," I said firmly. "We need to talk about other things. Like how we are going to handle this."

Cash shrugged. "We could call K."

"K?"

"Yeah. K. In the city. He disappears people. Mostly women who get themselves caught in bad situations. He's good at it. Been doing it for years. She needs to disappear. He will disappear her."

SEVEN

Summer

The sound of male voices woke me up. It wasn't an altogether unfamiliar sound and it wasn't the least bit comforting. I shot up in bed, surprised when my wrists didn't pull, before I remembered where I was.

Free.

I was free.

I was in Reign's house. And, for the moment, I was safe.

But there was still the sound of men's voices. Two, when there was only supposed to be one in the house. So I crawled out of bed, holding my pants up, and crept down the hall, listening.

I had barely made it around the corner when I saw the source of the other voice, the one that wasn't gargled glass sounding like Reign's. It was smoother, like whiskey or wine.

He was tall and thin, but muscular in black jeans, a white tee, and a black cut like Reign had been wearing when he picked me up.

But this guy was blond. Well, the half of his head that wasn't shaved was blond and long. His eyes were a deep green. But his face, his face was all his brother's. As in, they were actual brothers.

"Heya sweetheart."

That was all it took for me to know he was safe. He wasn't like V's guys. He wasn't even somewhat scary like his brother. He was warm and open and friendly. I could trust him.

And then he gave me a trenta mocha full fat with a shot and whip. And I think I fell half in love with him.

Not really, but ya know... it kinda made my day. Or month. Or year.

Then he told me they had conspired to get me clothes and soap and girl stuff. The tears I had kept inside for three months came springing to my eyes, stinging. I couldn't cry over clothes in front of two relative, but really kind, strangers. I couldn't do that. So I took a deep breath, accepted the bags, and rushed off to the bathroom.

Tears fell, hot and heavy, but not sad. I reached for the bags, pulling items out and placing them on the sink counter. There were three pairs of yoga pants: black, gray, deep green. There were three t-shirts: black, gray, white. There was one sweatshirt in pink and one sweater in white. There was a bag of socks and pretty patterned, but simple undies, five pairs of them.

Then there was the accessory bag which spoke highly of very in depth, intimate knowledge of women. In it I found: lavender soap, matching lotion, high end shampoo and conditioner, a leave-in conditioner, hair ties, a heavy-handled rectangle brush, shaving cream and razors, tweezers, face wash and a special moisturizer, a tube of chapstick, a toothbrush, paste, and floss. And, ha, a box of tampons.

**

Six weeks. I had been there forty-two days. My stubby, bloody nails had just etched the line into the wall when they burst in.

"Gonna go see V today."

Seeing V meant I was going to get hurt. Not by him, not usually anyway. The other guys did the actual hitting and kicking and cutting and branding. V just gave the go-ahead. He also called them off when he thought I had gotten enough.

My wrists were untied from the headboard but not released from the rope. No. Deke took those ropes and dragged me forward by them, making sure to jerk them every couple of feet to make them bite into my skin. Deke was a sadistic bastard, but Martin was the one who gave me pause to worry.

It was his eyes. He had black as night eyes. They were soulless, devoid of anything human.

Deke, the monster, had blue eyes, the bright kind. But there was still a person behind them. And that gave me hope on bad days.

I had a feeling it was going to be a very bad day.

The basement smelled like piss. It always did. Even though the half of it that I was taken to was always empty. Maybe the smell came from the other side. Maybe they did things to other people to make them lose control of their bladders. The windows gave a small amount of light but were barred. The walls were cinderblocks. The floors were cement. Cold; it was always so cold down there.

I was led over to the metal chair and dropped down. No one tied my hands to anything. There was no reason, because there was no escape.

Martin and Deke went a few feet away, leaning against the wall. Waiting. I'd catch them watching me with eyes that were expectant. A muscle was twitching in Martin's jaw. And Deke was impatiently tapping his foot. They were getting antsy, getting excited.

They lived for the days when they got to put their hands on me.

The door to the basement opened and footsteps came down the stairs and across the floor behind me.

"Miss Lyon," his cool, smooth voice said, coming around me. "How are we doing today?"

I learned not to answer his questions.

V was younger than you would expect for someone with his kind of criminal empire. He was somewhere in his mid-thirties with thick brown hair, tan skin, and brown eyes. He was good looking. He could be charming. And he always dressed in a suit, even when all he was doing was coming down to watch me be tortured.

"I have the paper you requested," he said, pulling a newspaper out from under his arm and giving it to me.

I never requested the paper. The paper was to show the date for the video he was about to film. A video he would record on my own cell phone. It would be of me getting tortured. It was a video to show my father, to try to blackmail him to do his bidding. Seven sessions and they were getting nowhere. I could tell they were all losing their patience. With him. And, therefore, with me.

I took the paper, holding it against my chest like I was supposed to.

"Your hair is filthy," he informed me like I didn't already know that, like it wasn't his fault.

"Not in the talking mood?" he asked, shrugging, pulling out my cell phone.

And it was about to begin.

"Who will it be today?" he asked the room at large. "Martin? I think it's your turn this time."

His dark eyes roamed over me, a smile tugging at his lips. "I think you're right V."

"Summer, darling. Why don't you say hi to your daddy?" V asked, holding the phone up.

"Go fuck yourself, V," I spat back.

I was never *that* girl, the one with the filthy mouth. I was not a headstrong, obstinate girl. I did what was expected of me. I went to private schools. I got good grades. I hung out with girlfriends from similar family backgrounds (meaning rich). I didn't date until I was eighteen, and even then only very selectively. I spoke to my father and his business partners with respect.

When I was twenty-one, I was moved into my father's never-used penthouse apartment in the city so I could have my freedom. I went to work at one of his many businesses, doing whatever was asked of me because it was important that I understood the value of hard work before I found a suitable man and settled into a housewife role.

I never so much as used the word "shit" in all my twenty-four years.

Until I was taken.

Until everything was stripped from me except my words and my will.

So I used them.

Even if it meant I got beaten worse.

"Oh, now that's not very nice is it, Mart?" he asked and Martin took the cue, slamming his fist into the left side of my face.

"This can stop," he said a few minutes later, watching me wipe blood from my face with the side of my arm, "if you would just tell you father to go along with the deal."

"Rot in hell, V. My father is never going to take the deal."

At that point, I was thrown down on the floor. Then there was kicking and punching and threats of worse. A lot worse. The kind of worse that they suggested when they crept in at night. I knew that would come eventually. There was no question about it. One day, I would be dragged down into the basement. And then I would be raped. By Deke. And Martin. And probably V.

That was my fate.

But I still didn't want V to win.

I didn't want my father to give in.

"What the FUCK!" Martin suddenly yelled, shrinking away from me.

"What?" V asked, putting the phone away.

"She's bleedin'," Martin said, his face twisted up in disgust.

"You beat her good," Deke agreed, his eyes small like he was trying to understand.

"No. Her fucking cunt is bleeding, you shit."

Then V got angry. *Angry* angry. It was not the cool, detached kind of angry he usually was. He flew at Deke, his hand at the man's throat, shoving him so hard against the wall that I heard a crack. "You fuck her? You fuck her, you stupid shit?"

I turned away from them, uncurling from myself, and looking down. And I *was* bleeding. Six weeks. I was overdue. Terror must have scared it off. But there it was; I had my period. And I was... *mortified.*

There were things they had done to me, awful things, painful things. They didn't feed me. They made me hold my bladder till bursting. And while they were traumatizing and cringe-inducing, there was something about having the dignity of a private menstrual cycle taken away from me that had humiliation rising up hot and sickening in my belly.

We were taught things as women about hiding our periods, about keeping clean. They stole that from me. And Martin was acting like I was disgusting.

And I *felt* disgusting.

And I hated them all the more for that.

"I didn't fucking touch her!" Deke screamed after V's fist landed true to his jaw. "She's prolly on the fucking rag. Jesus Christ."

V dropped Deke, looking back at me, his brows drawing together. "Right," he said, nodding stiffly. "I'll get one of the girls to get her some... tampons or whatever," he said, moving away. "Get her back upstairs."

"I'm not going near her," Martin said, cringing away as I pushed myself up.

V, to his credit (for which he had very little), rolled his eyes at Martin. "Never had a woman before? They bleed. Stop acting like such a bitch."

"I'll take her," Deke said, grabbing my rope and tugging me up the stairs.

Martin followed behind a few minutes later with a woman I didn't know, but who wasn't chained and who didn't look me in the eye. She carried a box of tampons which Deke took and shoved at me.

"Just leave her in there," Martin suggested, nodding toward the bathroom. "Tie her to the can or something. We'll let her out when she's clean again."

And with that, I was tied to a toilet for five days. I had enough give on my wrists to be able to get to the sink where I cleaned up. I scrubbed my clothes. I tried not to let the indignity of the whole situation get to me.

But it got to me.

**

I looked down at the tampons with a weird whimper sound in my throat, tucking them back into the bag and stashing the bag at the bottom of the linen closet. I was being given my dignity back.

They gave me that.

I shook my head, trying to fight the urge to take a shower and use my new soaps and shampoos and tweeze my eyebrows. They were waiting for me to eat. I jumped into a pair of black undies with cherries on them, pulled on the black yoga pants, the black tee, put on socks, and brought the pink sweatshirt with me in case I got cold.

Their voices hit me as soon as I stepped into the hall.

"We could call K," Cash's voice suggested.

"K?" Reign asked.

"Yeah from the city. He disappears people. Mostly women who get themselves caught in bad situations. He's good at it. Been doing it for years. She needs to disappear. He will disappear her."

Disappear me? What?

"Disappear me?" I asked, surprising myself and them, because they both jumped guiltily and turned to face me.

"We're just discussing your options," Reign said, shrugging.

"Like making me disappear?"

"It's just an option, sweetheart," Cash said, giving me a smile. "Why don't you come and eat and then we'll discuss it?" he suggested, carrying plates over to the dining table.

I grabbed my frap and followed, the smell of food making my belly growl even though I had eaten hours ago. I had lost time to make up for and my stomach knew it.

We all sat, unwrapping our food, taking first bites, before the silence got to me and I broke it. "Is that really the only option you think there is for me? To disappear?"

"It's the safest option," Reign corrected. "K has been disappearing girls for a long time. And save for one case, none of them ever get found."

"One case?" I asked, needing to know all the details if I was going to agree to it. Which I might, to keep my father safe. I would not let myself be used as a bargaining chip again.

Cash pushed a second hashbrown toward me. "Yeah. There was a big time H dealer who liked to beat and rape his girlfriend. She got away; she found K. K disappeared her. But the guy was relentless. She kept getting found."

"Is she..."

"Dead?" Cash asked, flat out, surprising me. "No. She got herself hooked up with some private investigator in the city..."

"Rhodes," Reign supplied, respect in his voice.

"Yeah, Rhodes. Anyway... she, ah, had the mob put a hit on her ex. Voila. All her problems gone."

"So you think it's the best bet even though he kept finding her? I don't know if you know V, but he's relentless too."

"I know V," Cash said and Reign sent him a look. It was a very 'what the fuck' kind of look. Apparently Cash had been keeping that from his big brother.

"The fuck?" Reign asked.

"It's nothing. I was on a run. Ran into him. He made it clear who he was. That was it."

"That fucking better be it."

Cash rolled his eyes at me in a very brotherly way, like we were both agreeing that Reign was being unreasonable. "I didn't have a shoe size," Cash said.

"I'm sorry?"

"A shoe size, sweetheart. For your feet."

"Oh, um... I'm a six," I supplied.

"Right. Next time I drop by, I'll bring shoes. Did I forget anything else?"

I felt myself smile a little. "No. You were very thorough."

"I know women pretty well."

"I can tell."

Reign rolled up his foil, drawing my attention. "Thanks for letting me stay," I said stupidly, feeling like I owed him more gratitude than I could even begin to share.

"It's no big deal," he said, getting up. "You got her? I'm going out for an hour."

"Sure," Cash said, waving a hand.

And with that, Reign was gone.

"Don't let him fool you," Cash said as the door closed.

"Fool me about what?"

"It's a big deal. Not that he's helping you. But that you're staying here. No woman has ever stayed here before."

"Oh," I said, picking at my hashbrown. "I mean... it's just for a couple days. I'm sure it's nothing. He's just trying to help..."

"That's just the thing, though," Cash said, sitting back in his chair. "Reign doesn't just do nice shit all the time. Does he seem like that kind of guy?"

"No," I admitted.

"'Cause he's not. He's got a lot of other shit on his plate. If he helped every damsel in distress, he'd never get a break. He's a good guy, don't get me wrong. Big heart underneath all that barbed wire. But it's usually for his brothers, the club. That's it. So, coming from his brother, this is a pretty big deal."

"Is that... a bad thing?" I asked, eating the last of my food, my belly aching it was so full. The sensation was still so new that I reveled in it.

"No, sweetheart," he said, getting up, shaking his head. "I think you'll be good for him. I'm gonna smoke," he said, moving toward the back door. "Keep trying to quit, but it never sticks. I'll stay where you can see me, okay?"

"Okay," I said, nodding.

I took the plates, carrying them to the sink where all the stuff from cooking and eating the night before were still piled. And I set to work.

If he was letting me stay and it was a big deal for him, the least I could do was carry my weight.

When Cash said he was going to smoke, he meant about half a pack. When I finished the dishes, leaving them in a dry pile on the counter, he was still out there, staring out at the fence, a cloud of smoke around him. I walked off toward the bedroom, making the bed. Then went to the bathroom, organizing all the supplies so they weren't strewn all over.

By the time I went back out into the main room, I heard Reign's bike rumbling up. Cash heard it too, turning to look through the door and giving me a smile.

The front door opened and in walked Reign, his hair all windblown, his eyes squinting to adjust to the dimmer inside light.

"Tell me Cash cleaned," he said in an odd tone, one I didn't know him well enough to decipher.

"I cleaned," I supplied, shrugging.

"Babe, you don't work for me," he said, piercing me with his hazel eyes.

My brows drew together. "It would be okay if Cash cleaned?"

"He works for me."

Oh.

Well that explained it.

"I was just... trying to do something nice. You're doing a lot for me. I just thought..."

"Babe," he said, cutting me off, his tone lighter than usual. "You don't owe me anything. You want to clean, you're bored... have at it. Don't do it for me 'cause you think you need to pay me back. Okay?"

"Okay," I agreed.

"You guys all set?" Cash asked, coming in, smoke clinging to his skin. "I got your text," he said, nodding at Reign. "I'll take care of it." He paused. "The boys are gonna get suspicious if they don't see you in church tomorrow though, bro."

Reign's eyes cut to me for a second. "I know. I'll figure it out," he said and Cash just shrugged.

Cash walked past me, winking. "See you soon, Cherry. I'll bring shoes."

"Thank you," I said, meaning it.

He hit his brother on the shoulder, then was gone. The rumble of a bike pulled away and Reign and I were alone.

"Car is gone," he told me, walking into the kitchen to put on a pot of coffee despite having downed the huge coffee Cash had brought him earlier. "Tree is still there, but the car is gone."

"Is that weird?"

"Township would have dealt with the tree too."

"But it's got to be a mess out there. Maybe they're just swamped."

"No, babe. V got his car towed."

"You can't know that."

"I know it," he corrected. "V wouldn't want people finding his car smashed up on the road."

"How far from the crash site are we?" I asked, trying to keep my voice calm. I had been so worked up the night before, I had no idea how long we drove. If it wasn't far from the site, then what were the chances that V wouldn't...

"I see those gears turning," Reign broke into my inner freak out. "Relax. We're about half an hour from the spot. There are plenty of houses between us and there. No one is coming here," he said, coming up closer. "I promise you're safe here. Okay?"

I looked up into his eyes, and I mean *up*, he was so much taller than me. I saw nothing but certainty there. If he was half as capable as he thought he was, then he was definitely someone I could trust. "Okay," I said, my voice oddly quiet. My air felt stuck in my chest with him so close, with his eyes on mine, watching me, and I swear he could see right inside.

"Okay," he repeated and his hand slowly raised, paused for a second in the air, then moved to tuck my hair behind my ear.

I think I shivered.

Okay. I definitely shivered.

And he definitely noticed.

"Good shiver or a 'get your fucking hands off of me you dirtbag' shiver?"

Surprised, I choked on a laugh.

"I'll take that as a good one," he said, giving me a small smile that I swear melted my new pretty cherry panties. His hand went away and he took a step back, running it through his own hair. "Shit," he mumbled to himself.

"What's the matter?" I asked, watching him.

"Nothin'," he said, going over to the fridge and grabbing a bottle of water. "I'm going to the basement. Stay in the house."

With that, he disappeared.

Yeah. Something was the matter. He just wasn't going to tell me.

And I had no right to feel indignant about that.

He was keeping something from me.

But I was keeping a lot from him too.

EIGHT

Reign

She was keeping something from me.

It had been something that had been rolling around in my head since I got up in the morning. Her story worked in an abstract kind of way. But it wasn't right. It didn't fit perfectly. V might have been a criminal, but kidnapping and extortion seemed beneath him. He had bigger business than that. It just didn't work.

So she was lying. Or at the very least lying by omission.

Though why she would do that was completely beyond me.

Unless she didn't trust me.

Which didn't sit right.

I didn't like that.

She trusted Cash. Right off. The second he greeted her, she trusted him. Rightfully so; he was trustworthy. But so was I. And I still hadn't won her over. She was protecting her full truth from me. Which was only putting her at risk. She needed to trust me fully.

Then I went and fucking tucked her hair behind her ear.

What the fuck was that about?

I wasn't a hair-behind-ear-tucker.

Then she shivered.

Shivered.

Fuck.

I threw myself down the stairs, going over to the bag. It was beat up, duct tape holding the guts inside it in more than a few places. I needed to hit something to get some of the sexual frustration out.

I'd been fucking half hard since I laid eyes on her.

Which wasn't going to get me anywhere in getting her to trust me. I needed to keep my hands off of her. And it wasn't going to be easy.

The ride hadn't helped. Usually it helped ease some of the tension. I spent a lot of time on my bike trying to clear my head, trying to sort through club shit. Sometimes the only thing that helped was taking off on the road, being alone. Nothing but the wind and the sound of my bike.

But it hadn't helped me make sense of Summer.

It certainly didn't help to come back and see her shiver when I touched her. Not flinch away. Not freak the hell out. No... she reacted. Not like one of V's girls would have reacted. Just like any woman would react.

I took to the bag, beating it until my fists felt raw. The kind of raw, burning sensation you got right before the skin broke open. I sat down on the bench, staring at the walls.

I didn't feel any better.

My phone blinked and I reached for it.

Cash: You're fucked.

I'm not fucked.

Cash: Saw how you looked at her.

She's hot.

Cash: More than that and you know it.

Nothin' gonna happen. What's up at the club?

Cash: Bitching about clean up. Hungover. Had a Blackout party last night.

No word on V?

Cash: Saw one of his guys in the ghetto looking around.

Keep me posted.

He was looking already. That was good. The sooner he ran through the area, the better. No one had seen her. He would move on.

Not that he would stop looking for her. She was important. I didn't know why she was important. And maybe she didn't even know why she was important, but I was going to make sure of that.

She wasn't going to keep shit from me anymore.

NINE

<u>*Summer*</u>

I heard the pounding and the sound of chains smacking together. I'd seen enough movies to place the sound. A punching bag. He had a punching bag. Listening, a weird sense of morbid humor came over me and I had to force myself not to laugh. Because it was twisted to even think it:

He had a punching bag in a basement. I used to *be* a punching bag in a basement.

What was wrong with me?

Then just as suddenly as it started, it stopped and I heard his booted feet stomping on the steps, then the door to the basement slammed shut.

Angry.

Even his footsteps in the hallway sounded angry.

I skirted around the bed, my heart flying into my throat, trying to put space between us. Because I knew he was coming. He was coming and he was pissed.

He stepped into the doorway, his hair wet with sweat, his hands clenched into fists, his shoulders tight. His eyes fell on me. And just like that... the anger seemed to deflate. His shoulders went slack, his hands unclenched, his eyes looked almost sad.

"Christ," he said on an exhale. His head ducked, his hand running across his brow before his eyes came up to me again. "I'm not gonna hurt you, babe," he said, his voice soft. "Never, okay?" he said, stepping into the room. I felt myself retreat and watched him wince. "Babe, eyes," he commanded and I lifted mine to his. "Long as I'm around no one will ever hurt you, okay?"

He meant that.

He didn't even know me, but he was going to make sure that never happened again. And I believed him.

"Okay."

"Okay," he said, nodding. "I'm gonna take a shower then you and me, we're having some words. You're gonna talk, understand?"

Shit.

He knew I was lying to him.

He knew and he wasn't going to let me get away with it.

"Yes," I answered, nodding, though inside I knew that couldn't happen.

I couldn't let that happen. It would put me at risk. It would put my father at risk.

"Give me ten," he said, then was off. Not ten seconds later, I heard the shower turn on.

I turned, grabbing the sweatshirt off the bed and throwing it on. I had no shoes. But there was nothing I could do about that. I took off my socks, stuffing them inside the pocket of my sweatshirt, then crept down the hall, wincing anytime a floorboard squeaked. I made it to the front door, unlocking it, then slipping out, closing it as quietly as I could manage.

Then I ran.

The field seemed like it was endless. The ride in hadn't seemed so bad. But then again, I wasn't doing it on foot. It was at least an acre. But I could see the gate. My heart was pounding in my chest, half from running and half from... well... the very strong feeling that I was doing the wrong thing. That it wasn't a good plan.

That I would only ever be safe with Reign.

But that was so ridiculous that I dropped to the ground beside the gate, looking for the button.

It wasn't there.

But it had to be there.

There was always a button. I had been in my fair share of gated homes in my past. There had to be a button to press to get out.

"The fuck you doing?"

Shit.

I flew back, falling onto my ass hard enough for me to yelp slightly. My eyes found Reign's well worn boots near my feet. I followed the line up, finding dark wash jeans slung low on his hips and... nothing else. He was shirtless again. My eyes crept upward to his face, his mouth parted slightly, his brows drawn together.

"Summer..." he said and the paralysis in my body flew away and I scrambled up on to my feet, brushing past him. "Babe," he said, his hand grabbing my arm from behind, "the fuck?"

Then he was turning me to face him, pushing my back against the hard metal gate. The hand that wasn't holding my arm lifted, knuckles sliding across my jaw and slowly tilting my face up to his.

"Why you running?" he asked, his voice soft. Well, as soft as someone who gargled glass could get.

I felt my lips part to answer, but the words didn't come as I looked into his hazel eyes. Watching, something crossed them. Something heated. Something that made his eyelids lower slightly.

"Fuck it," he said under his breath.

And then his lips were on mine, sending a jolt through my body. There was no hesitation, no softness. His lips seared into mine, branding me in a way that was almost painfully hot, but so consuming that I didn't even think about the fact that I was going to walk around the rest of my days marked by Reign. Even if it had crossed my mind, I don't think it would have mattered. Because I just... melted into him. My arms went up around his neck, pressing my body into his, my hands sinking into his wet hair. His tongue slipped across the crease in my lips. They parted and his tongue slipped inside.

I sighed against his mouth and the hand that was holding my arm slid down, curling around my back and holding me tight to his body.

And it felt right.

Which was stupid.

But it felt right in his arms. It felt safe. It felt like I belonged there.

Whoa.

What the hell?

That was absurd.

As if having a similar internal dilemma, Reign's head shifted and lifted, his breath warm on my cheek.

Free of the contact, I sucked in a shaky breath, trying to pull myself together. Because that was how I felt- pulled apart. Unraveled.

He unraveled me.

Okay. I needed to get a grip.

It was a kiss.

Just a kiss.

"Eyes," he commanded.

My gaze lifted and found his. Fierce. Mean enough to stare my demons down.

"Don't ever run away from me," he said, half-warning, half-pleading.

And I was so shocked to see someone like him, someone so strong and terrifying, begging for something from me that I didn't hesitate to agree. "Okay."

"Okay," he repeated, dropping my jaw, then releasing my hips. But his hand moved down and grabbed my hand and started pulling, practically dragging, me back across the field to the house.

He kicked off his boots inside the door, still holding my hand, then walked barefoot toward the kitchen, pouring himself a coffee, black. Then he turned to me, letting my hand go, grabbing my hips, and hauling me up onto the counter. "Think you can manage to keep your ass planted there for a minute?" he asked, his words hard but there was a trace of humor in his voice.

He turned back to the coffee, poured another cup, then went about adding cream and sugar to it before he handed it to me.

"You don't like it black, say something," he instructed as I took a sip and sighed. "Now why the fuck you running?"

I looked down at my coffee cup, lowering it onto my thigh. "You wanted to talk."

"And you didn't wanna explain the truth of what happened to you?"

"Something like that," I conceded.

"Babe, If I'm gonna protect you... need to know the facts."

"I don't even know where to start."

"At the beginning."

**

It was a bad day. I was on my second week at the new job my father had assigned me to and I felt like all I did was mess up then scramble to fix it before everyone else realized how incompetent I was. Before the rumors about nepotism started, as they always did. Until I couldn't take them anymore and asked my father to transfer me. It was a chicken move and I knew it, but I didn't like people knowing I had positions of power that I technically hadn't earned in the least.

So I wasn't in the best of moods. I had stormed into my apartment and went straight to the red. Wine, that is. And I drank a bottle. By myself. On an empty stomach. I was a stumbling mess going to my bedroom, reaching into my closet for pajamas. I settled on the pink silk shorts and the white tank top and struggled into them, falling once in the process and banging my shin hard enough to see stars and get an almost immediate bruise.

"Ow," I whined, sitting down on the edge of my bed, rubbing my leg. "Perfect end to my day," I grumbled, feeling the wine lead me steadily toward self-pity.

I crawled up to the top of my bed, sitting back on my heels for a second, staring out of the floor-to ceiling windows that surrounded me, taking in the view I far too often took for granted, before flinging myself forward into the soft pillows, slipping under the sheets, and having a pity party that ended in tear-covered pillows.

I heard nothing.

Whether that was from the wine or their abilities, I would never know.

All I knew was that one moment I was fast asleep, the next someone was on top of me, a hand over my mouth as I opened it to scream. The weight of his body held my pelvis in place and I was momentarily too stunned to do anything with my hands.

"Hurry the fuck up. V is waiting," another voice said and my foggy eyes searched around in the dark, not able to find the source of the other voice and feeling the panic well up strong. It was in the rolling in my belly, in my heartbeat that felt like it was lodged in the back of my throat, in the chill that sent goosebumps all over my body.

The guy on top of me reached behind him into his pocket.

Then I saw a needle.

And I remembered I had arms. And while they may have felt weak and heavy from wine and sleep, I reached out, raking them across his face, pressing as hard against his eyes as my squeamish stomach would allow.

"Fucking bitch," he howled, leaning forward and stabbing the needle into the side of my neck.

Things went slow and fuzzy for a second, but the last thing I got to see before I passed out was the claw marks I had scratched across his face.

I woke up slowly. The first thing that hit me was the cold. It was the kind of cold that settled into your bones, that made you feel like you would never be warm again. The second thing to hit me was the pain in my wrists. The third, the pounding in my head. The fourth, I was in a bed. A bed that wasn't my own. The fifth, the smell. Urine. It smelled like urine.

Then I remembered. My apartment. The wine. Hitting my shin. Crying myself to sleep. Men in my room. The pressure of his weight on my hips. His hand on my mouth. His skin under my fingers. The stab in my neck.

I flew upward, my shoulders screaming as I nearly yanked them out of their sockets before I realized they were bound to the headboard. I yelped, settling back down, twisting my head around to see the ropes holding me in place on a bed that smelled musty and old. The rope was tight, pulling at the delicate skin on my wrists. I rolled onto my side, pushing my wrists together, and looking around.

I didn't have much (okay, any) experience with basements myself. Not real basements. The ones that weren't finished and made into dens or exercise rooms. But I'd seen movies. Mostly horror movies. The girls always ended up in the basement with the thick cinderblock walls and the barred windows that were too high and too small to crawl out of anyway. It was always in the basements that they were brutalized in new and inventive ways. Because no one would hear their screams.

I was in a basement.

But I saved my breath.

Because I knew I wouldn't be heard.

I needed to focus.

I needed to fight through my hangover and get my wits about me.

There was nothing around except the bed and a staircase leading up. I could see that because the sun was shining through the barred windows. So it was morning, at least.

I needed to get my wrists free. I needed to get my wrists free and take a chance at the door. If I was tied up, maybe there wasn't someone standing guard. I could try it. It was my only shot.

I worked on the knots for hours, only accomplishing burns and making the ropes pull tighter.

I fell back on the bed with a cry of desperation.

Because when a woman is taken, there is only one reason.

Ever.

There is only one reason men take women.

And I had seen the news reports. I had watched the documentaries.

Human trafficking.

The skin trade.

I was going to be sold off and raped every day for the rest of my life. Or until I wasn't pretty anymore. And American women made for a pretty penny overseas. I would be popular. If I was too resistant, they would hook me on drugs so I was compliant.

I needed to escape.

And I tried. Hour upon hour. Day upon day. No one came. Not to let me go to the bathroom. Not to let me eat. Not to give one second of a break from the agony of not knowing.

Three days.

Three fucking days until I heard the door open. Until I heard footsteps on the stairs.

Three days and my captors had the sick, twisted opportunity to also be my saviors.

"Piss yourself yet?" a man asked, walking up. In another world, in another situation, he might have been attractive. He was tall and muscular with a thin well-proportioned face with bright blue eyes. But in my world, in my basement with my blood covering the pillow behind me, with my bladder so painful I was sure I had gotten a UTI, and my belly so hungry I felt sick, he was the ugliest thing I had ever seen.

"Come on," he said when I didn't answer. He stalked over to the bed, untying my hands. "Get up." But I couldn't. I couldn't trust my legs. "Suit yourself," he shrugged, reaching for the ropes and dragging me off the bed. A cry escaped my lips as the rope bit into my torn wrists. And I knew immediately that it was a mistake because he looked over his shoulder, smiling wickedly, then tugging me harder across the floor toward the stairs.

I scrambled up onto my knees, crawling up the steps so I wouldn't be dragged. As soon as we were up the landing, though, I was being pulled again. And we weren't alone. Wherever I was, there were people everywhere. There were a lot of men: standing around, lounging around, some with women on their laps, some with guns on their hips. Most of them looked over, their eyes blank, like girls getting dragged down the hall by ropes on their wrists was an everyday occurrence.

I got the painful, gut-wrenching realization that it probably was.

I was at the hands of real monsters.

It also didn't escape my notice that wherever I was being held was not some compound or warehouse. It was a home. An actual home. A huge, lavish one, but a home nonetheless.

We rounded a bend and I scrambled up to my knees to climb up the main staircase. It was huge. It felt like I climbed forever. At the landing, I was yet again pulled. Down a long hall. All the way to the end. There were two doors, one to each side. I was thrown into the one on the left.

"Five minutes," the man snarled, shutting me into a, yes... thank God, a bathroom.

Horrified with a time restriction, I counted in my head as I took care of myself. As I washed haphazardly in the sink. As I tried to clean out the cuts on my wrists. Then I guzzled as much water as I could, feeling so dry that my lips were cracking, but also almost painfully aware of how if I drank more, and didn't get a bathroom break again, it would mean more agony, more trying to hold it.

"Time's up, princess," I was told, my ropes grabbed again. And I was pulled into the hall and pushed into the room to the right.

It was a bedroom.

There were wrought iron head and foot boards, white dressers, and a mirror on the wall from the foot of the bed.

A mirror. Glass. I could use that.

Until I couldn't.

Because I was tied to the bed.

"Fucking shame to waste this opportunity," he said, shaking his head as he straddled my waist to tie me up. His hips shifted onto me and I could feel his hard-on through his jeans, pressing up against the juncture of my thighs. My hips jerked away from the sensation and he laughed. "Yeah, you want it too? Don't you, slut? Don't worry. I'll have you," he said, running his tongue across my neck. "I'll have you in every hole. I'll fuck you until you get hoarse from screaming. And then I'll fuck you some more," he said, grinding his dick into my pelvis. "Just not yet," he said, jumping off of me and ambling over to the door, shutting it and I heard a lock from the outside.

I tugged frantically but, ultimately, uselessly at the ropes. Then I turned my head into the pillow and screamed.

**

"They didn't come to take me out of the room for two more days," I told Reign, looking away from him, over his shoulder, out the window into the backyard. Because, despite my mind screaming at me that it was stupid to, I felt embarrassed.

"What happened after that? You met V?"

I nodded. "Deke and Martin came for me two days later, dragged me out of bed. Gave me my five minutes. Then we went down to the basement. The bed was gone. There was just a chair and I wasn't even tied to it. Then V came down the stairs. In a suit. He had a gray suit on and a newspaper under his arm. He told me he was going to video call my father, let him see that I was alive and well and then he told me to try to convince my dad to agree to his deal."

"What deal?"

Shit.

I didn't want to share that part. It was risky. For everyone involved.

"Summer," Reign said, and my eyes snapped to him. "You need to be honest with me."

Right.

Okay.

"My dad is an importer," I supplied, shrugging.

"An importer?"

"Yes. As in... shipping containers."

There was a pause, Reign looking at me with drawn-in brows. Then, not more than a few seconds later, the recognition hit. "Shipping containers?" he asked and I nodded. "For the girls? V wanted to import girls in your dad's containers."

"Yeah."

"Fuck."

"Yeah."

"And then?" Reign prompted, looking at me.

"And then I saw my dad on the video and... I don't know. I don't know what got into me. I freaked. I begged him not to take the deal. No matter what they did to me. I told him not to do it. Because those girls would suffer worse. I wasn't worth hundreds of them. I *begged* him, Reign," I said, my voice thick with the memory.

Reign nodded, his hand reaching out to stroke my hair. "I'm guessing that didn't go over well."

"I'd never been hit before," I admitted. "Not once. Ever. Not even kids on a playground. No boyfriend raised a hand to me..."

"Fuckin' better not have."

"So I just... I had no idea what I got myself into. And V was... pissed."

Reign's naturally hard face softened. "Talk to me," he urged. "Shit can't stay bottled up. Tell me. I can take it."

And then I did, my words half-running together, tumbling over each other for a chance to leak out of my system. I had never been a gusher, but I was gushing. I was bursting at the seams to tell someone my story. I needed to tell someone how it felt to have a fist collide with my jaw, eye socket, nose; how boots to the belly, to the ribs, felt; what it was like to have handfuls of my hair torn from my scalp; how it was to be left on a cold basement floor afterward, bleeding everywhere, too sore to move, too stunned to cry; then how it felt to be dragged back up a few hours later by one of my attackers who seemed to take a sick pleasure in jostling me every which way, getting off on my gasps and yelps, so much so that I bit hard enough into my lip to break it open, trying to keep the noises inside.

"Babe..." Reign's voice said, quietly, so quietly. His hand reached out, brushing over my cheek and it was then I realized I was crying. Not just crying, purging it all. For the first time. Before I could even react, Reign's arms went out, wrapping around my back, pulling me to his chest and holding me there.

Holding me.

The big, bad, scary biker dude with the guns and illicitly obtained money... was holding me.

And I was sinking into it. Into him.

My arms went around his back, holding on. My face was buried against his chest, warm, naked, smelling like soap and just... man. I took a shaky breath.

"Fuckers gotta pay."

Surprised, I jerked in his arms, but he just squeezed me tighter.

"What?"

"Those bastards who hit and kicked and taunted you... the fucker who ordered it and watched it... they gotta pay."

"It's over," I said, in the strange position of feeling like I needed to comfort him.

"It will never be over. That's the problem. You'll live with this on your soul for the rest of your life. Wakin' up screaming 'cause you feel guilty. This will be a part of you now. And they need to fucking pay for that."

"Reign..."

His body tightened, his arms releasing me enough to look down at me. "They're gonna pay, babe. You ain't gotta know nothing about it. But they're gonna pay."

"I can't ask you to..."

"You're not asking me. Still doing it."

"He's dangerous."

"I'm fucking dangerous," Reign said, a fierceness overtaking his features and I didn't doubt that was true.

There was no reasoning with him.

"You can't put your people in danger because of me."

"I'm not putting any of my men in danger. This is between me and V."

"Reign..."

"Like when you say my name, babe," he said, surprising me enough to shut my mouth. "Like it a whole lot which is why you're gonna step out of my arms and go plant your ass on my bed. And I'm gonna plant my ass on the couch."

"What?" I asked, feeling his fingers trace across my back in small shapes. And it felt good. Oh, my God did it feel good. Good enough that I almost asked why he wasn't going to bed with me. Almost.

"Gonna take ya if you don't get away from me. Don't want to fuck up your head any more than it already is. So I'm gonna let you go and you're gonna go in the bedroom and I'm gonna stay out here."

Wait. What?

He was going to take me?

As in... to bed? As in... sleep with me? Because I wasn't entirely opposed to that idea. To feel a touch on my skin that didn't want to hurt me. To feel pleasure at a man's hands instead of pain. I wanted that.

But also... fuck up my head any more than it already is?

My head was not fucked up.

In fact, I was pretty damn proud of how well I was holding myself together.

His arms slipped off of me, then reached to grab my arms, pulling them from around his back and dropping them. "Go," he said, nodding his chin toward the bedroom. When I didn't immediately step away, his brow quirked up. "Fucking go, Summer."

So I went.

The whole way to the bedroom, my belly was flip-flopping at the sound of my name on his lips. I closed the door, throwing myself down on the bed, putting a hand to my racing heart, trying to sort through things.

Reign wanted to go to some sort of underground criminal war with V.

He wouldn't listen to reason about it.

And I had spilled my guts to him. And then I cried.

I fucking... *cried.*

I'd never cried in front of a man before. Not in my life. Never. Not once. And I cried in front of him. And then he wiped the tears and he...

Held. Me.

Then, of course, there was that other little matter.

Reign wanted to have sex with me.

And I was pretty sure I wanted to have sex with him too.

REIGN

Fuck.

TEN

Reign

"You're fucking joking," Cash said, the beer he had been bringing to his lips dropping down by his side.

We were at the compound. It was something I wasn't too happy about. But it was also something I couldn't get out of. Cash had been right, the guys would freak if I wasn't in church on a Friday night.

So I was at the compound.

The building itself was a low, windowless structure that had been a mechanic shop before the recession took it down. It was surrounded by tall, barbed wire fences all around. I bought it dirt cheap and used it to our best advantage, building off the back and creating rooms for as many of the men as possible. The front had a garage door that lifted to reveal my baby: a hummer with military-grade weapons on the top. If someone wanted to fuck with us, they met my baby. So far, we'd only had to use her once. And we didn't even get a chance to *use* her. Once they saw her, they went scrambling with their tails between their legs.

The compound had a flat roof which was manned at all times. I didn't fuck around about security. We weren't exactly involved in legal activities and there was always some shit group trying to fuck with us, take what's ours, steal our guns and try to run them themselves. Suffice it to say, I am not a fan of being stolen from. So I was always on the offense, but with a strong as fuck defense if I needed it.

The waiting room and office that used to exist was ripped out and replaced with a bar, seating, and room for a pool table. A massive sound system and flatscreen was across from the seating area and metal was blasting loud as fuck from the speakers.

The meeting was long over and the probates were called in. Things were in full swing. All the men were around, a sea of jeans, tees, and black leather cuts.

The Henchmen cuts.

My cuts.

Before me, my father's cuts.

"You're taking this over," he told me when I was sixteen. "All this will be yours. The men will count on you. And you will reign. And Cash will be right there with you."

The old man had a lot of ideas.

Not least of which was naming his sons.

Reign and Cash.

Power and money.

The only things in life that were important.

If our mother had squeezed another of us out before she died, he probably would have been named some shit like Loyalty or Comrade.

Power. Money. Brotherhood.

"You fuck her?" Cash asked, bringing me out of my memories.

"No."

But Cash had a good eye. And he was the only person who really knew me. "Bull fucking shit."

"Kissed her. That's it."

'That's it' wasn't exactly the right way to put that.

Because kissing her had felt like being in the sun, like feeling the warm rays on your skin after being underground for your entire life.

Lame, but that's what it was fucking like.

Bitch was under my skin and I knew it. And Cash knew it. And it was a problem.

"Then why the fuck you all gung-ho to start a fucking war, man?" he asked, grabbing my arm, dragging me down the hall of bedrooms, past two bitches sucking face, and into my room.

My room was where I brought my bitches. It boasted a big California king bed, black sheets, dark gray walls, a dresser with some changes of clothes, and a flatscreen. There was a bathroom off the side. It was nothing special. It was streamlined, sterile almost. Because it wasn't home. It was a fuckpad. It was where I crashed when I tied on one too many to drive back to my place.

Cash slammed the door, leaning against it, his arms crossed over his chest.

"We're not going to war. This is just on me." I paused, shaking my head at his anger. "She told me some of her story, man," I told him, sitting down on the edge of my bed. "Just a small fucking part of it. She was cryin' tellin' me. They fucking tortured her. Beat her until she couldn't stand. Starved her. Threatened to rape her."

"This is V. This shit is nothing new," Cash said, shrugging. Sometimes, not often, but every once in a while, Cash could be the coldest fuck you've ever met. This was one of those times. Gone was the brother everyone knew - charming, funny, laid-back, womanizing. This was Cash, the criminal. And he was ice.

"Her father is an importer," I said, dropping the bomb.

All I got was a raised brow. "He's trying to scare her father into giving him access to the containers," he guessed.

"Yeah."

"To ship in girls."

"Yeah."

Cash bit down on the inside of his cheek, a habit he did when he was thinking, a tell he had when he played poker. His eyes cut back to mine, his voice low and hollow when he said, "You sure you want to do this? Think long and think hard. V has been trading skin since Pops was in charge here. You know that. I know that. Dad certainly knew that. This is not new fucking information. Going against him with the entire club behind you would be risky. Going after him alone is a fucking suicide mission."

I knew what I was asking him to accept. And I knew why he needed to remind me. That's why he was VP. Not because of blood obligation. But because he was the only one strong enough to stand up to me when he thought I needed it. And then back the fuck down and do his job when I gave him the go, regardless of his personal feelings.

That being said, he was still my brother. And he thought I was being reckless. And he wasn't going to give in easily.

The burden of power didn't rest easy on my shoulders. I wasn't dumb or careless enough to always believe I was right. I fucked up. I made bad decisions. But, ultimately, those decisions were mine to make. I had to do that. And I had to deal with the consequences. No one else knew how heavy that hung.

So I couldn't ask them to get behind me on a personal vendetta.

My teeth clenched together when I looked at him.

"She. Fucking. Screams."

Cash's eyes flashed and he sighed, running a hand across the shaved side of his head. "So he has to pay."

"He has to pay."

"When are you telling the men?"

"I'm not. They don't need to know this."

"Reign..."

I knew that voice. It was the 'you're being an idiot' voice.

"They don't need to know this. They know this, they'll want in and I'm not bringing another war on them. The new guys might not remember, but the last war cost us huge. It cost us Pops, man."

Cash ducked his head, nodding. "And now you're asking me to let you go ahead and get yourself killed. Think of the club, man."

"I die, the club has you. Case closed. But I ain't dying so stop worrying like a woman over it."

He sighed and his mouth opened, wanting to say more, before he closed it again. "So what the fuck we doing up here gabbing like bitches then?" he asked, giving me one of his lazy, easy grins. "There is whiskey and pussy down the hall and I got a taste for both," he said, wrenching the door open. "Ever lick whiskey off pussy, man?" he asked casually, walking back down the hall. "Fucking heaven."

Cash was back.

And there was nothing standing between him and his booze or his bitches. So I let him go, standing back against the bar, nursing my whiskey.

"Hey, Prez," Wolf said, moving to stand next to me. Wolf was a huge wall of a man. He was tall and solid. If he ran into a brick wall, the wall moved. He was a few years older than me, his dark hair kept in some obnoxious undercut style with a massive, but carefully groomed beard. His honey-light eyes caught mine and held. "What's going on?"

"Nothing yet."

"Hear things?"

"Feel it," I half lied.

"When you need me," Wolf said, tipping his beer at me.

Wolf was a quiet fuck. He never had more than five words to rub together at a time, but he was as loyal as they came. And he was his own brand of ruthless that came in handy in a lot of operations.

"I know, man. Appreciate it."

"Need a bitch?" he asked, no doubt sensing my sour mood.

I needed the bitch back at my house. In my bed. Holding my gun that I had shoved at her and told her how to use it, just in case. I needed her. But I wasn't gonna get her.

"Yeah," I said, throwing back my drink.

Fuck it.

ELEVEN

Summer

He left me.

I spent a full day with my 'ass planted on his bed' watching endless hours of television and falling asleep out of pure boredom. I only went out once, to use the bathroom and shower. And there he was with his 'ass planted on the couch,' wide awake, staring out the backdoor into the yard. He didn't so much as glance my way.

He didn't offer me food and I didn't ask.

I had already eaten enough to hold me over for a week.

He didn't come in to change or sleep in his own bed.

I smelled coffee in the morning, but I didn't go out to grab any. I heard him downstairs, the chain on the punching bag clang, clang, clanging away for the better part of an hour. Then he came up and showered. Then I found myself wondering what he was wearing since his clothes were in the bedroom and he hadn't come in.

I got a strong mental picture of him walking around naked and I didn't exactly push that thought away. Okay. I kinda relished in the thought for a few minutes. Alright. Maybe like half an hour. But no one would blame me. Knowing how good that man looked shirtless, one could only assume he was good looking everywhere.

I wasn't a man-crazy girl. Before V, before I was taken, before everything... I worked long hours and then made a lot of time for girlfriends. Shopping. Socializing. Coffee dates. Midnight margaritas on Thursdays. Pedicures on Sundays. I kept my time full. But very rarely with men. I dated casually when someone acceptable showed interest. But it usually didn't get very far. I had three relationships. And by "relationships" I mean we dated for an appropriate amount of time and then became exclusive and then had sex.

I wasn't a fling girl.

And I wasn't a girl who drooled over the opposite sex.

But I was drooling.

And I didn't understand it.

Maybe it was because he swept in all badass Prince Charming and saved me. Which was sort-of the truth. Even if his brand of saving came with threats of war and disappearing me.

Whatever the hell it was, it would pass.

Whatever my weird infatuation was, it would pass.

It wasn't like Reign No-Last-Name was a suitable choice for me.

Far from.

And I was ever practical about things like intimacy.

So it would pass.

I hoped.

And then around seven o'clock, after literally not a peep all day and half of the day before, he walked down the hall.

I felt my heart skip into overdrive as I frantically made sure my hair was an alluring kind of wild not the 'I rolled around in bed for an entire day and now birds could lay eggs in my hair' kind of wild.

Then he was in the doorway. Dressed. And I mean dressed. He had on black jeans, black tee, boots, and his cut. He also had a nasty looking gun in his hand.

"I have to go to the compound," he said as if it explained why he was approaching me with a gun.

I felt myself scramble up on the bed, slamming my back up against the headboard as he sat down on the mattress by my legs.

"I said I wasn't going to hurt you," he reminded me, holding up the gun by the side. "I'm going out and Cash has to go with me so I have to leave you alone. No one knows about this place but me and Cash. No one. So you won't have a problem. But for my peace of mind, I'm not leavin' you defenseless. I'm guessin' you ain't never used a gun before."

"No," I said, settling back into a more normal position.

He popped out the magazine, then pushed it back in, giving me a second to see the very shiny, very lethal golden bullets. "This is a gun," he explained unnecessarily. "Lotta cops use this. It's light but it might be wide for your little hands," he said, showing me the back of it. "It's loaded so you leave it on the nightstand unless you think there's trouble. If you think there's trouble, you pull this safety and you wrap your hands around the handle and you take your pointer finger and you lay it against the gun. You do not," he paused. "Look at me," he commanded and my eyes rose. "You do not put your finger on the trigger until you actually see a threat, understand? Finger stays on the gun so you don't accidentally fuckin' shoot me. You see a threat, you point for mid-body, you pull the trigger. And you keep fuckin' shooting until they go down."

"Okay," I found myself saying though I was pretty damn sure I would never be able to pick up the gun, let alone shoot someone with it.

Somehow, he picked up on that. He pulled the magazine and moved to grab my hand. "It's not loaded," he reminded me, shoving the gun into my right hand. "Now show me how I told you to hold it."

He was right. It was lighter than I thought a gun would be. But maybe that was only because the bullets weren't in it. I picked it up, wrapping three fingers around the handle, my thumb across the back, and my forefinger laying down the length of the side.

"Good," he said, getting off the bed and moving back toward the door. "Now aim it at me."

"What?"

"Babe, need to know you won't aim for my chest and hit my foot. Aim it at me." So I did. "Lower," he told me, and I lowered it slightly. "There. That's where you shoot," he said, nodding, making his way back toward me. He took the gun, loaded it, then handed it back to me. "Pick it up and point it toward the door. Now how do you pull the safety?" he asked, and I demonstrated. "Good. After that it's just wrapping your finger on the trigger and pulling. That's it. Got it?"

"Got it," I agreed, putting the safety back on and placing the gun on the nightstand. "So you're leaving."

"Just a couple hours. Wouldn't go if I didn't have to. You'll be fine."

And with that, he got up, walked out of the bedroom, slammed the front door, and rumbled off.

I jumped out of the bed, following my hunger toward the kitchen, rummaging around for whatever supplies Cash had dropped the day before.

And I found a lot of dude food: chips and glass jars of dips, peanut butter and jelly, white bread, boxes of cereal. With a shrug, I made a cup of coffee, grabbed a soda along with a bag of Doritos and a bag of corn chips and both dips: the salsa kind and the cheesy kind. I had been living on food I wouldn't have fed a dog for three months, I deserved to shamelessly eat junk food in bed on a Friday night.

So I did.

Then eleven rolled around. Twelve. One. Two. Three.

Still no Reign.

And then I heard it.

Awake and more than slightly freaked out about being alone, I had the TV down super low. And I heard it. Footsteps. But I hadn't heard a car or bike. There had been nothing. But there were footsteps. And then there was the front door closing. And then the footsteps were in the house.

My heart flew into my throat as I scrambled out from under the blankets and flew down onto the floor beside the bed. Then, realizing how girly and stupid a reaction that was when there was someone potentially coming in to drag me the fuck back to V, I stood up, grabbed the gun, pulled the safety, spread my legs wide, and aimed, my finger laying across the gun like I was told to.

And thank God it wasn't on the trigger.

Because not a second later, there was Reign in the bedroom doorway.

His head jerked up. Seeing me, his brow quirked, a smirk toyed with his lips. "Hey babe."

"You're drunk," I accused, still holding the gun aimed at his chest. My insides were starting to feel shaky from all the unnecessary adrenaline. But on top of that, I was pissed. He made me almost fucking pee myself in fear because he was too drunk to fucking think of announcing himself when he walked in the door?

"Yep," he agreed, still watching me, still looking amused.

And then it wasn't just my insides shaking. My arms were shaking so bad the gun could barely stay in focus. "You scared me," I accused.

"Baby..." he said, his voice dropping. He moved forward, wholly unconcerned about a shaking woman holding a loaded gun pointed at him. He got closer, clamping a hand on the top of the gun and pushing it downward before taking it from my hand, putting the safety back on, and putting it down on the nightstand.

"I didn't hear your bike and then there were footsteps..."

"Couldn't drive," he shrugged. Close up, I could see why. Well, no. I could smell why. He reeked of alcohol.

"Couldn't say it was you? You just let me have a fucking panic attack thinking someone was here?"

"Wasn't my brightest plan," he agreed.

"You could have..." the rest of my argument got muffled against the material of his shirt as he pulled me forward and wrapped his arms around me. And damn if I didn't melt right into him again, my arms going across his lower back as his stroked up my spine and into my hair.

"Won't do it again," he murmured and I felt his warm breath on my hair.

I nodded, relaxing into him, feeling my wobbly insides settle. I took a deep breath, expecting to inhale Reign: soap and man and the barest hint of manly detergent. But that wasn't what I got. What I got was smoke. And alcohol. And... perfume.

Perfume.

I felt myself straighten immediately, stiffening, my arms falling from around him.

"What's up?" he asked, squeezing me and suddenly I wanted him off of me. Away from me.

"You need a shower," I said, jerking away. My eyes fell as I stepped away from him, crawling back in the bed. "You stink of smoke and booze and perfume," I snapped, reaching for the remote and turning the volume back up.

I could feel his gaze on me for a long minute before he stepped away, walking over to the dresser, grabbing sweatpants, and going into the hall. The bathroom door shut and the shower water turned on.

And I drowned my very strange, very unwelcome feelings of jealousy in half a bag of Doritos smothered in cheesy dip.

Because jealousy was ridiculous. It was so ridiculous that they needed a new word for how ridiculous it was. He wasn't mine. He wasn't even close to mine. He was a random guy who did something nice for me. So what he kissed me? He was the hottest guy in five states wide, he probably kissed every half-bangable babe he crossed paths with. I wasn't special. I was just ready lips in close proximity to his.

Augh.

I was so stupid.

The shower stopped, the door opened, there was fiddling in the kitchen, and then I heard footsteps coming closer. Like, as in, he was coming back to the bedroom.

I kept my eyes on the TV, eating even though I felt ready to burst.

"Doritos in cold salsa con queso sauce?" He asked, putting his coffee cup on his nightstand.

"Dip," I corrected, my tone a little snippy.

"What?"

"It's dip, not sauce."

I could practically *feel* the eyebrow lift I was getting. I couldn't see it because I was refusing to look at him.

"What's got your panties in a bunch?"

Oh, the asshole.

Who asked women things like that?

"Nothing."

"Really? 'Cause you're acting like I'm some lazy house husband who forgot to rinse out his beer cans before he recycled them."

"Trust me," I said, my voice cold, "you have no effect on my panties, Reign."

That was the wrong thing to say.

Like... really wrong.

Like... he saw it as some kind of challenge wrong.

Because he was coming toward me, around the bed, sitting down by my hip. "I have no effect on your panties, huh?"

"Nope." Aside from the fact that anytime he got within five feet of me, I was turned on as all-get-out for no good reason.

"You're sure about that?" he asked, his voice dipping even lower than usual, the sound feeling like it slipped under my skin and reverberated against all my internal organs. His hand moved outward, stroking up my thigh, slipping slightly inward as he rounded my hip. And I should have pushed him off. I really should have. But I was too busy watching his big, beat up, scarred hand move over my pants, slide up toward the waistband, but not slip under. No, he stroked across my belly, sending a shock of wetness between my legs. As if sensing it, his hand moved downward, pressing hard between my thighs, making me arch up against him, and causing a throaty gasp to escape my lips. "No, no effect at all," he said, giving me a grin that would have just... melted my panties if I didn't get a very clear flash of him doing what he was doing to me to another woman. Just hours before.

And I was definitely not that girl.

The girl who was okay with that.

I jerked upright. "You want me," I started, making my eyes hold his even though the heat there made me want to lay back and tell him to *take me*, "you don't come to me with hands heavy with the scent of other women," I snapped, swinging my legs off the bed and storming toward the door.

I half expected him to follow me, to argue with me, or try to change my mind. But he didn't. I took myself out to the couch and settled in, staring at the empty fireplace until I finally passed out.

I woke up sometime later from a nightmare, being jostled up. My eyes shot open to find Reign looking down at me as he carried me back down the hall.

"You were screaming," he said gruffly, watching my face.

I rested my head against his shoulder, enjoying the feeling of his arms across my back and under my knees.

"Sorry I woke you up," I murmured, breathing in his scent.

His arms squeezed me tighter, and then I was being lowered into the bed, the sheets still warm from his body. I curled up on my side, pulling my knees to my chest. The lights dimmed. The TV stayed on, but low. Then the mattress depressed behind me as Reign climbed in. The blankets got pulled up.

And then I was in his arms. He scooted in behind me, his body curling around mine, his arm going across my belly, pulling me backward into him.

I was almost asleep, warmed by his body, comforted by his closeness, when he said softly in my ear, "Sorry I'm an asshole."

I fell asleep smiling.

TWELVE

Reign

Sorry I'm an asshole? Sorry I'm an asshole?

What the fuck had gotten into me?

I didn't apologize. Ever. Not ever. That was another thing that was brow beaten into me and Cash from a young age-apologizing was admitting weakness. We were not weak. We did not apologize for anything. We did what we damn well pleased and everyone else just had to man up and deal with that.

And then there I was... fucking apologizing to some chick I knew for two point three seconds for just being myself? For drinking and screwing around like I always did? For coming home late? For making her see she wanted me?

Alright. Maybe that was a dick move.

I hadn't even fucked the clubwhore.

She sat on my lap, reeking of perfume, and whispering dirty things she'd do to me.

But I had a vision of Summer flash into my mind and I lost any desire I had to fuck the bitch.

I could blame that unused desire for what happened.

But fact of the matter was, she was traumatized and abused and didn't know me.

But, fuck, walking in on her holding up that gun like she fully intended to use it, legs spread, arms steady... hottest shit I'd ever seen.

Then she started shaking and I felt like shit for being so fucking stupid. I was trashed. And I never had someone in my house to worry about scaring. It just didn't even cross my mind until I walked into the doorway and there she was.

But, fuck, she was wet for me.

That was something I stayed up awake thinking about for hours. Those thin yoga pants did nothing to hide how much she wanted me.

Then she was screaming again. The sound was something that sank into my skin, that lodged itself in my brain, a sound I was worried I would always hear. Even when she was gone. When she was safe and happy and away from me, I was pretty sure her screams would keep me awake at night.

I had to go out and get her. I couldn't just let her lay there alone, working through some shit memory because she wanted her space. She shouldn't have had to deal with any of that, least of all alone.

So I brought her to my bed, tucked her into my side. And there was no more screaming.

I got up early that morning, making coffee, trying to get away from her. Her scent was all over me. That lotion that Cash had bought for her. The shampoo in her hair. It was covering me. It was all over my skin. I needed to get the hell away from her before she woke up to me groping her all over.

"Hey," she said, her voice a sleep-filled whisper as she padded out toward me.

"You alright?"

Her head cocked to the side, her brows drawing together. "Yeah. Why?"

"Nightmares," I said, shrugging, throwing cream and sugar into a cup for her.

"Oh," she said, biting into her lip.

"Wanna talk about it?"

She shrugged her shoulders, taking her coffee, careful not to let her fingers touch mine. "Just the same old stuff," she said, trying to brush it off, but I could see the pain lingering there behind her eyes. "The dreams will fade eventually."

No they wouldn't. But I didn't want to tell her that. Instead, I reached into my pocket, grabbing the burner I had pulled out of the safe and charged. "Here," I said, holding it out to her.

She gave me a smile, reaching for it, her brow lifted. "Big bad biker guys don't spring for smart phones?"

"It's a burner. Call your father."

Her eyes widened. "What? You sure that's a good idea? I mean won't that like... put us or him at risk or something?"

"If his phones are tapped, yeah. Which is why you're going to keep it short and sweet. Say hi. Tell him you're safe. That he should not give into V's demands because he doesn't have you anymore. Tell him you'll be in touch when you can. Then hang up. Got it?"

She nodded, putting down her coffee cup, opening the phone and typing in a number. "Are you just going to stand there?" she asked, looking uncomfortable.

"Yep," I said, watching her hit the send button and bring the phone to her ear.

There was a long pause, her face seeming to crumple more and more as each ring went unanswered. "Dad?" she asked, finally, her voice a weird whisper. "No. Dad. Stop. I'm fine. Dad. Dad!" she said, almost yelling. Trying to talk over him, I imagined. "I got out. I got away. Yeah. I can't..." she said, looking over at me. "I can't tell you that but I'm okay. So don't agree to the deal, okay? No matter what. I, ah, I have to go. Yeah. I know. No, I have to go. I'll be in touch when I can. Okay. Love you too. Bye, Daddy."

I held out my hand and she gave me the phone, tears clinging to her lashes, but not spilling down her cheeks. I took the phone, removing the battery and SIM card and tossing them. "Good reunion?"

"He was confused and kinda... frantic. But he said he wouldn't do anything until he heard from me again."

"You did..." I started, then the rumbling caused me to cut off and look toward the door. Because I wasn't expecting Cash. And while, on occasion, he would drop by, it was never after a Friday night at church without some kind of communication about it. Two seconds later, he slammed through the front door and I knew something was wrong. "Fuck is it?" I asked, moving away from Summer.

Cash looked pointedly over at Summer. "It's a full-on fucking manhunt, man. There are men everywhere. Talking to everyone. Putting up a quarter mill for word on her."

"Two-hundred fifty thousand for me?" Summer croaked, looking pale.

"You'd be worth five times that in just over a year if your father went through with the deal," I supplied.

"And you were right," Cash went on, ignoring Summer which was so unlike him that I felt unease settling in. If he was ignoring a woman, his mind must be on more important things. And there was only one thing more important than women for him. "He's got the cops. They're all over with posters of her, claiming some missing person bullshit. They were at the club early this morning, starting shit."

I felt my back straighten. "What kind of shit?"

"Wanting to look around kind of shit. No warrant so they didn't get to see shit. But still. Not normal. We don't get heat from them. Why are they snooping?"

That was a good question. And there was no good answer. Unless someone saw me driving that night. Someone saw me with some bitch on my bike. Unless V had some clue. And if he had some clue, it wouldn't be long before he figured out I had a house. And that my house had very little to no protection.

"Fuck," I growled, running a hand down my face.

"Gonna have to move her," Cash said, watching me.

"Tell me some shit I don't already know, man."

"It's time to bring in the club on this."

"We ain't telling them, Cash. Understand me? We'll bring her. She's just a bitch I'm fucking with. That's it."

"Fine. But... do it now man," Cash said, his tone firm.

"It's that bad?" I asked, feeling too cut off from everything. Not liking it. Not liking Cash having to be my eyes and ears.

"Not yet. But it could be if they somehow have something to go on," he said with a nod.

"Can someone stop talking in weird badass 'we don't need to use complete sentences' lingo and tell me what is going on?" Summer asked, her voice strong if not with a hint of fear in it.

Cash looked over, his features softening. "Heya sweetheart," he started, giving her a small smile. "For some reason, V is sniffing around The Henchmen. And if he has a hunch on some chick he values in the millions, well he ain't gonna give up on it. So we got to move you out of here. There's no protection."

To her credit, she didn't freak. She barely even winced. "Where are you taking me?"

"To the club," I told her.

Then she freaked. Her voice got high and almost squeaky. "To the *club*?" she repeated. "Didn't he just say that the cops were snooping around? What's to stop them from going to get a warrant and doing some real snooping and finding me there? Or from V just charging in there looking for me?"

"First," I said, my voice calm. "Probable cause is what is stopping them. They don't even technically have a missing persons report." Which, speaking of, was something I hadn't considered before. Why wasn't there a missing persons report? Richard Lyon should have filed one. No matter what bullshit V fed him about not involving the cops. Good, upstanding citizens called the cops.

"And the part about V not charging in?" Summer persisted.

"No one charges into the compound," was my answer.

"That's it? That's all you got? No one's done it before so no one would try? Pardon me, but that is an asinine reason and you know it."

"You want protection? You stay with me. V might be a criminal, but he doesn't start a war by charging into someone's territory because he thinks something. He gets information first. And he ain't gonna get shit from us," I said, shrugging. "So pack your shit and be ready in twenty." She glared at me, arms crossed over her chest. "Fucking now, Summer."

Her eyes lowered, but she went to do what she was told.

"She's not wrong," Cash reasoned.

"I know that, but the compound is likely safer than here is at present. Not saying we're staying there."

"You want me to call Wolf? Get him to get here with the truck?"

"Yeah," I said, nodding. Though having to explain to him how I managed to keep my personal house from him all these years was not going to be fun. Or why we were sneaking a bitch into the compound for that matter. And why that bitch had her face plastered all over (fake) missing persons reports.

THIRTEEN

Summer

It was a stupid plan. It was a supremely stupid plan and he knew it and Cash knew it and I damn well knew it so I couldn't understand why we were all going along with it. Well, okay. I had very little choice. I didn't even have shoes for God's sake. And V was looking for me everywhere. A redheaded woman walking down the street wouldn't exactly go unnoticed.

So I had to go.

But why they were bringing me there, yeah, that made no sense whatsoever.

I grabbed the stuff off the floor in the bedroom, looking over at the gun, then pulling out the magazine and tucking that and the gun into a sweater that I rolled up. He had a whole arsenal. He wouldn't miss it. Besides, if there came a time when I couldn't tolerate their reckless stupidity and needed to take off on my own, having some kind of weapon would be a major asset.

I dragged everything into the bathroom, piling it into the shopping bags Cash had dropped off.

There was the sound of a car outside that had my heart spasming in my chest as I grabbed my bags. The front door opened and closed. And then there were three voices. Three.

Creeping over to the door, I pressed my ear against it, trying to see if the voices were raised or anything. Hearing only calm, deep tones, I opened the door and stepped out.

And then there was a giant hulking mass of a man standing between Reign and Cash, somehow managing to almost dwarf them with his size. And given that they were both their own tall piles of muscle, that was saying something.

The new guy was solid. As in... I was pretty sure he could pick up a truck like it weighed nothing more than a Matchbox. He had his hair in an undercut which was surprisingly fashion forward for a biker, and a long but groomed beard.

His eyes shifted, as if he had sensed my presence, and I was pinned under the intensity I saw there. Not just because they were a pretty honey color that I had never seen in person before, but because they seemed almost... empty. But in a different way than Martin's were empty. They were a haunted kind of empty.

"This is Wolf," Reign informed me, nodding to the guy who was still pinning me with his gaze. Seriously. I wasn't sure I could move forward if he didn't look away.

I swallowed hard against the dryness in my throat. "Ah... hi... Wolf." Who the hell was named Wolf? Seriously. That was not a name. Then again, neither was Reign. Or Cash for that matter. Were they even their real names? Oh, God... did I not know the real names of the men I was entrusting my life to?

"Woman," Wolf said, nodding at me, then looking away.

Woman? *Woman*? Did people actually greet other people like that? Was I supposed to just nod my head at bikers and say "man"? Seriously. Who taught them how to...

"Summer," Reign said, his voice frustrated like maybe he had called me more than once. Which was a possibility.

"What?"

"Gonna get your ass over here so we can go or what?"

"Well since you asked so nicely," I said dryly, moving toward them.

"Wolf is gonna take you in his truck." Oh, great. That was just wonderful. "He's got blackouts but you're gonna lay on the floor of the backseat."

"Seriously?" I asked, my brow shooting up. "Why not just throw me in the trunk like a corpse?"

"Ain't got a trunk," Wolf answered so seriously I almost laughed. Almost.

I sighed. "Fine. Backseat it is," I said, brushing past them toward the door. I glared at Cash as I passed. "You said you'd bring shoes the next time you visited," I said, looking down at my bare feet.

"Got them," he surprised me by saying. "Just couldn't bring them on the bike. I'll bring them by the compound later."

Seeing as he took the wind out of my sails, I walked outside to find a massive black pick-up truck, Reign's bike tied down in the bed of it. All three of them went toward the back, I imagined, to get the bike down. I threw all my bags on the seat, pulled my sweatshirt on, pulling up the hood, and attempted to haul myself upward. And I say 'attempted' because it was like a million feet off the ground and I couldn't even reach the grab bars to help myself in.

"Short," Wolf's voice said behind me, making me jump. And then, his huge hands went to my waist, almost spanning it completely. And I was off my feet, then flying into the backseat of the car. The door slammed as soon as I was inside and I sighed, getting down on the floor of the backseat which was, thankfully, clean. Almost brand new kind of clean.

The bed slammed closed, someone banged on the side of the truck. Then I heard Reign and Cash's bikes rumble to life and start to pull out. Wolf climbed up, slamming his door, and turned over the engine. "You aight?"

"Oh, yeah. Backseat floors are super comfy," I said, annoyed at myself for complaining.

"You're small," he said as if that made slamming into the front seats more comfortable.

Then we were moving. And there was no more talking. Not that that was surprising since Wolf seemed to have the vocabulary of a toddler.

To say I was anxious about going to this "compound" or "church" or "club" or whatever the hell it was called was an understatement. I liked it less that I was not really being given a choice. I had the distinct impression that if I refused to go with them, I would have ended up trussed up like a pig and deposited onto the floor regardless.

We drove for a while, my body bouncing none too gently over the bumps in the road before I felt the car idle for a minute and then pull in and park. Not given any directions about what to do after we arrived, I stayed on the floor and waited.

And waited.

And waited.

Finally, the door flew open at my feet and there was Wolf. "Woman," he said and I swear he was somehow able to communicate in that one word the phrase 'come on, we're here. I'll help you down'.

So I scooted out toward the door, slipping my legs down. Before I could even reach my feet down to the step-up bar, Wolf's huge mitts were around my waist and pulling me downward.

"Wait... I need to get my bags," I objected as I was pulled downward.

"Got 'em," Wolf said, putting me on my feet. And I took that as 'I will get them, don't worry about it.'

"Hands off," Reign's voice growled. Yes, growled. At Wolf. Whose hands fell from my waist which, admittedly, did not need to be there, but he had me pinned with those strange eyes of his again and I didn't even think to squirm away. Wolf made some kind of non-committal sound in his throat, reached into the backseat, and gathered my bags. "Bags," he said, holding them out to me.

"Thank you, Wolf," I said, giving him a genuine smile. I don't know why, what with the hollow eyes and weird lack of words, but I liked him. I understood him in a strange way. "I appreciate it."

He jerked his chin at me. "Later, woman." Then he ambled off into the building.

A building, I might add, that was or had been at some time, a mechanic shop. It was low, long, and windowless. It was also protected by huge fences with barbed wire on top. There were men on the flat roof with what looked like guns strapped around their backs. Off the back was a massive newer construction. Again, oddly windowless. The grounds were on the large side, picnic tables and chairs strewn about, a massive grill set up, a shed in the back.

"Babe," Reign's voice reached me. My eyes found his. "Gonna keep gawking all day or get your ass inside where it's safe?"

"Right," I said, stiffening as I fell into step beside him. I was led to the front door where music was coming from, loud for the early morning. Cash fell into step behind me. Wolf had already gone inside. I got two feet inside the door and froze. Because every eye, literally every eye, had fallen on me. There were dozens of rough and tough bikers. Some were young and attractive like Reign, Cash, and Wolf. Some were older, rougher, road-weary.

Cash's attention must have been elsewhere because he plowed into my back, making me stumble forward on a weird 'omph' sound.

"Sorr..." Cash started, but then Reign's arm went around my waist, pulling me tight up to him, and Cash and everyone else fell silent.

Apparently that was more of the weird biker no-words-needed conversations.

"Get everyone in here," Reign demanded. "We have church in ten," he said, then hauled me away.

He walked me through a doorway then down an amazingly long hall, all the way to the end where he unlocked a door and led me inside.

"You're tense," I observed as he stepped inside, letting my waist go. "I'm getting you guys in trouble," I said, my voice small as I looked around. There was a huge bed, dresser, door to the bathroom, and a T.V. That was it.

"Couple cops snooping around. No big deal. Don't worry about it."

"But I am worried about it," I countered, dropping my bags. "This is my mess, not yours. You shouldn't have to do this. To drag your men into this. It's pointless. You can just call that K guy. Disappear me. I'll take care of myself."

"Not an option."

"You said it was an option."

"Not anymore."

"That doesn't make any sense, Reign," I said, trying to catch his eyes but he kept his gaze lowered. "No one else should have to deal with V because of me."

"Did you ask me to?"

Augh. This again. "No."

"No. You didn't ask. You have no part in this. This is my business. And I see you don't know much about my kind of business, babe. But I can tell you one thing, we don't involve women in it. So keep your opinions to yourself. Stay in here. Lock the door. Don't open for anyone but me."

With that, he was gone.

And I was alone feeling my hackles rising, and staring at the giant bed that I had absolutely no plans on sitting on. Lord knew how many different deposits of bodily fluid were on those sheets.

So I went into the bathroom and sat on the edge of the bathtub.

And waited.

But I'd be damned if I got up and opened the door whenever he deigned to show back up again.

FOURTEEN

Reign

I started off small, soothing their nerves about the cops snooping around, about the heavy presence of V on our streets. Then I launched into a cover story for Summer. Because they'd seen her. They'd see her again. They needed to know she was under our protection.

"Cops want her. She's got a past," I said vaguely. It was true enough.

"You been keeping shit from us?" Vin, an old timer, a man who had practically helped raise me and Cash when Pops was busy, also the only person with balls enough to question me, asked.

Alright. I had been. I had been keeping a lot from them. And I was going to continue doing so. Because this wasn't going to involve them.

"I know they got pictures of her going up all over, calling her a missing person. But she ain't a missing person. She's my bitch."

My bitch?

My bitch?

What the fuck?

She wasn't my bitch. She wasn't anywhere close to my bitch.

I glanced over at Cash who had his arms crossed over his chest and was giving me the biggest fucking shit eating grin I'd ever seen.

Vin nodded.

It was that simple.

No one fucked with a Henchmen's old lady. No one. Not even the cops.

The only problem being that soon, and there was no telling how soon, but soon, I would have to explain why she wasn't my old lady anymore. And that just wasn't going to go over well.

"Anything else we forgot to discuss on Friday?" I asked.

"We got a big run in two weeks," Vin reminded me. "Meeting with the Russians. They need to see your face."

Yeah, they did. Unfortunately. *Fucking Russians*. "I'll be there. Cash will stay behind and keep an eye on things." Vin nodded, satisfied that I was handling business as usual. "Anyone have any other concerns?"

"What the fuck are we supposed to say to the pigs, man?" Dean, a headstrong kid in his mid-twenties, just patched-in a few months ago, asked.

"The cops aren't a problem since there isn't a real missing persons report. They're on a fishing mission. Don't give them shit and we won't have an issue with them."

"Aight," he said, looking less than comforted. He needed to be toughened up. It had been too long since the club had any real trouble. The young bloods hadn't had enough action to harden them.

"I want you guys on the probates. Keep an eye. Make sure they don't fuck up. Now's not the time to find out we have weak links." This was met with some table banging and beer raising.

Cash grabbed a bottle of Jack and raised it in the air. "Time to party. Call the bitches!"

I stayed with them for two rounds before slipping away, everyone occupied with the women or pool or conversation.

I knocked on the door. Waited. Knocked again. Waited.

Nothing. No noise inside. No nothing.

My heart started to slam in my chest as I reached for the key, jabbing it in the lock, mind running to the worst possible scenarios. Someone getting in while we were all busy in the meeting. Or, possibly, her sneaking out. It hadn't escaped my notice that she hadn't been very happy about moving. And she seemed obstinate enough to actually think she could make a go of it alone.

"Summer!" I shouted as soon as the door was open. Empty bed. Empty bedroom. "Fucking hell. Summer!" I rounded the corner to the bathroom. And there she was. Sitting on the edge of the tub. Pretty as you please. Looking up at me with a haughty chin lift. "Didn't fuckin' hear me knockin'?"

"I heard you."

That was it. She heard me. Her tone with a very strong 'so what' underneath it.

"Couldn't get off your ass and let me in?"

"You obviously had a key."

"Fuck's your problem?"

"No problem," she said, her voice with a strange edge to it. "Just sitting here... keeping my opinions to myself. As instructed."

I snorted, watching the fire rise in her eyes. So that was it. She didn't like taking orders. Well, that was just too fucking bad.

"Fuck you doing on the tub?"

Her head tilted. "I'm not sitting my ass on that science experiment you call bedding."

Well, she wasn't exactly wrong there. But I didn't fucking wash sheets. "Really? Then where you sleeping tonight?"

"You're an asshole," she said, standing up, and brushing past me. No, not brushing past. She plowed into my shoulder as she went. And, well, I couldn't very well just let her get away with that, could I?

FIFTEEN

Summer

One minute I was walking out of the bathroom, the next I was slammed against the bedroom wall hard enough to see stars for a second. But only for a second because the next second, Reign's lips were on mine. Hard. Hungry. Bruising into mine until I whimpered against him and his tongue slipped between my lips. His hands were planted on either side of my head, caging me in, his hips pinning mine to the wall.

And I kissed him back.

With everything I had.

Until my hands were grabbing the front of his shirt.

Until I was moaning and writhing against him.

Only then did he pull away.

My eyes opened slowly to see him looking down at me.

"Now go wash the sheets or you'll be sleeping on the floor tonight."

Then he was gone.

As I was still sputtering.

Sputtering.

Because what the hell was that?

Also, no way was I sleeping on the floor. So I did actually have to wash the sheets. Without knowing where the washing machine was. Or how to use it even when I found it. But I guess I didn't have a choice.

I walked over to the bed on wobbly legs, cursing Reign No-Last-Name seven ways to fucking Sunday. Because, really, who kissed you until your damn toes tingled and then told you to wash the sheets and then left? Assholes. That's who. So much for thinking he was a decent guy.

I stripped the bed, gathering the sheets inside out and still feeling like I was going to need to burn my clothes after they came in contact with his skanky bed sheets. I walked along the hallway Reign had led me down earlier, trying to ignore the strange sense of unease in the unfamiliar area.

"Oh, yeah, fuck, yeah. Fuck me, harder. Harder!" My eyes widened, my head snapping to the side and then immediately regretting doing so when, inside one of the rooms with the door open, there was a woman spread eagle and a man clothed from the waist up and naked from the waist down plowing into her.

My head dropped immediately, a blush creeping up my cheeks, as I ran forward. And slammed into someone.

I struggled straight, my head snapping up when two hands landed on my shoulders to steady me. My eyes met the hollow honey ones belonging to Wolf and I almost wanted to cry in relief. He looked down at me for a second. "Laundry?" he asked.

"Yeah," I said, finding myself gushing yet again. "Reign went all bossy asshole on me and told me to clean them since I said I wasn't sleeping on his disgusting sheets. Then he neglected to tell me where I could go to do the cleaning of the sheets because, as I said, he's being an asshole."

Wolf's head tilted and for the barest of seconds, I thought I saw light in his eyes before it got quickly extinguished. "Basement," he said and lumbered away.

Basement.

The word left me frozen in the spot for longer than I cared to admit.

Basement.

And I was sure it wasn't going to be the comfy finished kind. It was going to be the cinderblock and cement kind. And, knowing their illegal status, likely barred.

I could do it.

Hell, I had to do it.

I took a deep breath, moving toward the far end of the hallway where I had seen a staircase when we came in. I reached up, flicking on the light, and very slowly descending the narrow wooden steps, my heart wedging further into my throat with each step. I reached the bottom landing, seeing the two sets of washers and dryers. Keeping my focus on them, I quickly went about figuring out the buttons, putting the sheets in one machine and the comforter in another. I stared at them for a long time before I turned back around.

And froze.

Froze froze.

Because there at the other end of the basement, was a metal chair. And that metal chair had three sets of handcuffs attached.

**

"You're only making this harder on yourself, Summer," V said, raising a hand to Martin who had me by my throat on the chair, pushing my neck so far back I was worried it was going to snap. "All you have to do is tell your father you changed your mind. To go along with the deal."

Martin's hands were pressing hard enough to bruise and make my throat feel like I swallowed razor blades, but not hard enough to be of real concern. They didn't want me to pass out. They wanted me to suffer. His hand lifted and my head snapped to face V.

"Fuck you, V. He's never going to take your deal."

"All this could stop," he offered, waving a hand at Martin and Deke.

Deke had already had a go at me and was standing against the wall, smoking, enjoying the show. If you looked, you could see how hard he was through his jeans.

I tried not to look.

"Doesn't matter what you do to me. He won't agree," I spat.

And it was the wrong thing to say.

I knew this when V nodded at Martin and suddenly the ropes were gone from my wrists and Martin was pulling handcuffs from his pocket. Three sets.

"No where obvious yet," V warned, his voice unaffected.

Martin nodded and I was dragged out of the chair, turned around, and made to straddle it.

The handcuffs opened.

One set was for each of my ankles, the metal way too small, cutting painfully into the skin there. And then one set for my hands which were pulled forward to hug the chair, but cuffed so low down that the pressure of the chair on my chest made it hard to breathe.

This was new.

There had never been cuffs before.

I had never been restrained to the chair before.

So I knew it wasn't going to be good.

Then Martin reached into his boot and came back with a knife.

A knife.

He flicked it open, the blade long and dangerous.

Then he was coming toward me.

Nowhere obvious.

My tank top was hauled up my back, tucked up near my shoulders. I barely had a moment to register the genuine fear before the blade started slicing into my skin.

And it burned. It *burned.*

And it was everywhere.

It was unrelenting.

I clamped my eyes shut, forcing the tears away, biting the insides of my cheeks until they bled to keep myself from screaming.

But it wouldn't stop until I screamed.

Then the knife found a spot it had already torn open and slipped back into the cut, digging it deeper.

I screamed.

**

"Cherry? Hey, Cherry. Summer!"

I was vaguely aware of the voice. It was newly familiar and close to me. But my focus was on the chair and the cuffs. My body felt unbearably cold, goosebumps all up and down my arms and over my chest. On my back, the scars felt raw. They felt like they were new and bleeding. They felt like they were being aggravated by my tank top rubbing against them.

"Summer!"

Then I was being pulled away, back toward the stairs, my head twisting over my shoulder to stare at the chair as it slowly slipped out of my field of vision.

But that didn't make the memory fade. It didn't make me hear the sounds of music and men and women as I was pulled into the main area of the building where everyone was happily partying.

"Reign!" Cash's voice called and it was then that I realized who had been pulling me along. Cash.

A silence fell.

Followed by, "What the fuck?"

Reign.

That was Reign.

And, for some reason, that slipped through.

My head snapped upward to find him storming across the room toward me, his eyes hot, his brows drawn together.

"She was washing the sheets," Cash supplied.

"So why the fuck does she look like she's seen a fucking ghost?"

"Reign," Cash said, waiting for his brother's eyes to find his. "She was washing the sheets. In the basement." Realization started to dawn on Reign, but Cash continued. "The chair. The cuffs..."

"Fuck," Reign growled, turning back to me. His hand reached out, rubbing his knuckles against my jaw. "Fucking stupid," he said to himself. "Come on," he said, his hand moving behind me to slide up my back and I shrieked, arching away from him.

Reign's eyes flew to Cash who shook his head, confused.

"Okay," Reign said to me, pulling his hand away, putting it on my arm instead. "Okay, babe. Come on. Let's go back to my room. Okay?"

He didn't give me time to answer as he started steering me back toward the hallway, pulling me into his room and locking the door.

He paused, looking at me for a minute, before he came toward me, turning me, and pulling my shirt up.

"Fuck," he said quietly. "Fuck," he repeated, louder, his fingers moving out to stroke over the raised scars. "Babe... talk to me," he said, letting my shirt fall, and turning me again.

I swallowed hard wanting, yet again, to purge it all to him. "The handcuffs," I said.

"The handcuffs," he prompted.

"In your basement," I went on. "They had handcuffs in the basement. But only..." I took a shaky breath. "But only on the days when the knife came out."

"I'm so fucking stupid," he said, shaking his head, not able to look at me.

"It's not your fault," I said, shrugging.

"I told you to wash the sheets," he countered.

"Yeah but you weren't the one to cuff me to a chair and cut me up."

He sighed, running a hand over the scruff on his cheek.

Then he came at me. Fast.

So fast that I expected to be crushed to his chest.

But his arms went slowly around me. He moved us toward the stripped bed, sitting on the edge and pulling me into his lap. "He's gonna pay," he said into my hair.

I felt myself straighten. "Reign..."

"He's gonna pay. No one fucks with what's mine."

His?

His?

What was that supposed to mean?

I wasn't his.

I wasn't anybody's.

"Reign..."

"What'd I say about you sayin' my name?" he asked.

My brows drew together. "You like it?" I asked.

"Like it a lot," he agreed. "So now you're going to go plant your ass in the bathroom. And I'm gonna go get the sheets. Then you're gonna plant your ass on the bed. With me."

With that, I was pushed off his lap. And he was gone.

And I was left with the distinct impression that being in bed with him, this time, didn't mean sleeping or watching TV reruns.

SIXTEEN

Summer

Reign came back an hour later, slamming the door, locking it, and not even bothering to look my way. So I had been worrying myself to near ulcers about him potentially wanting to have sex with me (okay... maybe it was less worry and more... anticipation) for no reason.

He shuffled around. I imagined, making the bed. Then I heard his boots hit the floor.

"You sleeping in there tonight or what?" he said, his voice casual.

I got up, pulling off my sweatshirt, and moved back toward the bedroom where Reign immediately flicked off the light and laid still.

So, yeah, we were *sleeping* sleeping together.

I squished the weird surge of disappointment, trying to convince myself that it was for the best. He was bad news. I was a good girl. Not to mention the fact that I really wasn't in a place where I should even be considering such things. I had just been kidnapped, beaten, and starved for months. *Months*. And I was considering having sex with a relative stranger just days after getting away? *Days*.

I was having some pathetic White Knight syndrome.

Except Reign couldn't be further from a White Knight.

I slid into the empty side of the bed, curling up on my side away from him, staring into the relative darkness of the room. Behind me, Reign was still. Still for long enough that I figured he had fallen asleep. I let out a long breath that sounded suspiciously like a sigh, and closed my eyes.

But they sprang right back open a few seconds later when Reign's hand landed hard on my hip, pulling it backward until I was lying flat on my back. Then his body was half covering mine, his forearm pressed into one of my sides, his palm flat on the mattress on the other side.

"What are you doing?" I asked, feeling my heartbeat speed up, his warmth sinking into my skin and sending a small shiver through my body.

"They hurt you?" he asked, making me jerk back unexpectedly.

"What?" I asked, my voice airy.

"Those fuckers... did they..."

"No," the word rushed out of me, frantic to be shared. Of all the things that had happened to me, of all the things that were whispered promises of what was to come, it never got there. "No," I said again, more firmly. "It never got that far. They came in at night, drunk, and would... grope me and threaten me. But they weren't allowed to... do that."

"Thank fuck," Reign said, his breath exhaling, his body losing some of its tension.

"Reign," I said again, looking up at his face, seeing the unfair perfection there. His hazel eyes were lowered and I found my hand reaching out, stroking down the side of his face. His gaze flew to mine, intense, searing into me. "What are you doing?"

As an answer, his head lowered, turning to the side, his lips landing on the sensitive skin of my neck, making my body buck slightly under his, my hand flying out to land on his arm. His tongue slipped out, sliding upward toward my ear, his mouth closing over the lobe and sucking on it. I felt a surge of desire, wetness dampening my panties, as his warm breath tickled across my ear.

His head shifted, his lips moving to my jaw and kissing downward slowly. My lips parted seconds before his found mine. There was none of the teasing sweetness at the contact. His lips were bruising into mine. Hungry. Urgent. My belly curled in on itself, my hand going to the back of his head, slipping into his hair and holding him to me as my lips responded, parting, letting him slip inside, his tongue desperately seeking mine. My back arched upward into his chest and his body shifted, coming fully over mine, his thighs pressing mine apart so he could settle there.

I moaned against his lips and his head lifted, looking down at me with heavy-lidded eyes. His mouth opened to say something, then thought better of it, and closed. He pushed himself backward, sitting back onto his ankles and my body felt the absence like a physical pain.

His hands moved downward, grabbing my sides, and pulling me upward toward him. As soon as my eyes were level with his chest, his hands slipped to the hem of my tee, grabbing it, and quickly pulling it up and over my head.

His hands went to the skin of my back and I stiffened, feeling a surge of insecurity at the scars his hands were running over. But his fingers didn't hesitate. They ran over the marks gently, like he was trying to memorize them, before his hands settled up on my shoulders and pressed me back flat against the mattress.

His eyes stayed on my face for a long moment. My bare breasts ached, heavy, my nipples hardening in anticipation. His hands moved to my belly, stroking upward, teasing across the sensitive skin underneath my breasts.

"Perfect," he said quietly, his hands moving upward and cupping my breasts, squeezing hard. I arched up into his touch, a groan escaping my lips. His hands left me, replaced with fingers, rolling and pinching the hardened points until I was writhing underneath him.

I expected him to bend forward, to take me in his mouth, for his tongue to continue the sweet torment his fingers started.

Instead, he moved backward, his hands slipping into the waistband of my pants and pulling them down, pulling them off completely, discarding them off the side of the bed.

He moved toward me again, his fingers stroking up my thighs, over my hips, up my belly. They ran over my breasts again, then disappeared.

Then he was down, stomach on the mattress, propped up on his forearms. His hands went to my thighs, pulling them open, pressing them down hard, making me immobile.

Then his mouth was on me.

I mean... *on me.*

His tongue stroked up my slick cleft slowly, making my breath catch in my chest. He moved upward, circling around my clit, but not touching it until I was writhing, my hands reaching down and slipping into his hair, until I was struggling for breath.

"Reign..."

His tongue pressed down hard on my clit and I was pretty sure I flew out of my body for a second before crashing back down into the sensation, my hips rising to meet him as he started working fast circles around the sensitive bud, his pace quick and unrelenting.

I felt the pressure building, a tight, coiled feeling deep inside, making me beyond need, beyond shame as I moaned loudly, my hands tugging hard at his soft hair.

"Reign... please..." I begged, my thighs starting to shake, my back arching off of the bed.

Then he finally put an end to the torment.

His tongue slipped away, his lips closing around my clit and sucking hard.

I crashed through my orgasm, my sex clenching almost painfully as he kept sucking, his tongue stroking out at the same time. My entire body did one hard shudder as his name moaned out of my lips.

I came down slowly, Reign's tongue lapping gently over my clit a few more times before he slowly pulled away, kissing up the center of my belly.

His lips found my neck for a second then his head lifted, looking down at me. "Sweet fucking pussy," he said, and I felt a surprised, half-horrified laugh escape my lips, my face blushing painfully. Because the men I had known, the few I had been intimate with, would never have said something like that. I wasn't sure I had ever heard a man I was with even say the word 'pussy' let alone tell me that mine was sweet.

"That's funny?" Reign asked, his lips quirked up on one side.

I put a hand over my mouth. "Unexpected," I said through my fingers.

"Yeah?" he asked, looking like he was considering that. "Don't know why. Could eat that pussy for breakfast, lunch, and dinner."

"Oh my God, shut up," I groaned, covering my face with both my hands, feeling at once embarrassed and so turned on it was painful. Because, well, Reign eating me out three times a day... *yum.*

Reign chuckled, the sound low and deep and so sexual that I felt a rush of heat between my thighs. I felt him move, the mattress shaking slightly, before his hands came down on top of mine, pulling them from my face.

"You're done being shy," he said. Said. It wasn't a question. He let one of my hands go, and it fell down by my side. He pulled the other one forward and down. *Down.* Until I felt him curl it around his hard cock.

Alright.

It was official.

Reign was pure, magical, masculine physical perfection.

His hand squeezed mine and pushed it down the long path to the hilt. And I mean long. And thick, my fingers barely meeting around him. His hand slipped away and I felt mine stroking him, wanting to touch every inch of his hardness, my hand slipping up and my thumb stroking over the wet head.

"Yeah, you're done being shy," he said, his voice sounding husky as I started stroking him fast and hard.

His body shifted, his legs going on the outside of my chest, his hips pivoting and lowering toward my face. His hand went back over mine, pushing it to the base, and then pushed his cock against my lips until I opened around him and his cock slid inside.

He let out a low, growling sound, pushing his hips forward, his hand slipping down the side of my face and grabbing my hair.

Emboldened, my lips tightened around him, my tongue stroking over the head in lazy circles until his hand yanked hard at my hair and his hips shoved forward, his cock pushing deep, lodging up against the back of my throat. My gag reflex clenched then subsided as he rocked into me.

"Eyes," he commanded, his voice a harsh whisper. I opened my eyes, looking up at him. "Fuck," he said, closing his eyes for a second, then pulling away from me.

His body lowered back down, pushing between my legs. His lips found mine, hard and hungry, his teeth biting into my lips, making me gasp. He reached out and I heard the drawer in the nightstand open. I heard the crinkle of the wrapper as he released a condom. His hips lifted from mine as he made quick work of protecting us.

Then his body pressed back down, his cock pushing against my inner thigh, making me arch up against it. His arms slipped under my back, coming up around my shoulders and holding them hard. His face lifted. "This ain't gonna be soft and sweet," he warned, sounding about as far gone as I felt.

My mouth opened and my lips found words they had never uttered before, words I felt down to my soul. "Fuck me, Reign," I commanded, my hips grinding up against him.

His eyes heated, his hand going between us. Then his cock was pressing against me, pausing, waiting. My hands went around his back, my legs up around his hips. "Reign... now... please..."

His cock slammed forward, pushing in completely. So deeply it ached. His thickness stretching me to accommodate him. I let out a gasp, my hips bucking up in surprise and the barest twinge of pain.

"So fucking tight," he said, his mouth clenched.

His face lowered, taking my mouth, his tongue pushing inward as he withdrew and thrust forward. Not soft. Not sweet. Hard. Fast. Like promised. My legs wrapped tight against him, rising up to meet his thrusts- a clawing need like I had never known before overtaking me, making me cry out against his lips as he slammed into me over and over, my entire body jerking with the motion, his fingers bruising into my shoulders, my nails clawing into his back.

"Reign... fuck... I'm..."

"Come," he commanded against my mouth, raising his head up to watch me. "Don't fucking close your eyes," he said as I felt them get heavy as I suspended on the edge before toppling over. "Come for me, Summer," he growled.

Then I did. Hard.

Then he did. Just as hard.

And I felt shattered. Broken open. In a million little Summer-shaped pieces.

And nothing had ever felt more right.

SEVENTEEN

Reign

She held on after, her legs around my hips, her arms around my back. The back she had clawed open. Her body shook in aftershocks and I buried my face in her neck until she slackened. I leaned down, kissing her lips hard before pulling away, walking into the bathroom to deal with the condom and get myself together.

Because some shit went down in that bed.

Something I didn't understand.

Didn't even want to try to.

But something happened.

And I needed to get my fucking head on right.

It wasn't just the sex. Though, fuck, the sex...

I'd had more than my fair share of women. I had had two or three at a time. I'd shoved it in one chick's ass while she ate out another chick. I'd had two bitches fight over sucking my cock. I'd done every sordid thing you could imagine, letting the filth settle in my soul.

I knew good sex.

But being inside Summer, in her mouth, in her pussy... being inside her was a whole other level. A level I didn't know existed. A level I planned on spending a lot of time exploring in the future.

But it wasn't the new level sex. It was something else.

It was something that made me want to get a "Property Of Reign" cut made for her. It was something that made me want to grab her, throw her on my bike, and take the fuck off with her. Away from V and his memories. Away from my men. Just away. Just the two of us. No more responsibilities, no more fear.

Because I knew one thing about Summer Lyon.

She wasn't meant for a man like me. With a life like mine.

She was meant for penthouse apartments and designer clothes and safety.

She was meant for the clean life.

And I was nothing but violence, blood, and filth.

I sighed, washing my hands, going back into the bedroom. She was up under the sheets, her legs to her chest, her face half on my pillow. I slipped under the covers and she made a murmuring sound, half asleep, snuggling up onto my chest as I lay down.

She slept.

I lay awake.

Later. A lot later, closer to morning than night, two knocks sounded on my door. Then there was a short pause. Then three knocks.

Fuck.

I slipped out from under Summer, watching her mumble something in her sleep and curl up again, dead asleep. I grabbed my pants, hauling them up my legs, and made my way to the door.

And there was Cash. And Wolf.

"Fuck is it?" I asked, rubbing a hand over the stubble on my face.

"Boys caught someone on the grounds," Cash said, his jaw tight.

"Who?" I asked, moving back inward, grabbing a shirt out of the dresser, then grabbing my key and tucking it in my pocket.

"We think it's one of V's guys."

"What?" I half-shouted, tensing, looking back over my shoulder, to see Summer still fast asleep.

I stepped into the hall, closing and locking the door.

"Dunno, man. He ain't talking. But who the fuck else could it be?"

I nodded, making my way down the hall. "Well I guess we have to fucking make him talk then, don't we?" I asked. "He in the shed?" I asked and Wolf nodded his head at me. "Who is with him?"

"One of the probates," Cash said, looking as uneasy as I felt with that prospect. "He's cuffed."

I tore through the compound, taking across the field at a dead run, unlocking the door Cash or Wolf had remembered to bolt on their way to find me.

The shed was a normal wooden one that we reinforced with soundproofing material and cinderblocks. I also had plumbed a drain into the floor.

A lot of blood got spilled in the shed.

And it looked like that night there would be a lot more.

Inside, the probate was standing three feet away from the man cuffed to the chair, his legs wide, one hand curled into a fist, one holding a bat, his knuckles white he was gripping it so hard. He had a taste for blood. I liked that in my men.

"Probie," I said, my voice gruff.

He turned. He was young, but strong, fierce. I didn't know much about the probates until they got patched-in. But this one had a past. You could see it in the hardness in his dark blue eyes. You could clearly see it in the scar that ran down the side of his face, cutting off at the sharp jut of his jaw. He'd seen some shit. He had done some shit. He was going to make it into The Henchmen. No question about it. "Prez," he said, nodding his chin at me and moving back to lean against the wall.

"You catch him?"

He nodded his head. "Drifter spotted him, but he got taken down."

"He breathing?"

"Doc's got him," he nodded.

"Good job..." I trailed off, not ashamed of not knowing his name.

"Repo," he supplied, nodding, silently going to the door and letting himself out, knowing it was official business and he wasn't in the inner circle yet.

I looked down at the guy on the chair. He was tall and muscled with brown hair and bright blue eyes. "Fuck you doin' on Henchmen turf?" I asked, feeling my tiredness slip away, replaced with the charging blood in my veins.

"Taking a little early morning stroll," he said casually, smirking.

Great. He was gonna be difficult.

Well, at least I could enjoy my time with him.

My fist cocked back, swinging forward, and landing hard enough into the man's jaw to hear a crack. His neck flew in the other direction, but he simply snapped it back, grinning with blood in his mouth.

"Not getting shit from me, man. You might be bad. But I've known worse."

"You work for V?" I asked, my fist landing on his nose before he even had a chance to think about answering.

All I got was a laugh.

And I saw red.

And then I spilled it.

A lot of it.

"Prez," Wolf said, his hands grabbing my arms and pulling me backward. I fought against his hold for a minute, my blood surging too hard in my ears to think straight. "Gettin' nowhere," Wolf reasoned.

I took a breath, settling down enough for Wolf to let me go, staring at the punching bag I had made of the trespasser. Who was still just sitting there, grinning away.

"Fuck," I growled.

"Bro," Cash cut in, leaning against the wall, arms crossed. "Think maybe you should bring her down?" he asked.

"Bring who down?"

"You know who," he answered, a brow lifted. "She might be able to give us proof."

"No fucking way," I said immediately, thinking of the sleeping Summer up in my bed- peaceful, happily fucked.

"Only way," Wolf reasoned.

They were right. I knew they were right. And that was the worst part.

I wanted there to be some other choice. Any other choice.

But they were right.

I had to ask that of her.

And she might never forgive it of me.

"Fine," I growled, taking off toward the door. "You stay here," I told Wolf, slamming the door.

But I ended up slamming it into Cash as he followed me out. "Yo slow the fuck down," he said, looking up at the slowly rising sun.

"What?" I growled, stopping short to glare at him.

"Think maybe you should at least wash your hands before going up there?" he asked.

I looked down. And again... he was right.

I went into the club, scrubbing best I could, but there was nothing I could do about my shirt. So I took off toward the rooms.

Where I met a crowd of men and half-dressed women, standing in the hallway, all looking alarmed.

"What the fuck you all..." I started, and then I heard it.

Screaming.

Summer screaming.

I took off toward the door at a run, stabbing the key in, throwing the door open, flicking on the light. And there she was, still under the covers, curled on her side, fast asleep. Screaming.

"Fuck," I said quietly.

"She alright?" one of the bitches asked, sounding worried.

"Got a past," I said vaguely, slamming the door in their faces.

I walked over toward the bed, kneeling beside it, and reaching out for her shoulder. The second my hand touched her, her eyes flew open: wild and unseeing for a moment.

"It's alright. You're alright," I said, trying for soothing but my voice was too on edge to pull it off.

"What's the matter?" she asked immediately, sitting up, the blanket pooling around her hips, giving me a lush view of her perfect tits. Her eyes drifted over my face, then down to my shirt. "You're bleeding!" she gushed, eyes going wide.

"Not my blood," I said, reaching out to stroke my knuckles down her cheek.

"What's going on? Whose blood is it?"

I sighed deeply. "I was hoping you could help tell me that."

Her eyes squinted for a second. "How?"

My hand went to her thigh, squeezing it. "My guys think they caught one of V's guys," I started and her entire body went taut as a bow. "Relax. He's not gonna touch you," I tried, but if anything she only got more tense. "He won't talk. I've tried."

"That's his blood," she said, looking down at my shirt.

"Like I said... I've tried. We need confirmation that he's one of V's." Her head dipped, looking at the bed, her teeth biting into her lip. "If you can't do it..."

"I'll do it," she surprised me by saying, her tone hard. Hard. I had never heard her voice like that before.

"Babe..."

"I said I'll do it," she said, brushing the blanket off and going in search of her clothes.

"Summer..." I said, watching her fumble around, dragging her panties up her legs and struggling into her pants. "I ain't bringing you in there when you're shutting down on me."

"I'm not shutting down. I'm getting dressed," she growled back. Growled. And it was so unexpected, I found myself smiling.

"Babe. If your head isn't on right..."

"Oh my god," she said, ripping a black tee down her body and turning to glare at me. "Stop worrying about my head. My head is fine."

"The weird look on your face says different."

"I just got fucked into unconsciousness then woken up from a nightmare to you telling me one of the monsters from that nightmare is here. Sorry if my face is a little off. Are you taking me to see him or what?"

Maybe I was wrong about her. I smiled, shrugging. "Yep. Let's go."

EIGHTEEN

<u>*Summer*</u>

I wasn't lying when I said he fucked me into unconsciousness. I could barely keep my eyes opened afterward. I hadn't even known he left until he woke me up. Then I woke up from another screaming nightmare to find him sitting there covered in blood.

My heart flew up into my throat.

I had gotten used to seeing my own blood. So much so that it didn't even worry me after a while. But seeing someone else's blood, seeing Reign's blood, yeah, that did something to me on the inside that I didn't quite understand.

But it wasn't his blood.

"My guys think they caught one of V's guys."

I couldn't accurately describe the feeling that came over me at that declaration. That rolling in the belly, sweat coming from your pores, goosebumps all over your body feeling.

"If you can't do it..."

"I'll do it," I said, my tone stronger than I thought it would be. One mention of V and his men had my insides turning to acid. But identifying him would mean something. It would mean they could get information. It would mean I was a step closer to being safe. So if all I had to do was waltz in and nod my head, well then... I was going to do my damn part.

I jumped out of the bed, finding my panties and pants and quickly getting into them.

"Babe. If your head isn't on right..."

Jesus Christ.

What was with the comments about my brain? That was what? The third time? First because I was in a little car crash. Then because I had been through some trauma. And now because I was willingly, happily, going to help him and his men find out where their trespasser came from?

"Oh my God," I said, dragging a black tee down my body and turning to glare at him. "Stop worrying about my head. My head is fine."

I took a deep breath as he finally (I mean, seriously, who fights you when you agree to do what they came in and woke you up and asked you to do in the first place?) led me out into the hall. Things were still quiet in the compound, most people sleeping or screwing.

Reign's hand went to my lower back, pressing hard. It was reassuring, and at the same time, predatory. My insides went liquid.

Then we were walking out into the yard and I turned my head to look at him, brows together. "Where are we going?"

"The shed," he said, nodding forward.

The shed. Right. So they had more than one place for torture. That was, sort of, good to know.

We walked up to find Wolf standing outside the door. He nodded his head at me, but there was work going on behind his light eyes. "Woman," he greeted me, taking the bar off the door and going in.

Reign followed him in, pausing in the doorway, his hands going to my shoulders. "Eyes babe," he said, his tone soft. "I'm right here," he said, surprising me. "And Cash and Wolf are in there too. You're safe. He can't touch you. You don't even have to say anything. Just nod your head and walk out if you need to. Okay?"

Something about his gentleness made me feel like steel. I nodded my head at him and watched him turn his back and move in.

I took another deep breath.

I could do it.

I was going to do it.

I wasn't the one chained up this time.

He was.

I had the power.

I went in, slamming the door behind me.

The first thing that hit me was the smell of blood. It was a scent I was intimately acquainted with.

And in that small shed, it was almost overpowering.

The second thing that hit me was his eyes. The bright, bright blue. The kind of blue that could be light even in the dark. Like how a cat's yellow eyes pierce the black of night. That was what his eyes were like.

Deke.

They had fucking Deke.

And I was frozen.

I couldn't say why. PTSD or just plain old shock.

But all I could do was stare.

He had been beaten. Badly. And from the look of Reign's shirt, the beating had come from him. I took a sick sense of satisfaction from that. His lip was split open, his eye bloodied, his nose broken. And that was just what I could see. I was sure there were body shots. If I pulled up his shirt, there would be bruises, blue and purple, the heinous red of busted ribs. A part of me really wanted to see.

But that thought flew away when his eyes landed on me.

And he smiled.

Smiled.

No fear. No pain.

Pure amusement.

Dare I say... condescension?

That mother fucker.

He was supposed to be scared. Shaking. Begging. He was supposed to feel trapped and terrified.

He was supposed to feel even the slightest bit how he made me feel for months.

He was looking at me like he was still crouching over me in V's basement, getting ready to slam his fist into my face.

Well...

Fuck. That.

I'd known anger in a sort of detached way. I'd had a little flare up every now again when my father said something out of turn or a girlfriend said something that seemed unnecessarily bitchy. Or when someone cut me off in traffic and then forgot how to use the gas pedal after. Little things. Daily things. The kind of things that caused a little bit of heat, a few snippy words.

But this wasn't anger.

This was rage.

My hands curled into fists at my sides, my air huffed hard out of my nose, heat rose to the surface of my skin, and every inch of me felt like it was buzzing.

"Summer?" Reign's voice reached me, sounding almost concerned. But it came to me as if from a distance. Because, for me, he wasn't there anymore. Neither was Cash or Wolf. It was just me and one of my demons.

And I wasn't cowering and screaming anymore.

"Cherry, you alright?" Cash's voice breezed past me.

Before the decision was even made in the rational part of my brain, I flew at him. I was across the floor before anyone could even blink. My closed fist cocked back and swung with every bit of my (admittedly not much) weight. But lack of girth aside, it landed with a satisfying crack, making his head snap, and sending a shock of pain through my knuckles and up my arm.

But pain was nothing new.

And it sure as shit didn't stop me.

"You *mother fucker*," I growled, slamming my fist hard near his eye socket.

Then it was just pure adrenaline and instinct. My hands, nails, fists, hitting, scratching, punching everywhere within reach: face, chest, stomach. One hard knee to the groin which finally made his smile slip and a groan escape his mouth.

I felt like I went at him forever, finding a deep well of rage underneath the surface, filled with the memories, the nightmares. Filled with every moment of helplessness and humiliation. Filled so full that I was sure I would never get to the bottom of it. That I could beat him into a unrecognizable pile of flesh and not even expend half of the anger.

Then an arm went around my waist, tight, squeezing, pulling me backward as I tried to keep hitting.

"Guess that was my nod, huh?" Reign's amused voice said in my ear.

The sound made the red taking over my whole body subside, moving quickly backward, making me acutely aware of the pain in my hands, the blood on them, the reality of what I had done, the fact that I had an audience.

My eyes snapped over to Cash and Wolf. Wolf looked downright amused, his lips turning up ever so slightly, crinkles next to his eyes.

Cash shrugged a shoulder at me. "Guess you earned that, huh?" he asked, giving me a smile.

I looked back down at Deke, whose smile seemed permanently missing. His eyes were on me.

"You're gonna kill him?" I asked, my voice almost hollow. Because I didn't care. I should have cared. He was a human being. He was bound. And I was pretty sure they were going to take his final breath from him. A normal person would be horrified. All I could feel was hope.

"Yeah, babe," Reign said in my ear, still pulling me backward.

My eyes went back to Deke. "Rot in hell you sick sonovabitch."

Then I was hauled outside, the door slamming and locking.

"Let me go, Reign," I struggled, only to be pulled up off my feet and carried across the field by my belly.

How he managed to walk backward, holding a struggling woman against his chest without missing a step was totally beyond me. We stopped walking and I felt Reign lean back against the wall of the compound. My feet touched back down, but his hand stayed around my waist.

"Take a breath," he demanded, his voice low.

I sucked in air, feeling it settle me inside. "You can let me go. I'm not gonna make a run for it."

"I'll hang onto you for another minute," he said. "How are your hands?"

"They're fine."

"Summer..." his voice said, sounding like he was trying to reason with me.

"Fine. They hurt like a bitch."

His chuckle made the hair next to my ear move, his body shaking slightly against me. The sound was doing all kinds of things to tamp down the rage and replace it with something else. "Of all the things I had expected to happen in that room," he started, his hand loosening around my middle a little. It didn't need to be there. I was leaning my back against his chest. "That was one I had not counted on."

"What were the other options? Me to freeze? Or to start freaking out and crying or something?"

"Pretty much."

"You think I'm that weak?" I asked, feeling a strange rush of sadness overtake me. In my life before everything, maybe I would have been okay being seen as soft and feminine. Maybe I even would have taken a small amount of pride in that. But that was *before*. That was before I was taken and drugged and beaten and starved. That was before I knew what softness meant- powerlessness. That was before I learned that the worst thing a woman could ever be in life is weak.

"I don't think you're weak," he said, his voice firm.

"Right," I said, dryly.

His arm tightened around my belly again. "Summer. You're not weak. You've been through shit that most people would never even have the imagination to dream up in a nightmare. You've suffered and you've survived. You're not weak. But I figured you would feel like he still had some kind of power over you. That isn't weakness. That's trauma."

"I didn't feel under his power," I said, losing some of the tension in my shoulders. "I felt powerful. And I wanted him to know what it felt like to be under my power. I wanted him to hurt like he used to hurt me. And I know it's wrong of me. It's like... evil... but I'm glad you're going to kill him."

"Fucker has to pay," he said simply, repeating his vengeance mantra.

"Hey Reign?" I asked after a silence fell.

"Yeah, babe?"

"When you catch Martin..."

"Yeah?" he asked when I trailed off, biting my lip, feeling all kinds of twisted inside.

I took a deep breath and just... said it. "Knives."

His arm tightened painfully. "Done," he said, his tone a promise.

And then his hand was gone from my belly, both of his hands grabbing my waist as he slipped out from behind me, then slammed me back against the wall. Hard. Hard enough to see stars for a second. But I didn't care. Because then his lips were on mine. Hot. Searing. The kind of kiss I was sure no one else on Earth was capable of. It burned. It burned in through my skin and into my soul.

His hands went to the side of my face hard, feeling like he was crushing my bones underneath them as his tongue slipped into my mouth.

"Reign..." I moaned against his lips.

But then his hand slipped from my face, making no show at flirtation as his fingers slid right down under the waistband of my pants and into my panties, stroking over my clit.

"Oh, my God," I rasped out, my head tilting up to look at the sky as his mouth went to my neck, biting hard enough for me to yelp, then sucking.

His finger slipped down my cleft, pressing inside me fast and thrusting hard, making my legs feel weak underneath me.

Nothing had ever been like that before.

I thought I understood the different kinds of sex.

The slow, sweet lovemaking.

The fun and mostly satisfying quickies.

The angry sex.

But this was a whole other league I didn't even know about.

This was hard and fast and raunchy and so hot that I thought my panties were going to catch fire.

His finger slid out of me and my fist slammed down hard on his shoulder. "No," I whined, feeling the need like a clawing sensation inside.

Reign said nothing, just grabbed me, turned me, and pushed me against the wall. His hands went to my waistband again, but this time they grabbed and pulled my pants and panties down fast, his fingers scratching down the backs of my thighs as he did.

"Spread your legs," he commanded in my ear, his mouth sounding like it was clamped tight.

My legs widened.

I put my arms on the wall of the building, pushing slightly off of it. Only to have Reign reach out and push the side of my face flush against it again, holding me there by the back of my neck. His other hand went down behind me, slapping my ass hard once.

His feet went between mine, kicking them wider.

Then his cock slammed inside me.

Unexpected.

Hard.

Hard enough to make my hips jerk forward and slam against the wall.

"Fuck," I groaned, pushing my hips backward, arching my ass up to give him better access.

His face tilted toward mine, his mouth by my ear. "I'm gonna..."

I felt my head shake. "Shut up and fuck me," I said, cutting him off.

His chuckle made my stomach flutter.

Then he was fucking me. Hard. Deep. Deeper than I thought was possible. His hand stayed on the back of my neck, the other going to my hipbone and curling into it, hard enough for me to bite my lip to keep from complaining.

"I want to hear you," he said near my ear as he thrust deep.

"Cash and Wolf..." I started to object, knowing they were just a couple yards away.

"Fuck Cash and Wolf. I don't care if the whole fucking compound hears you scream while I fuck you."

His thrusts came faster, his hand slipping off my hipbone and snaking around my waist, holding me still as he slammed into me.

"Fuck... oh fuck..." I found myself groaning, no longer caring about Cash or Wolf hearing. Not even aware that such people even existed anymore. All there was was me and Reign. All there was was his hand pressing into my neck, his cock slamming deep inside me, his breath hissing into my ear.

My body was jerking upward with each thrust. "You like it hard, don't you? That's my good little slut," he said, his cock fast, unrelenting, not giving my budding orgasm a second to play peekaboo. "You want it harder?"

It could *get* harder?

"Yes," I gasped, pressing back toward him.

"Fuck," he growled. "I'm gonna fuck you so hard that anytime you move tomorrow, you're going to remember my cock in your tight little pussy," he warned.

And then he did.

My moans became a string of curses, of pleads, of cries of his name.

Then my sounds got caught and his hand went from the back of my neck to the front, pressing down on my throat hard, cutting off my air supply as the orgasm wracked its way through my body, the pulsations so strong they were almost painful. His hand loosened slightly and I screamed out his name.

Yes. Screamed.

I was too far gone to care.

His cock slammed forward hard, burying deep as his body jerked. "Fuck," he growled, crushing his arm around my belly.

I came down slowly, all my senses seeming dulled.

Holy shit.

Holy. Shit.

I thought I knew a thing or two about orgasms. I'd had my fair share over the years. By the select few men I dated. By my own hand. By vibrators. But nothing had ever felt like that. Like it tore me apart. Like it put me back together.

I heard the crickets chirp. The wind blew. And I was suddenly acutely aware that I was standing in the middle of a biker compound with my pants down around my ankles. I felt myself tense and Reign chuckled, leaning forward and biting into my earlobe before pulling out of me. He went down on his knees, grabbing my pants and panties and pulling them back upward, kissing my ass cheek before it disappeared under the material.

"Turn around," he said when I didn't immediately go to do so.

I took a shaky breath and turned, not entirely trusting my legs to keep me upright. I sank my hips back against the wall, wincing a bit at the already tender sensation between my thighs.

"Shit," he said, his eyes getting worried.

"What?" I asked, eyes going wide.

His hand went upward, stroking my hair back behind my ear before trailing a finger down the side of my face. Which suddenly hurt. His finger came away with a slight hint of red. "You alright?" he asked.

My hand went up automatically, touching the small cut on my temple from being pressed against the wall. I looked up at his worried eyes. And I couldn't help it.

I laughed.

His brow raised, watching me. "Summer..."

"Oh, don't 'Summer' me in that tone," I smiled. "I'm fine. This is my first sex-related injury," I declared, finding myself laughing again.

Reign's eyes lightened and his lip started twitching. "You've been missing out," he declared.

I found myself nodding, my head slipping to the side slightly, my lashes fluttering. Flirting. I was fucking flirting with the man. What was going on with me? "You gonna help me make up for lost time?"

The twitching turned to a smirk. His hand reached out, pressing between my legs. "Sore yet?"

"Yeah," I admitted.

"Mission accomplished," he said in all his satisfied male pride. "Tell you what. Tomorrow morning, I wake up to you sucking me off... I'll happily see how many different ways we can mark you up. Sound good?"

It did. It sounded good.

And I was pretty sure that was not normal.

But I didn't care.

"Sounds good," I agreed, smiling.

"Good. But now... I have some business to take care of," he said carefully, as if cautious to bring up the topic of the man cuffed to a chair a few yards away.

"Okay," I said, my voice a little orgasm-cheery.

"You want me to walk you back..." he started.

"I think I can find my way," I said, pushing off the wall, grabbing the back of his neck and hauling him toward me for a kiss. Which he gave me. Happily.

I stepped into the doorway of the compound. "See you in the morning," I said, my voice full of innuendo.

"Yeah, babe," he said, giving me an odd look.

"Have fun," I added.

And then he gave me a really odd look followed by a small smirk. "Okay."

NINETEEN

Reign

Have fun? *Have fun?*

That was all I could think of as I made my way back to the shed.

She told me to have fun while I... killed a man? Granted, he was a low life piece of shit, but still.

Fuck.

Apparently I really underestimated her.

I really had expected her to break when she walked into that shed. To look at me with tears on her lashes. To turn and run. Anything. Literally anything but watch the rage overtake her perfect features for a long minute before she just fucking... flew at him.

My eyes went straight to Cash who was grinning his fucking ass off, shaking his head. Then to Wolf who had a brow raised, his lips pursed slightly, nodding his head at her.

They liked her.

That meant something to me.

Why that meant something to me was completely fucking beyond me. But it did.

I was going to let her go apeshit on the man until she ran through her shit. She earned that right. She wasn't given a reprieve. Why should he get one? But Cash had cleared his throat and shrugged his shoulders. "She's gonna hurt herself," he said quietly.

And he was right. The way she was going at it, throwing her whole weight into every punch, she was going to end up breaking her hands. So I had to pull her off. Regrettably. But I planned to make up for it later.

I was absolutely going to have some fucking fun with the shithead.

I was just completely floored that she told me to.

I was so damn wrong about her.

I walked back into the shed to find Wolf already getting started without me. Cash had some blood on his hands as well.

"Get anything?" I asked, leaning back, watching the show. It had been too long since I let any of them shed some blood. They were due.

"Just that they want her back."

"Too fucking bad," Wolf growled, slamming his huge fist into the man's stomach.

"I get to end it," I warned Wolf, knowing his reputation for letting his anger, his ghosts from the past, get the best of him and send him into some damn trance only to snap out of it later to find someone dead, their features bashed unrecognizable.

He sighed, the wind being taken out of his sails and stepped back. He huffed out his breath. "A word," he said, taking off toward the door.

I nodded at Cash. "See what you can get."

Outside, Wolf was pacing.

Wolf pacing was never a good sign.

"Wolf?" I asked, hearing the metal chair inside scream across the floor. Cash, for all his jocular ways, was a violent son of a bitch himself.

"V?" he exploded, rounding on me. His control was slipping. And if he lost it, there was really no telling what he was capable of. "She's V's?"

Yeah. It was time to fill in Wolf.

Or I was going to be the one he went into a trance around and later realized he accidentally killed.

"Alright. I know. Looks bad."

"Bad? Bad!" He was sucking in giant gulps of air, his hands clenching and unclenching.

"She's not one of his whores," I went on, ignoring his ticking jaw, but keeping a close eye on him. "V wants her Dad to give him shipping containers. Took Summer to coerce him into it. She got away during the hurricane. I found her. That's all there is to this."

"The... club..."

"Doesn't need to know this," I clarified, my tone firm.

His eyes flamed. "His. Men. Here."

"Yeah. I know. That's why as soon as I am done with the run, she's moving somewhere else. I just need three weeks, Wolf. That's all I'm asking of you. Help me keep her safe. Keep the rest of the men out of this."

"Repo," he reminded me.

"Yeah, Repo is going to have to earn my trust by keepin' his fuckin' mouth shut," I said.

"Why?" he asked, his breathing slowing, his pacing stopping suddenly.

"It's personal. Not going to war over a private vendetta, man. Not worth the risk."

"Why?" he repeated, shrugging a shoulder.

I let out a breath. "She screams," I told him.

His eyes went to the floor, looking at his feet. "Mom screamed," he told me.

"I know," I said, nodding. I was the only one who did. Outside of Pops who was dead and didn't count. His mom screamed. So his father had to pay. Brutally.

"When you need me," he said, slamming his hand down on my arm.

"Appreciate it," I said, watching him lumber away.

I turned back toward the shed, going inside. I nodded at Cash who put the chair back on its feet and watched me. "Wanna go work off that extra energy with one of the bitches?" I asked, knowing that was his M.O. After a fight, he needed a fuck.

"Yeah," he said, hitting my shoulder on his way to the door. "You good?"

"Oh, I'm gonna have some fun," I said, smiling.

--

I woke up to Summer's tongue sliding over the head of my cock. My hand went down, moving her hair out of the way, holding it in my fist. Her eyes rose to mine. And fuck if she didn't fucking grin up at me then take me deep.

I let her suck me for a few minutes, the velvet wetness of her mouth the best way to wake up. Hearing her throaty moans as she worked me only served to make me harder.

My fist grabbed her hair and pulled it hard, making my cock slide out of her mouth. And there was that smile again.

"All fours."

Her brows drew together. "Wha..."

"All fours," I growled, knifing up, grabbing her, and throwing her down on the mattress. She hit with a grunt, then rose up on her hands and knees, laughing. I reached into the nightstand, rolling on a condom while I watched her perfect ass. "How far you want to take this?" I asked, squeezing her ass.

She flipped her hair, looking over her shoulder at me. "As far as I can handle," she said simply.

And it was the fucking right thing to say.

She wanted it.

I gave it to her.

I spanked her ass until the pale cheeks turned an angry red and her body jerked with each slap. Then I buried my cock deep in her pussy, holding her hips, and not giving her a damn thing but the fullness. Not moving. Not letting her move. Until her pussy started clenching around me, trying to get some relief, until every breath she took was met with begging.

I only slammed into her twice before she came hard, her moan loud enough to wake the entire fucking compound.

I flipped her onto her back, dragging her to the edge of the bed, and pulling her legs up onto my shoulders. "Whose pussy is this?" I asked, lifting her hips upward and burying deep.

"Fuck," she groaned, slamming her hands down on the bed as her back arched.

"Whose is it?" I demanded, thrusting forward hard again.

"Reign..." she tried, her cheeks getting pink. So I could spank her. I could say dirty shit to her. I just couldn't get her to dirty talk back.

Yeah, she was gonna have to fucking get over that.

"Tell me or you don't get to fucking come again," I warned her, meaning it. "I mean it, Summer. I will fuck you to the cusp ten times in a row and not let you finish." She made a unhappy choking noise. "Tell me."

"It's yours."

"That's not what I want to hear."

She covered her face in her hands, her eyes closed tight. "It's your pussy, Reign," she said, sounding horrified at her admission.

"Damn fucking right it is," I agreed, fucking her fast. Not hard. Just fast. My hips slamming into her thighs faster than she could draw in breath to gasp.

She came hard, shooting up on the bed, flying at me, her hands grabbing onto my shoulder so hard she drew blood. And sending us falling off the side of the bed.

I grabbed her as we went down, holding her to my chest. I hit the ground with a grunt. Her face was buried in my neck, laughing.

"What?" I asked, swiping her hair out of my face.

She pushed up on my chest to look down at me, smiling. "I thought I was the one who was supposed to be getting sex-related injuries."

I snorted, rolling my eyes. "We'll get there," I said, patting her sore ass hard, making her jolt. "Got time. Got nothing better to do with it than throw you around my bed." I pulled her down toward me, kissing her plump lips hard until she was writhing above me again. "Now be a good little slut and ride my cock, would you?"

She lifted her head and smiled down at me.

And then she rode my cock.

And she walked away with bruises on her neck and thighs to match the little cut on her face.

And she was pretty fuckin' happy about it.

Fuck me.

TWENTY

<u>*Summer*</u>

"What do you mean you're leaving?" I asked. Okay. It was more like a screech, but I really just hated that I sounded so shrill.

But, the fact of the matter was, Reign started to mean something to me.

Not just because of the life changing, headboard breaking (literally, we broke the damn headboard) sex. Though I am not naive enough to not realize the sex was definitely a factor. But it was more than that.

It was that after our morning of sex, he brought me in the bathroom and cleaned the cut on my head. He slathered on triple antibiotic.

He kissed my forehead.

He kissed my forehead.

Then he took my hand and brought me down to the kitchen, scrambling up eggs and buttering toast and giving me coffee the way I liked it.

It was the fact that no matter what was going on at the compound, he came back up to the bed at night and made time to kiss me, to fuck me, to fall asleep next to me.

It was about how his arm automatically went around me when one of his men walked by.

It was the way he didn't coddle me, but still managed to be sweet.

Two weeks.

Two weeks of morning sex, for the first time in my life too caught up in another person to not care about morning breath.

Two weeks of at least one shared meal a day. Of his very demanding, very alpha, very panty-melting sex.

I tried to remind myself that it was *just* two weeks.

Two weeks was nothing.

You could barely know someone in two weeks.

But I knew him.

I *knew* him.

And he was leaving me.

"Summer..." he started, his voice hard. He was leaning against the closed bedroom door, looking down at me sitting on the edge of the bed.

"Where are you going?" I asked, trying to make my tone less hysterical. I was being pathetic. And needy. And so not like myself.

"On a run."

"A run?" What the fuck was a run?

"A business trip," he clarified. His face was unyielding, his hazel eyes giving away nothing about what was underneath. That wasn't Reign my bed buddy, that was Reign The Henchmen president.

"How long will you be gone?" God, I sounded like a nagging wife.

"I'm making it as short as possible."

He was giving me nothing. He was leaving me alone at a compound that I never walked around without him and he wasn't even going to give me a roundabout estimate of how long he was going to be missing?

"Summer..." he said, his voice softer, walking toward me. He crouched down in front of me, his hands going onto my knees. "I can't tell you how long it's gonna be because I don't know. Two days drive each way. Then the meeting, I have no idea. Expect five days, accept that it might be more."

Five days.

That wasn't that bad.

I could deal with that.

I was pretty sure I could deal with that.

"I'm leaving Cash here with you."

My brows drew together. "Isn't he supposed to go too?"

"Yeah, but he isn't. He's staying here so he can keep an eye on you. You know him. You're comfortable with him. And it's good to have someone here who knows about your situation so they can keep an eye out."

Keep an eye out because things had died down. After Deke got disposed of (good riddance to bad rubbish), things had died down. And by 'died down' I mean everything stopped. There were no more of V's men on the streets. There were no more cops flashing around my picture on posters. There were no more men snooping around Henchmen grounds.

Instead of comforting me, it made me worry all the more.

And while Reign wouldn't talk about it, telling me instead to 'leave Henchmen business to him' (the arrogant ass), I knew it wasn't sitting right with him either. Because no way was V scared away by one lost lackey.

"Shut those gears down," he commanded, squeezing my knees. "You'll be fine here. Safest place possible for you. Even if I'm not here."

I got the strong, irrational, ridiculous thought that I would never be safe without him around.

Then I squashed the fuck out of that irrationality.

Because I wasn't going to let myself be that weak.

"Alright," I said, shrugging a shoulder. "I understand."

His eyebrows lowered, like he could see right through my bullshit. But I lifted my chin and worked to make my face as passive as possible.

"You understand?"

"Yep," I agreed, pulling my hands out from underneath his. "Though I'm going to miss the sex," I said, standing up and moving away from him.

I didn't get far.

He snagged my belly from behind, hauling me back against his chest. "You'll miss the sex?" he asked, his voice sounded half-amused and half... something else. I couldn't quite place it, especially not being able to see his face.

"Yeah," I said, my voice a little breathless he was holding me so hard. "The sex has been pretty good. I'll miss it."

"Pretty good? The sex was... pretty good?" he asked, his tone amused. He knew I was fucking with him.

"Well," I said, making my tone sound sweet, "it's been... almost a full day. I think I'm starting to forget if it was any good or not."

That was all it took.

I was turned, my pants and panties were whipped off me and I was thrown on the bed, shirt still on. Then, a moment later, he was on top of me, shirt and pants gone. And a second after that, he slid inside me.

"You need a little reminder?" he asked, biting hard into my lip as he started thrusting, his rhythm unhurried.

My back arched, my hands going to his shoulders, digging my nails in. "Harder," I demanded, trying to grind my hips into his.

"Nope," he said, looking down at me, continuing his torturous pace.

"Reign, please," I tried. Yeah. I begged. Shamelessly.

"I'll fuck you as hard as you want," he started and I felt my hope raise, "when you admit that you'll miss *me*."

What? No. Hell to the no.

I would. Oh, my God. I was going to miss him.

But I was trying to convince myself that I wouldn't. So I couldn't exactly go and admit it to him, could I?

"Stubborn," he said, shaking his head, rocking his hips into mine. His lips lowered to mine, soft and sweet, lots of tongue and lip nibbling. "I'm gonna miss this sweet pussy," he admitted and my belly fluttered. "You're gonna miss my cock," he informed me.

"Yes," I admitted, breathlessly, feeling my orgasm building slowly.

His tongue went to my neck. "And you're gonna miss my tongue licking and my lips sucking on that sweet clit of yours."

Oh, God, yes.

But I was beyond words. I was at the throaty whimpers stage.

"And when I get back," he said, his mouth by my ear, his voice getting strained, "I am gonna claim your ass. Bury deep in there until you are screaming my name."

Ohmygod.

"Reign..." I moaned, pushing my hips against him faster, feeling my orgasm budding.

"Just like that," he crooned, pushing in deep.

And I crashed.

Down.

Hard.

My sex clenched hard around him, my legs shaking with the sensation, as I started gasping, my fingers digging into his shoulders.

Reign followed me a moment later, my name on his lips, as he buried in me, his face in my neck.

I drew a shaky breath, my hand moving up into his hair. "I'll miss you," I admitted quietly.

He pushed up to look down at me, a slow, lazy grin on his face. "Yeah, you will."

--

"Open up, Cherry," Cash demanded.

He had a key. I knew he had a key. But he didn't use it. No matter that I hadn't stepped out of Reign's room in two days and he was worried, he still didn't open it on me.

"Leave me alone," I said, rolling over in bed.

"I have a present for you."

Well.

He certainly knew how to get a girl's attention.

"What kind of present?" I asked, already sitting up.

"Open the door and see."

Augh.

The things a girl would do to get a surprise.

I climbed off the bed, unlocking the door, and drawing it open.

And there was Cash, charming smile on his face, looking fresh as a daisy at seven (yes... SEVEN) in the morning. "Nice bed head," he said, grinning harder.

"Shut up and give me my present," I said, lowering my eyes at him which only served to make him chuckle.

He moved into the room, leaving me to follow behind, eying the bag in his hand. He sat down at the foot of the bed. "This present comes with a condition."

Of course it did.

"What condition?" I asked, crossing my arms over my chest.

"You come out and eat something," he said simply.

At the mention of food, my belly did a small grumble. Cash refused to bring food up to my room and I refused to go out. We were at a standoff.

"Reign is pretty pissed you aren't eating."

"You talked to him?" I asked, cringing at the neediness in my voice.

"Yeah, sweetheart. I talk to him every day he's on a run. He checks in on things around here."

"Right," I said, sighing. "Fine. I'll go down. Just for breakfast," I clarified.

"Alright, I'll take it," he said, putting the bag down and reaching inside. "As much as you like those hideous flats you've been wearing around," he said, nodding toward the pair of black ballet flats he had brought me on my second day at the compound, "Henchmen bitches wear these," he informed me, pulling out a pair of badass leather combat boots.

Alright. I had always been a girly girl. I had a closet full of pricey heels. And I mean... heels. Ankle breakingly high and thin. I wore them like I was born to. Day and night.

But the boots in his hands filled me with a surge of something I could only describe as excitement. I held out 'gimme' hands and he smiled, handing them to me. I reached down, slipping into them, tying them loosely, and admiring them. "What do you think?"

"Some black jeans and a nice cut and you'd fit right in, baby," he agreed, nodding.

I'd fit right in.

I felt a thrill.

Because, I realized with blinding clarity, I wanted to fit in with them. With Reign's men and women. I wanted to be a part of their life.

Shit.

I wanted to be a part of Reign's life.

In a sort of permanent way.

Which was crazy.

"Uh oh," Cash said, watching me. "Your happy scale went from an eleven to a zero pretty fast. What's up?"

"Nothing," I said, shrugging it off.

"Nuh-uh. You aren't getting off that easy. What's up?"

I let out a loud sigh, sitting down at the foot of the bed with him. "I miss Reign," I admitted.

"I can tell. Not many women take to their bed in nineteen-fifties dramatics over guys they don't miss."

"I'm that obvious, huh?"

"Yep," he agreed, not bothering to stroke my pride. I liked that about him.

"Why don't you run a brush through that hair and we'll go get you some coffee and food?" he suggested, nodding his head toward the bathroom.

I got up, nodding, making my way inside and locking it.

He was right. I was being obvious. Painfully so.

It was pathetic.

It was beneath me.

If I wanted to fit in, if I wanted Reign to maybe, just maybe, accept me as one of his people, I needed to start acting like it. Not like some silly heartsick girl. I needed to go out there and get to know some of his men, incorporate myself into their lifestyle.

Maybe he wouldn't disappear me.

Maybe when things blew over with V... maybe I could stay.

I ran a brush through my hair, pulling it into a ponytail, brushed my teeth, and went to my pile of folded clothes. Courtesy of one of the "club bitches" who showed up to strip the bed and take any laundry down and do it. Like... it was her job or something.

I slipped into a fresh pair of black yoga pants and the black tee. I reached for the sweater, unraveling it.

And there was the gun.

I don't know what made me do it, but I grabbed it, making sure the safety was on, and slipped it into my boot. After I loosened the laces, there was plenty of room.

I trusted Cash. I knew he was capable of protecting me, but a part of me was getting a little sick of relying on others to take care of me. At least if I had the gun, I would *feel* like I could handle myself. No matter what.

"Alright," I said, moving into the bedroom. "Feed me."

—

I was sitting in the lounge area of the compound, watching some God-awful action movie on the television. There were lots of explosions and blood and cursing. On the couch beside me was Vin who had taken it upon himself to be my personal Henchmen guide for the past three days.

That made a total of five days.

Five days.

He had been gone five days.

I still hadn't heard from him.

Cash did.

When I asked what was going on, I got an oddly guarded face and, "Shit happens," as an answer.

Let's just say that didn't inspire the warm and tinglies in me.

I was worried freaking sick.

"Hey, Summer," Flee, one of the probates (Vin taught me that meant they were prospective members, but weren't 'patched-in' yet and therefore had the menial jobs like walking the grounds) came in the back door, tall with stringy blond hair, on the ugly side, but he had a nice, smooth voice.

"What's up?" I asked, looking away from the movie.

"Want some fresh air? It's nice out." I felt my lips twitch, watching him shuffle his feet. Like he was nervous. Like maybe... he had a little crush on me.

I gave Vin a smile and he patted my knee in a fatherly way and I got up to follow Flee outside.

"Where are we going?" I asked, falling into step beside him.

"Over by the picnic tables," he said, shrugging.

I didn't even get a chance to scream.

TWENTY-ONE

Summer

One minute I was walking, hearing the sounds of crickets, feeling the rustle of the wind moving my hair around.

The next minute, I was flying onto the ground face forward, knocking the wind out of me for a shockingly long moment. Then there was a weight on my back, a hand over my face.

My heart was slamming alarmingly hard in my chest as I flashed back to memories of my apartment. As my mind flew through each and every terrifying moment in V's clutches in a matter of five seconds.

Before I finally remembered to fight.

I bucked hard, twisting and flinging an arm behind me, wiggling forward.

"You're making this harder on yourself. Stop fighting," someone growled in my ear, then there was duct tape over my mouth to replace his hands. His hands that he needed because they pulled my struggling ones and cuffed them at the small of my back.

The weight lifted and I was hauled back onto my feet.

I watched as Flee eyed me, then ran out through a hole in the bottom of the fence.

Fucking traitor.

"Walk," my captor commanded from behind my shoulder.

"Summer?" a voice reached me. My head snapped around to find another of the probates standing there, hands clenched at his sides for a second. He was the one with the scar down his face. Reign liked him.

Repo.

His name was Repo.

My captor followed my line of vision.

One second he was behind me, the next he was pummeling into Repo. And while Repo was young and strong and wiry, the man was huge and hulking, reminding me of Wolf in terms of size.

I should have run.

I should have run into the compound and found Cash or Vin or... anyone.

That would have been the smart move.

But all I could focus on was the blood starting to pool out of Repo's face. His body struggling to help me. Trying to save me. Then a fist landed hard in the side of his face and his body went limp.

And I fucking flew at the other guy.

I threw my whole body weight into him from the side. Caught off guard, his body flew off of Repo. I scrambled onto my side, pushing myself up as fast as possible, and took my boots to the man's side hard. Unrelenting.

I felt my blood in my ears.

I felt rage that put my outburst with Deke in the shed to shame.

I felt a surge of pleasure when I felt a crack and heard a muffled curse.

It was short lived as he grabbed my legs and I flew onto my back hard. Hard enough that I couldn't draw a breath.

Then he was standing, hauling me up, tucking me under his arm and running.

It was a short lived victory, but I made the fucker hurt.

I twisted my neck as we reached the fence, looking at Repo's prone body, watching as hard as I could. Waiting, praying for a sign of life. Then, just a second before I was thrown through the fence and into Flee's traitorous arms, I saw his chest rise and fall.

I felt a wave of relief even as I was hauled through a field and shuffled into the backseat of an SUV, and thrown down on the floor. Flee was in the passenger seat. The other guy in the driver's. And then we were moving.

I fought through the hysteria.

I needed to get out. I needed to get free.

I couldn't fucking go back.

I twisted, looking down at my boots, feeling the gun pressed comfortingly against my sock. If I could just get to it...

But that was useless with my hands cuffed behind my back. Even if I got to the gun, I would never be able to shoot anyone.

I had to wait. Oh, God. I had to wait.

I breathed hard out of my nose, trying to calm myself down. I would get a chance. To get to my gun. To get away again. I would get a chance. They never patted me down. They would never think I had a weapon on me. Least of all a gun hidden in my boot.

I would take whatever I had to take. Whatever beating. Whatever torture. I would endure. I would wait for my opening. And then I would get the gun and I would get myself free.

I wasn't a God damn victim anymore.

And, in Reign's words, they were gonna' fuckin' pay.

—

The drive felt endless with nothing but Flee's and the other guy's sporadic comments about what direction to turn in to keep me from going crazy.

Then the car pulled over and the driver turned to Flee. "Get out."

"What? No man. I need to see him. He needs to know I did my part."

"You need to get your fucking ass back to the compound and take care of business. Make sure no one knows shit."

"Repo didn't see me, man."

"Did anyone see you with her?"

Vin. Vin saw me with him.

At Flee's silence, the man cursed. "Shit. Fuck. Can you not handle the simplest fucking instructions? Get out. Now I have to make it look good."

I got a pit in my stomach at those words.

The doors slammed and not ten seconds later, I heard Flee grunting, yelling, groaning.

Apparently, '*making it look good*' meant making it seem like Flee wasn't involved.

Shit.

Fuck.

He would go back to the compound. He would continue spying on them. Who the hell even knew what the plan was. To kill them all? For getting involved?

Thank God Reign wasn't there.

But, fuck, Cash was still there.

Cash was there and he was clueless.

And so was Vin.

I needed to get away.

I needed to get in touch with them and warn them.

"No. Fuck. Lee... let me g..."

Silence.

But I had a name.

Lee.

Not a minute later, Lee got into the truck, slamming it into reverse, and we were off again.

Lee reached for a cell, shooting off a quick text with one hand while keeping a one hand feel on the steering wheel.

But the car only drove for maybe another five minutes before we paused. I heard beeps, like a code being punched into a gate, then the sound of said gate opening. There was a short drive up a driveway. Then we parked. Lee got out. Then the door by my feet opened and I was being pulled backward.

I slammed down on my feet. Lee got behind me, holding the chain between my cuffs and shoving my head forward so all I could see was my own two feet as he pushed me forward. Into a garage. Through the garage into some other room, tile floor. Through to a hardwood floor.

And it was familiar.

But it wasn't V's house.

Holy fucking shit.

"Baby girl," a voice said and the hand on the back of my head released.

My head snapped up, my eyes going wide.

And there was my father.

Richard Lyon.

Smiling at me like I just got off a plane after a long vacation.

What the hell was going on?

"Lee," he said, shaking his head. "I think the duct tape can be taken off now, don't you?"

Lee made a grunting noise then reached for the tape and pulled it off roughly.

I sucked in air, turning to look at my captor.

I was right, he was built like Wolf. But he was older. He had a buzzcut and hard black eyes. Everything about him, the way his shoulders were pulled back, the way his feet were spread, his hair... it screamed of ex-military.

"I'm going to fucking *kill* you," I spat at him and was rewarded by a slow, amused smirk.

"Summer," my father's voice reached me, sounding shocked. "You should be thanking Lee."

My gaze went to my father. "Thank him? *Thank him*? For what? For knocking me onto the ground? Twice? For beating an innocent kid half to death? What, exactly, should I be thanking him for?"

His head tilted to the side, watching me. "Baby... he saved you."

Saved me.

He... saved me?

The truth hit me like a kick to the gut.

He thought The Henchmen were holding me against my will. He sent someone in to get me out.

Shit.

That changed... everything.

"Baby, are you feeling alright? You look positively ghostly."

I felt positively ghostly.

"I'm..." I started, shaking my head. "Daddy... I need to sit down."

"Of course. Of course," he said, jerking his head at Lee. "I think you can take those cuffs off now," he told him. Lee reached into his pocket for a key and released my hands which I pulled toward my front and rubbed at my wrists. While I was doing so, my father slowly approached me. His gaze went to my wrists and he paled. "Oh, Summer..."

"It's fine. I'm fine. I survived. I got out."

"Trading one prison for another," he went on, his tone sad. "Come on, let's get you up to your room so you can clean up. Looks like you got a little gash on your cheek," he said, giving Lee a hard look over his shoulder.

I took a deep breath, not entirely sure how to handle the situation. I couldn't exactly tell my father that I was willingly staying with an outlaw biker gang. He had been worried sick about me. He sent some big, macho ex-military guy in to get me out and home safely.

"Daddy..." I started as we made our way up the staircase.

"It's okay, baby. You don't have to say anything. I'm just glad to have you home," he said gently, putting an arm around my waist and giving me a small squeeze. "Here we go," he said, leading me to my childhood bedroom door and opening it. His hand moved to my lower back. "I'll leave you to freshen up. Then maybe you can come down and have some coffee with me? Tell me your story?"

I gave him a small smile, feeling very much like a little girl again suddenly. "Yeah, Daddy," I agreed.

"Okay, baby," he said, kissing my temple and closing the door behind me.

He had kept it exactly as I had left it when I was eighteen: pale lilac walls, canopy bed with white, billowing fabric draped over the top and a plush white comforter laid over the bed. There were two shabby chic white nightstands with lamps. There was a small golden jewelry box on top of one of them. On the other was the remote for the television which was hidden away on the wall across from my bed in a huge white cabinet. To the left behind the door to the hallway, was a door to my walk-in closet. Far on right was the door to the en-suite bathroom which boasted a huge soaking tub and a shower bay with four shower heads along with a huge round tufted ottoman and a vanity across from the sink and mirror.

The whole thing was bigger than most New York city apartments.

It wasn't unfamiliar over time. I had stayed in my old bedroom on many occasions when I visited my father. The brushes on the vanity in the bathroom I had used over the last Christmas season. The drawers under the sink cabinet were stocked with the products I used as an adult woman, not the ones I had used as a teenage girl. Complete with my perfume and cosmetics.

I had actually forgotten about makeup. It had been so long since I had put any on.

I turned into my closet, looking for something even remotely suitable to wear. I settled on a pair of light wash skinny blue jeans and a white long sleeved t-shirt. And, oh yeah, a bra. I forgot about bras too. I grabbed fresh panties and socks and made my way to the bathroom, locking the door behind me.

I gave myself an hour to relax. To shower, dress, fix the cut on my face, apply a little mascara and lip gloss. I dried my hair.

Then the worry set in.

Worry about Cash. And Vin. But mostly Reign.

What was he going to think when he got a call from Cash saying I was gone and two of his men (technically one of his men, and one traitor, but he wouldn't know that) were busted up?

I couldn't imagine how that would make him feel.

Because he would think V had me again.

He would want to storm in there looking for me.

I couldn't let that happen.

I had to do something.

I rushed out into my bedroom, full of possible ideas. Because I had no phone numbers. Not Reign's or Cash's. Not the compound's. Not Reign's house. I had no one to call. But I was sure I could find some way. Call information. Go do a quick search online and find something. There had to be a way to contact them.

Then I froze as I reached for the phone. The pretty, white replica of an antique rotary phone.

Because the phone wasn't there.

It wasn't there.

My heart immediately started thudding, the swirling feeling in my stomach instantly telling me something was wrong. I couldn't say what, but something was wrong. Something was off.

I turned, moving toward my television cabinet, intent on dragging out my laptop for a search. But when I opened it, the laptop was gone. The laptop. And the TV. And the DVD player.

The swirling turned into a solid lead sensation in my stomach.

I glanced around, my throat feeling tight, looking for anything else that was wrong or out of place or missing.

I went to the windows, pulling the lock on top, then trying to haul them up. But they didn't budge. Not one of them.

Heart in my throat, I walked slowly toward the door to the hallway, already knowing. But I reached for the handle and tried to turn it. Tried. Because it was locked. From the outside.

I backed away like it would burst open at any moment, feeling sick. Sick. I felt like I was going to throw up all over my own feet.

I was trapped.

My father had me trapped.

I looked over my shoulder into the bathroom, seeing my boots laying there discarded and I flew at them, shoving my feet in, lacing them loosely, giving me a gap to slip my hand in and grab my gun if I needed it.

I sat back down on the ottoman.

What. The. Actual. Hell. Was. Going. On?

There was a soft tap at my door a few minutes later and I rushed to my feet. I caught my reflection in the mirror, seeing the wide eyes, seeing the shock and alarm.

I needed to tamp it down. I needed to play it cool. I didn't know what the fuck was going on, but whatever it was, was not good. And I needed to act like I had no idea about the missing phone and laptop. The locked doors and windows.

For all my father knew, I was happy to be home. Relieved. Thankful.

He couldn't know I was freaking out.

And he damn well couldn't know about a gun tucked into my boot.

"Baby girl?" he called, opening the door.

"Coming," I called, sounding cheerful as I walked into the bedroom. "Sorry... I got carried away. It's been so long since I had... my stuff."

He gave me a smile. "You look much better. All that black," he said, shaking his head. His gaze went quickly over my outfit and landed on my feet, a brow raising.

"They're comfortable," I offered. "I, ah, had some nasty cuts on my ankles." That was not entirely untrue, though it was several weeks before. "These don't hurt."

His eyes got sad and I knew I said the right thing.

"Come on, honey," he said, holding out an arm for me to step into. "Let's go get you some good food."

I gave him a small smile, every bit of energy going into not trying to run the fuck away from him. Because something was wrong. Something was off about him. I couldn't put a finger on it. But it was there.

"Coffee?" he asked, already grabbing a cup and pouring for me.

"Yes, please." I needed every bit of energy I could get. That being said, I watched every movement his hands made. But he didn't do anything to my drink. I took it and sipped, enjoying the kick it gave to my system.

"Darling girl," he said, standing across from where I was sitting at the enormous kitchen island.

"Dad... where's Mae?" I asked, looking around. I don't think there had ever been a time in my entire life that I went into his kitchen and she wasn't there. Cooking, cleaning, looking over recipes, writing letters to her family.

Her missing was another huge red flag.

"Oh," he said, looking around. "Her daughter is getting married," he supplied with a shrug.

Yeah. Right.

Her daughter was a thirty-five year old virgin with an attitude problem and a hatred of all things masculine.

"Oh, good for her," I said, smiling.

"You seem... worried," he said, his blue eyes watching me. Keen. I had never known he was so observant before.

"Sorry Dad, I've... it's been a really bad couple of months."

At that, his face fell.

Fell.

With genuine sadness.

"Summer if you want..."

"I don't," I said immediately. "I just... it's too soon. I'm just happy to be here. Away from it all."

"Thank God I found you," he said, nodding at me.

"I knew you would," I said, giving him a smile. "The whole time... while things were... bad... I just kept thinking that you would save me from it all."

"Of course. I was never going to stop until I got you back," he said. "I've taken... precautions to ensure you stay safe this time," he supplied.

"Precautions?"

He nodded. "I've hired more men like Lee to keep an eye on the property. I've had your windows sealed so no one can get in that way. I've had your doors locked."

I couldn't help it.

I really tried to keep my mouth shut.

I just couldn't.

"From the outside?" I asked, my tone sharp, watching him.

And it was good that I was watching so hard. Because if I hadn't been, I would have missed it. It was there and then gone faster than a blink. But it *was* there. And I saw it: a darkness, a hardness, a side of my father I hadn't known had existed. All my life he had been good, over protective, kind, worried. Perhaps a bit stern about my life choices, but always out of kindness, out of fatherly concern.

But whatever passed his face, it didn't belong to the man I had known for twenty- some-odd years.

"You're a sharp girl, Summer," he said, surprising me. "Always were."

"Sharp enough to know that if someone was coming for me, that having the door locked from the inside is the only way to keep them *out*. Having it locked from the outside, Dad, that is how you keep someone *in*."

The look was back.

But that time, it was stronger.

No longer needing the Dad-mask.

He was just... another person.

Someone I didn't know at all.

"I can't have V getting you back. And I can't have you running back to that lowlife Henchmen you are in love with either. I am covering my bases."

What.

The.

Fuck?

"Lee," he called and Lee appeared out of nowhere, nodding at him.

I noticed a small wince as he moved and felt my spine straighten, felt my pride surge. "How're those ribs, Lee?" I asked, smiling over my coffee cup.

To my surprise, he winked at me.

"I raised you better than that," my father shot at me, making me almost shrink away from his disappointment before I remembered what was going on.

"*You* didn't raise me," I clarified. "A man who was sweet and good and loving raised me. I don't know who the fuck you are."

"I see you've picked up the crassness of those base creatures."

If he was looking for a compliant hostage, he was going about it wrong by calling my saviors names.

I looked down at my cup and before I thought about it, I flung it hard across the room toward him, watching it shatter directly behind his shoulder, pouring the rest of the hot liquid over his suit. He didn't even flinch. "Rot in hell, *Dad*," I spat.

"Lee," he said calmly, "I think it's time my daughter went to rest."

And with that, I was grabbed and dragged toward my room, fighting it the whole way, managing a few elbows to his center, which were rewarded with grunts of pain from his busted ribs.

"You've got spirit, I'll give you that," he said calmly.

"You're going to be sorry you're working with him," I warned as I was thrown into my room, slamming hard against the pillar of my bed.

"Who is gonna make me pay, princess? You? For trapping you in your little girl bedroom?"

"Reign is going to make you pay," I supplied and saw the slightest trace of worry mark his eyes before it got pushed away.

"Reign won't be a problem for long."

Shit.

TWENTY-TWO

Cash

"Cash! Mother fuck fuck fuck!" Vin's voice yelled and I flew out of my bedroom, down the hall, into the main room. Because Vin sounded freaked. And Vin was a tough old fuck, he never sounded freaked.

"What's..." I started, seeing him dragging a beat and bloodied Repo in from outside. "What the fuck?"

"They got Flee too. Q found him out in front of the gates, bleeding the fuck out. Got him to the hospital."

"Who was it? Did they get..."

"Cash," he broke in.

"We need to know what the threat is. We need..."

"Cash!" he hollered.

"What?" I asked, looking over at him.

"She's gone."

"What? Who is gone?"

"Summer. They got Summer," he said through clenched teeth.

And that, I was pretty sure, was how I died. Heart stopped. Right then and there.

"What?" I asked, my voice a strange raspy whisper.

"They got Summer. She was out back. She's gone. She's fucking gone."

"Fuck!" I yelled, turning and slamming my fist into the wall, watching it slip under the plaster past my wrist. I pulled it back out, reaching into my pocket for my phone.

It was the last thing in the world I wanted to do. It was the worst news I had ever had to bring to someone. And he was still a fucking day out. A day away. Fuck.

"What?" his voice growled at me, impatient.

I sucked in air. "Someone got on the grounds, fucked up two probies and, fuck," I said, lowering my head, "they got Summer, man. They got her."

The silence on the other end of the phone was the worst sound I had ever heard in my life. It was the loudest kind of noise.

It felt like it lasted forever.

Then, "No."

And there was so much in that word. Desperation. Anger. Disbelief.

"Yeah, yeah, man. She's gone. She's fucking gone."

"I'm on the road."

Disconnect.

I turned back to Vin, feeling the weight of leadership in a way I never had before. That was always on Reign. Even when he was out of town and I was technically in charge, it had never been real. I had never needed to make decisions. I never had to deal with consequences alone.

"What the fuck do we do?" Vin asked, mopping some of the blood off of Repo's face with a torn piece of his shirt.

I ran a hand over the shaved side of my head.

Shit.

Fuck.

What the fuck were we going to do?

Reign was a day out.

A whole fucking day.

A day where fuck-all knew what was happening to Summer back at V's. Reign told me about the scars on her back. I'd seen the ligature marks on her wrists and ankles myself. When she had her hair pulled up, I'd seen the wisps where her hair was growing back after being pulled out.

She had been through fucking hell.

And she was going through it again.

And we had to fucking sit on our hands for a whole day?

"We need to call in all the men. Tell them we had a break-in. We need to double up men on the perimeter. Not just fucking probies. The men too. We need to find out how the fuck they got in. And we need to see if we can find any leads. Tire treads. People who saw something. Anything we can. When Reign gets here, we need some fucking answers," I concluded, going through my phone and shooting off a group emergency text. I turned back to Vin. "How bad is he?"

"Looks like broken eye socket and nose. A rib or two. Prolly a concussion. He'll pull through."

"He need a hospital?"

"No. Doc can deal with him when he gets here."

I nodded, going behind the bar and grabbing one of the semi-automatics. "I'm checking the mother fucking grounds."

Outside, I took a breath that I hadn't realized I had been holding.

"God damn it," I said to the night as a whole.

Reign was probably shitting bricks on the road, pushing the bike as fast as it would go. And I knew why even if the stubborn fuck didn't know himself. He fell hard for Summer the first night he met her. It was pathetic storybook shit. But it was real. Every single second he could spare, he spent with her. I saw it. The men saw it. The bitches definitely saw it.

And fucking Summer looked at him like he hung the moon.

He would go on a suicide mission to get her back.

He would bring on a full-blown war to get her back.

And, for once, I wouldn't fight him on it.

--

Twelve hours. Twelve fucking hours.

I was sitting on top of the bar, hand clenching at my gun, sick of inactivity. The men were everywhere. We'd found the hole. We'd found the tire tracks. The car was something heavy, a truck or an SUV. That was it. No one knew shit. Repo was still unconscious in one of the bedrooms with Doc. Flee was still in surgery at the hospital with Q standing guard.

There was nothing to do.

Vin's eyes kept flashing to mine and I could feel the tension in his body match mine.

Then the door opened.

And Reign was there.

Twelve fucking hours.

I didn't even want to think of the speed he'd had to travel to make a day's journey in half the time.

He looked like hell. His entire body, head to feet, was tight. His face was hard. His fists were clenched. His eyes though, his eyes were burning.

Wolf came in hot on his heels and his eyes had that edge to them. That edge that said he was barely holding it together.

Hell, it looked like all the men had fallen for Summer.

"What do we know?" Reign asked through clenched teeth.

"Not much," I started. "Hole in the fence. Tire tracks. Something heavy. Flee is in surgery. Repo is unconscious in one of the rooms. There are signs of struggle out back. No witness. Nothing. We got shit, man."

He nodded his head tightly. Then he turned to Wolf.

"Find something," he demanded. The words were barely out of his mouth when Wolf nodded and took off.

"We'll get her back, man," I said, attempting comfort.

"I told her she was safe here," he said, staring off into the room. "I shouldn't have fucking left her."

He was barely holding on.

I'd seen Reign in a lot of situations in our time together. I'd seen him leaning over our father's dead body, riddled with bullets. I'd seen the horror slowly getting replaced with a thirst for revenge. I'd seen him look into the eyes of traitors, the look of rage so strong it was catching.

But I'd never seen him like that before: utterly wrecked.

Vin was the one who broke the silence. "You had business," he told Reign, subtly reminding him that club business trumps all.

On a normal day, that would have snapped Reign out of his inner struggles.

But on the day when the only bitch he ever gave a shit about in his entire life went missing, falling back into the hands of men who made her scream in her sleep every night... yeah... it only served to uncage everything he was keeping buried deep.

His hand reached for the closest thing, a stool my feet were resting on, picking it up, and hauling it at the flatscreen.

It shattered quickly, the metal stool slamming loudly back onto the ground.

Five men came running from different directions, guns at their sides, looking around for some kind of threat. Seeing Reign, they stood down, looking at the destruction, looking at their president, understanding spreading over their faces.

Chuck, a man around the same age as Vin, stepped forward. "Go hit something," he told him, clamping a hand on his shoulder. "Gotta run through this energy if you want to handle this clear-headed. Go hit something."

Reign nodded stiffly, taking off toward the basement.

When he was gone, they all turned to me.

"We got shit," I said, shrugging. "Wolf is out trying to find some news."

"Nothin' worse than nothing to do," Chuck said, nodding.

"Should we be worried about our families?" one of the others asked.

I shook my head. "This is personal," I decided to share. "Your women and kids are safe."

"Someone is fucking with the prez and we ain't handling it?" Vin asked, looking a mix of confused and angry.

"He said it's personal. He's not involving everyone in his shit."

"That ain't how we handle things, man. Someone fucks with one of us, they fuck with all of us."

I nodded. Because that was true. It was how it had always been.

That being said, the people who fucked with us in the past were nothing compared to V.

I shrugged a shoulder.

"He has his reasons. We'll all get more information when he's ready to give it. Right now he doesn't need us all sitting here acting like bitches 'cause you're feeling left out. Do your jobs and wait for orders."

Their heads jerked back, surprised, chastened. Then they nodded, and filed back to whatever the fuck they had been doing.

Half a day in charge and I was feeling heavy. Physically, emotionally heavy. It was new, foreign. My life had always been different from Reign's. He got the burden, I got the fun. Booze and bitches and runs. I never had to deal with the weight of the questions from the men, their anger, their nervousness.

Half a day.

And he had been dealing with the shit for years.

It was no wonder he needed to escape to his cabin, he needed to spend so much time on his bike alone, sorting through shit.

Fuck.

I hopped off the bar, making my way toward the basement where the chain was swinging viciously.

I stopped at the bottom step, watching him fly at the bag, his fists moving fast enough that they were hard to keep your eyes on.

He had been down there for a good twenty minutes and he didn't seem any less tense. If anything, he seemed all the more worked up.

He needed his woman back. He needed her there to soften his sharp edges, to give him what comfort he could get, to let him have one piece of good in the shitstorm that was his life.

"Don't think it's working, bro," I said, moving across the floor.

He stopped punching, shaking his head, his breath coming out hard. "They fucking have her again," he said, looking up at me with haunted eyes.

"I know man... we'll..."

I was interrupted by the sound of boots on the steps, hard, heavy.

Wolf was back.

He walked across the floor, his body tense, his eyes hot.

Then he looked at Reign and strung together more words than I had ever heard him speak at one time.

Nine words.

Nine words that changed everything.

"There's something you need to know about Richard Lyon."

TWENTY-THREE

Summer

Two days. *Two days.*

I scratched the marks into the wall like I had done at V's house. But not with a bloody fingernail. No. I ripped one of the lamps off the nightstand and used the square edge to etch huge, three foot tally marks on the wall beside my bed. Mostly because it would piss off my father. He had always been a freak about the house being in good order.

There wasn't much I had control of anymore, but at least I could tick him off a little bit.

Fact of the matter was, Richard Lyon, the man in the house with me, the man who had taken me from The Henchmen, the man who had locked me in my room... he wasn't the man I knew.

He was a whole different monster and I felt sick that I had spent my entire life not seeing who he really was. It wasn't like there hadn't been warning signs. There had been fucking warning signs. I had just... ignored them, brushed them aside, pretended to not see them.

There were more times than I could count in my life where he had let the Dad-mask slip. Where I had seen pieces of the man underneath the persona. When I caught sight of the coldness, the deadness in his eyes.

God, how had I been so freaking clueless?

All my life I had been living some kind of elaborate lie.

And, sitting alone in my childhood bedroom twenty some-odd hours a day, I had nothing to do but beat myself up for being so stupid.

There was a soft knock and I sat up on my bed, glaring at the door when it slowly opened.

"Hey, darling girl," he said, giving me a kind smile. His eyes drifted, looking over at the ruined wall. I got a head shake and pursed lips. It wasn't much, but it was something. "I'm afraid I can't do dinner with you tonight. I have some business to attend to. But don't worry," he went on, his words slick, "Lee and the other men will be here to protect you."

Right.

Protect me.

From escaping.

But still. It was a small victory. Not having to sit across a table from him, trying to figure out what I could haul at him while he tried to keep casual conversation with me like he hadn't kidnapped and held me hostage. Like I hadn't been held for three months at some psycho's house. Like I hadn't found salvation in Reign's arms.

"Works for me," I said, my tone cold.

At that, he sighed. "One day, baby girl, you're going to see that I did this all for your own good. I mean... a biker? Summer, I raised you better than that," he told me, shaking his head, moving back into the hallway. "I'll see you in the morning," he told me, shutting and locking the door.

I lay back on the bed, my feet hanging over the edge because I still had my boots on. I never took them off. Not even to sleep.

I had considered grabbing for the gun, using it.

Two things stopped me.

One, there was the mini military he had walking the grounds. Even if I managed to get a shot off, there was not much chance I would escape. And then... who the hell knew what kind of punishment I would get if he lived through the bullet?

Two, okay. He wasn't the man I thought he was. But he was still the man who came and checked under my bed for monsters as a kid. He was the man who bought me a pony of my sixth birthday. A pony. He was the man who encouraged me with my school work. He was the only person in my life who had given a damn about me. He was the only parent I had. And I just... couldn't bring myself to shoot him.

But I kept the boots at the ready just in case.

I wasn't taking any chances.

The thing about being held captive that they don't tell you, is that it's boring. Sure, it's nerve-racking and scary for a while. But mostly, just fucking dull as hell. No television. No books. No one to talk to to keep yourself from going crazy. I spent a lot of time showering. And staring at the walls.

The night got late, darkness coming through the windows.

I rested back, falling into a purely boredom-induced sleep.

Again, I didn't get a chance to scream. I woke up with a hand over my mouth.

My eyes flew open, arms swinging to fight when I felt a body come over mine, knees pinning my forearms, a man's full weight settling on my chest.

Then I saw him.

Martin.

Fucking fucking Martin. With his dead eyes.

And he was smiling at me.

He reached behind him, pulling out duct tape.

Again.

In what universe did boring, good girl Summer Lyon end up kidnapped three fucking times in four fucking months?

That was all I could think as I felt the duct tape slide over my cheek, his hand moving little by little so he could cover my lips without me being able to open my mouth and scream.

Which I would have. I would have screamed bloody fucking murder. Because no matter how frustrating and ick-inducing being held captive by your own fucking father was, it was nothing compared to being dragged back to V's. To being tied to that bed. To being beaten and starved and carved up. To, very likely, being raped.

I would have moved heaven an earth to get Lee's attention.

But my mouth was covered and then I heard the handcuffs slide open. An arm was wrestled up and the bracelet went around my wrist, then the same was done with the other wrist.

"V has been missing you," he informed me, lifting off my body and hauling me up by the chain between the cuffs. "Said I could have all kinds of fun with you if I brought you back," he informed me, pulling me across the room and toward the door.

Not quietly I might add.

He wasn't whispering or murmuring.

He was talking just as loud as he pleased.

And I was getting familiar enough with the seedy underworld of society to know that that wasn't a good sign.

Then, to prove my point, we went into the hall.

And there was Lee. He was slumped up against the wall on the floor, his body in weird contortions. Blood was spattered all behind him from the bullet hole he had in his forehead.

I felt the bile rise up in my throat and was forced to swallow it back down.

I'd never seen anything like that.

A man dead like that. Horrifically. Brutally.

And, not entirely understanding why considering he was one of my captors, I felt unbelievably sad. He was dead because of me. I was dragged down the stairs and out the front door and before I was shuffled into the trunk (yes Martin, unlike Wolf, had a trunk), I saw the devastation all around. My father's entire mini-military was dead. Shot dead. Blood everywhere.

I gulped back more sick as the trunk slammed closed.

Bodies were piling up because of me.

And maybe they weren't all great men, but they were people. People who had their lives ripped away because V wanted me back.

So maybe he should have me back.

Maybe me dealing with the torment was worth keeping others alive.

My father.

The Henchmen.

Reign.

Oh, God, Reign.

When I wasn't busy hating my father or trying to find a way to escape (there were none), I was thinking about Reign.

Seven days. I hadn't seen him in seven days.

And I missed him, like he told me I would.

Like I had never missed someone else before.

I missed him like a limb suddenly ripped away.

Like something vital.

He had to know that I was gone by then.

And he would think it was V all along.

And he would come for me.

Fuck.

I wished I had a way to contact him. To tell him to let it go. Tell him it wasn't V. Lie my ass off. Tell him I took off. I needed to get away, start a new life. Tell him to move the fuck on.

Because I might have been able to live with a whole militia dying because of me, but I couldn't live with Reign dying for me. Or Cash or Wolf or any of the other men for that matter.

I thought about the gun in my boot.

And then I thought something awful.

It was something I never thought I would think.

It was something that, on a normal day, seemed weak and cowardly.

But in my situation, it seemed noble and brave.

It seemed like a very viable option.

I could take myself out of the equation.

Permanently.

I could save myself the beatings, the starvation, the brutality.

I could save my father from getting involved with V.

And, more important than all, I could save Reign.

I drew in a shaky breath, feeling my body roll around as the car drove away.

The cuffs would come off eventually. The cuffs would come off and the ropes would go on. And the ropes would be untied for me to use the bathroom. Or right before my beatings in the basement.

Hell, maybe I could take V out with me. Or, at the very least, Martin.

Even as I thought that, I knew I couldn't. Yes, I had the gun. Yes, I knew how to use it. But I wouldn't be able to. Not to take someone else's life. Not even people as sick and twisted and undeserving of breath as V and Martin. I couldn't do that.

But I could turn the barrel on myself.

I could do that.

Resolved, I kicked out my legs, pressing them against the back seats of the car to hold my body still.

I should have been freaking out. I should have been breaking into a cold sweat. I should have been feeling sick to my stomach. I should have been running over all the things I would never get a chance to do: get married, make babies, grow old, have a good, safe, sweet little life. I should have been devastated that I was going to take that away.

But I wasn't.

I felt resigned.

I felt like I had a mission.

To save people from trying to save me.

And dying in the process.

I wouldn't have been able to live with that anyway.

For the first time in almost four months, I was going to be in control of something.

That was something to cling to.

To comfort myself with.

The car stopped. I heard Martin's door open and close. I felt the trunk pop. Then he was looking down at me, a smirk toying with his lips. "Welcome back," he said, reaching in and hauling me out. He set me on my feet and I turned to see other cars pulling in. V's men got out in varying degrees of dishevel. And it hit me that V had sent his own mini army to get me back.

I swallowed hard, looking away from them.

"I think we can remove the duct tape now, don't you?" a voice hit me and I turned to see V walking out of the house, wearing a pristine blue suit with a white shirt and striped blue tie. He looked like he was walking out to meet an old friend, giving me a smile.

A fucking smile.

The sick fuck.

Martin reached up and ripped the tape off my lips, the skin smarting as he did.

"Summer, Summer, Summer," V said, coming up toward me, his head tilted to the side slightly as he looked me up and down. "You look well. All plumped up again."

Okay. I knew I was in a kidnapping situation. And I knew that these people had hurt me in countless ways over months. And I knew that I was pretty set on taking my own life at the first opportunity, but somehow... being referred to as 'plumped up' was offensive. It was stupid and girly and insecure, but it stung.

"Yeah, that happens when people *fucking feed you,*" I spat angrily to cover my ridiculous inner battle with my self-confidence.

V's shoulder shrugged, his smile spread. "Still got a lot of fight in you, huh?" he asked, turning his smile on Martin, sharing something silently.

Martin spoke next, to V, "Yeah, it's gonna take double the effort, I think, to break her this time."

Break me.

They never broke me.

And I felt the need to let them know.

"Break me, huh?" I laughed a little hysterically. "Is that what you think you did? Because I'm pretty sure a broken person doesn't escape her tormentors and then get the pleasure," I said, twisting my head to glare at Martin, "of beating the ever loving shit out of one of the men who used to beat *her*." I paused, watching Martin's eyes get tight. "And then order his death. Happily."

There was a spark of surprise in his eyes before he tamped it down. I turned my head to look at V whose smile, somehow, had widened even further.

"We figured Deke had met with some... difficulties."

"If by 'difficulties' you mean had the life beaten out of him, then yes. Yes, he did."

V laughed, waving a hand. "He was disposable," he said casually.

I felt Martin tense behind me, knowing, I guessed, that he realized that if Deke was disposable, so was he. That must have hurt his pride a little. "Hear that, Martin?" I asked, carelessly poking the sleeping bear, "It sounds like you're disposable too."

I was rewarded by being thrown forward.

Wrists cuffed, there was nothing I could do to break my fall but round my shoulders so my head didn't crack fully onto the pavement of the driveway.

I might as well not have even bothered.

My head smacked hard, sending a swirling blackness through my consciousness that I fought hard as the pounding started in my temple and I felt the hot trace of blood running down the side of my face.

"That was hardly necessary," V said casually as if Martin had just spoken out of turn instead of given me a fucking concussion.

I saw V's feet move and knew that he was the one who pulled me back onto my feet. I pulled my lip in slightly, licking the blood off of it. "I don't know, V, it looks like you're losing control of your men."

To my surprise, he threw his head back and laughed. It was full. Hearty. Like he hadn't heard a joke that funny in ages.

"Oh, sweet girl," he said, looking at me, still grinning like a mad man, shaking his head like he was talking to a silly child. "I had thought you would have figured it out by now."

Figured it out? Figured what out? What was I missing?

"Hey, I don't think..." Martin broke in, sounding like he was uncomfortable, like V was saying something he shouldn't.

V waved a hand, brushing Martin's concerns aside. "Things have changed, Mart," he informed him. "Time the truth came out."

"You're sure that..."

"I'm sure," he said, his words firm. Then he turned his focus back on me and the smile picked up again. "You're not as clever as I thought you were. That's unfortunate."

"Oh, please let me tell you how much it hurts that you low life pieces of shit are disappointed in me," I said dryly.

To that, he chuckled. "At least you found that spunk. I knew it was in there somewhere."

I rolled my eyes, suddenly realizing I would rather endure a beating than useless freaking banter in the God damn driveway. "Are you going to bring me to the basement or stand here gabbing all day, V?" I asked.

His head tilted, his smile falling to a smirk. "That's just it, Summer. That's just what you have missed." He paused, letting his words sink in. "I'm not V."

I felt my face fall. My mouth opened slightly, my eyes got wide. He wasn't V? What? How was he not V? Everyone called him V. That made no sense. At all.

"In fact, I believe it is time for you to meet the real V," he informed me, jerking his head at Martin who started shoving me forward.

So I followed Not-V up the pathway, into the entrance, past the huge staircase that led up to my old prison upstairs. Not-V turned down the hallway that I had a vague recollection of leading into the kitchen. I felt myself pause, my legs not willing to keep moving. My mind was just simply... not ready for any more surprises. Any more shocks to my system. I just couldn't do it. I couldn't deal with any more. I was done.

Martin made a grunting noise, bringing up his knee and hitting it hard into my lower back, making me stumble forward a few steps.

I had no choice, so I kept walking. The kitchen was a massive area of warm brown tile, stainless steel, and a huge island. Not-V was standing in the doorway, half blocking it, a weird smile on his face. Like he was enjoying it. Like he was anticipating my reaction. Which could only mean that whoever I was about to face was going to scare the ever loving shit out of me. That was the only explanation.

Then he moved to the side, watching my face hard. "V, here she is," he said.

And then there was V. And I just collapsed back against Martin. "Mom?"

TWENTY-FOUR

<u>*Summer*</u>

V.

Vanessa.

Vanessa Lyon.

My mother.

No. No fucking way. No no no no.

Martin shoved me away, making a strange disgusted noise, moving to go stand next to Not-V who was smiling like a maniac still. Like this was the most entertainment he had gotten in months.

I looked at my mother. A mother I had no actual memory of. A mother who was nothing more than a single picture on the mantle in the formal sitting room. A picture that was taken with her smiling beautifully, her gray eyes shining bright, her red hair flowing around her shoulders.

I had no memories of her. Of her brushing my hair or kissing my skinned knees. I didn't know what her voice sounded like. I didn't know what perfume she wore.

She was a ghost to me.

She was some story my father told me when I had finally asked about her. She was his sad eyes falling on mine, his hand landing on my shoulder. "Your mother didn't want to be with us, baby girl. She had other plans for her life. And they didn't include us. That doesn't say anything about us. It doesn't say anything about you. It says she was a very selfish woman. Do you understand me, Summer? It was her loss."

That was what I knew of my mother.

Aside from knowing that I had her eyes and hair.

That was it.

She was selfish.

She didn't want me.

But there she was, standing five feet from me.

She didn't look that different from her picture. Her face wasn't as full as it had been when she was younger. She had some crow's feet beside her eyes. But she looked mostly the same. Youthful. Beautiful. Her red hair was pulled into a loose barrette at the base of her neck. She was short, like me. She was slight, like me. In fact, she was a perfect representation of what I would look like in twenty or so years.

Except I wasn't going to live that long.

She was wearing a pair of black slacks, heels, and a tight white long sleeve t-shirt. Her head was tilted, looking me up and down.

"Daniel, darling," she said, looking over at Not-V. Daniel. His name was Daniel. That was somehow so much less terrifying. And also, my mother's voice was nothing like mine. Mine was smooth, girly. Hers was more throaty, lower, a bedroom voice. It was really weird to be learning that while I was standing cuffed in her kitchen, years after I gave up thinking I would ever meet her. "What has happened to her face?"

Daniel cleared his throat. Martin shrugged and answered. "She tripped."

"Oh, is that what it's called?" I asked, glaring at him.

To that, my mother laughed.

The sound shocked my attention back toward her.

"Summer," she said, giving me a smile. "It's so nice to finally meet you."

Alright.

Let's just say my anger managed to break through my shock.

"Couldn't have dropped by when I was chained to a chair in the basement having one of your lackeys carve into my back? Or perhaps late at night when they would come into my room, climb on top of me, grab at me and tell me all the ways they were going to rape me?"

At that, her face hardened. As did Daniel's, I noticed, as his eyes shot daggers at Martin.

"Deke, man," Martin said, shaking his head like he wasn't a part of it.

"Really? It was Deke who told me that girls like to get it from both ends at once? Funny, cause that sounded a lot like you," I shot back. I was beyond caring about pissing anyone off.

"Summer, darling, no one was going to rape you," my mother soothed.

"Really? Because judging by the look of surprise and anger on your face, you had no fucking idea what was going on under your own roof at night. Please do try to convince me you have any kind of control over the situation. Or your men for that matter."

To that, she smiled. Warmly. It could only be described as warmly. "You know, I was worried about leaving you behind. Leaving you with Richard. I thought he would squeeze every bit of independence and spirit out of you. I guess I was wrong."

Oh, God.

She was right though.

She was so right.

He had done that. He had done that without me even realizing it.

I was his little yes-man. I did what he said. I never fought him. I never even thought about disobeying him. I was terrified of the prospect of letting him down. I was his God damn trained puppy.

The only reason I found my independence and spirit was from being held captive. By her. How fucking sick was that?

At the same time though, whatever my father had done to me, nothing, literally nothing would even come close to being held against your will and starved, beaten, sliced open, and humiliated at the hands of your own mother.

"Whatever Dad may or may not have done, he never had someone lay a hand on me," I said, my chin lifting.

"Oh, darling girl," she said, reminding me of my father. They both called me that. And it was, on both of their lips, incredibly condescending. "Haven't you learned yet that there is far worse damage to inflict on people other than the physical kind?"

"Sounds like you're speaking from experience. How's the skin trade, Mom?" I asked and saw a flash cross her eyes before she pushed it away.

"Martin," she addressed instead, looking at him. "Would you please show my daughter to her room? It seems she needs some time to think about how to speak to her mother." She paused, her eyes going to Daniel as a second thought. "You go with them," she said pointedly, obviously no longer trusting Martin alone.

Thank God for small miracles.

"Will do, V," Daniel said, jerking his head at Martin who walked up to me, shoving me back toward the hallway.

I stumbled up the steps, Martin's hand banging between my shoulder blades every few steps while Daniel followed a few steps below. And I found myself wondering about the man I used to think was V. The man who delivered the orders about what was to be done with me. They weren't his decisions. They were my mother's. And he only put his hands on me once. Then jerked back from me like I had burned him.

What the hell was his deal?

He wasn't the vicious skin trader I thought he was. But he was someone important, someone my mother trusted.

And if he was part of the inner circle, why wouldn't he get his hands dirty?

Were the higher-ups like... above that?

The door to my room was opened and I was pushed inside. Martin reached into his pocket, getting a key to the cuffs and unlocking one of my wrists.

And, well, let's just say I was getting a little sick of being a good prisoner. The second my wrist was free, my arm swung out, the bottom of my palm slamming upward underneath his nose and I heard a sick, satisfying crunch before he reared back, cursing.

"Fucking bitch! The fucking bitch broke my fucking nose!" he yelled, as the blood started pouring.

He advanced on me quickly, but Daniel's hand at the back of his shirt pulled him backward. "Go deal with your face. I'll lock her down."

He'll lock me down?

I was too stunned to swing out again, my arm falling down at my side.

Martin glared at me then stormed out, slamming the door so hard I was shocked it didn't splinter down the center.

"You gonna hit me too?" he asked, his head tilted, watching me.

"I haven't decided yet," I answered honestly.

At that, he nodded. "Do you need to use the bathroom?"

I should have said yes.

I should have taken the opportunity, one arm free, to get my gun and get done with the whole dying thing. But I couldn't bring myself to. Not yet. Not when things had changed so quickly. It shouldn't have mattered that V was my mother. She was nothing to me. But I found myself needing answers.

After I got those answers, I was going to follow through with my plan.

Which would, hopefully, be before Martin got his hands on me again.

I shook my head. "No."

Again, I got a nod. "Are you going to fight me?" he asked, motioning toward the bed.

"Are you going to threaten to rape me?"

He flinched.

Flinched.

The second in command to a skin trader, aka: someone who routinely sold women to be raped, flinched.

What the hell was his deal?

"No, I'm not," he said, his words firm.

"Then I guess I don't have to break your nose too," I said, sitting down on the bed, moving to press my back onto the headboard. I didn't want to be cuffed lying down. I had been cuffed lying down for months. I lifted my hands above my head.

Daniel came toward the bed, kneeling beside me. "No," he said, pulling my arms down. "Put them behind your back instead. It'll hurt your shoulders like hell but it won't make your arms fall asleep." Agreeing to his logic, though wholly uncomprehending why he was trying to offer me comfort, I put my arms behind my back. He reached around me, slipping the chain through a rail, then putting the bracelet on my other wrist and clicking it closed. Then, to my utter disbelief, he grabbed one of the pillows, turning it longways and slipping it behind me to cushion my back from the hard headboard.

"Who are you?" I found myself asking his profile.

His head snapped to me, his eyes flashing for a second before it was gone. "Someone who doesn't get off on pain," he said simply, moving off the bed and toward the door.

He was half in the hallway when I found my voice again. "Is it a good or a bad thing now that she knows I know?" I asked, not sure why I was bothering.

But he turned back to me, hand on the doorknob. "Honestly?" he said, shrugging a shoulder. "There's no way to know that. V is unpredictable on good days. But I can guarantee that no one will be coming into your room at night anymore."

Well.

That was something.

"Thank you," I found myself saying.

His brows lowered, looking confused, before he shook his head at me like I had lost my mind. "Don't thank me, kid. There's no telling what I might have to do in the future. Don't be getting all your hopes up that I can protect you."

And with that, he was gone.

Okay.

I needed to focus.

In the matter of three days, my entire life had been turned on its head. Everything I had accepted as facts were wrong. People I thought I knew were relative strangers. People I thought were strangers were somehow family.

It was a fucking lot to try to digest.

While cuffed to a damn bed.

But then again, being cuffed to a bed left me with nothing to do but think about things.

Like... my mother.

My mother who I had always pictured off living on some white beach somewhere, her days spent drinking margaritas and getting fanned by cabana boys. Then spent her night praying on unsuspecting men like a parasite. Bitchy, childish, maybe. But that was how I saw her. Far away. Wholly unaware of me growing up, becoming my own person.

I didn't think I would have been able to handle knowing she lived within an hour of where I grew up. That would have hurt. More than the abandonment in the first place. More than knowing she loved herself more than she loved me. The fact that she could have made an effort to get to know me, if not as a child, then as an adult, and she tossed it away. Yeah, that burned.

Then there was, of course, the matter of her being a complete and utter monster. A psychopath. Or sociopath. Whatever the psychological term for her might be. She was inhumanly evil.

Never mind that she had me kidnapped, starved, and tortured. Let's forget that for a moment.

She was a woman.

She was a woman who was in the skin trade.

She had other women kidnapped and then she sold their bodies over and over again.

It was disgusting when men did it. Stupid, clueless, careless men.

It was downright evil when a woman did it. Women who knew the horror of rape. Women who, even if they hadn't experienced it, knew the ever-present fear of it. The reality of it possibly happening in their future.

For a woman to subject dozens or hundreds or lord-knew how many innocent women to that, daily, for however long they brought in money... that was so horrifying that I couldn't think of a word to describe it.

My mother bought and sold women into prostitution.

Jesus fucking Christ.

And my father... I didn't know what the hell was going on with my father. But something was up.

My life was crumbling underneath my feet.

I slammed my head back against the headboard to keep the tears from coming as my mind wandered back. To the compound. To the days that followed Reign bringing me there.

**

I was pressed up against Reign's side, his arm laying across my hip, my head on his chest. "Tell me about your past," I'd said, my voice quiet, post-orgasm contented.

"You don't want to know about my past, babe," he'd said, his tone casual, his fingers drawing circles over my hip.

I turned my head to look up at him. His chin ducked and he looked me in the eye. "Tell me," I'd tried again.

He'd rolled his eyes, letting the air out of his chest. "What do you want to know?"

"Everything," I had decided. Because I did want to know everything. The big things, the little things. Everything that made Reign who he was.

He'd shook his head, his hand pressing my head back on his chest. "Not much to tell, babe. What you see is what there is. I'm prez here. It's booze and bitches and brotherhood. You're not stupid. I'm sure you put two and two together and figured out what I do."

"You sell guns," I had put in.

"Yeah, I sell guns. So I meet with a lot of unsavory types. I bust skulls when I need to. Which is more often than you would think. But that's it, babe. That's my life."

I wasn't giving up that easily. "What was your childhood like?"

He'd made a short, weird chuckle. "Seriously?"

"Yeah, seriously," I'd said, mocking his tone.

"It was this too. Dad was prez. We grew up on the compound. Me, Cash, Wolf, a few of the other guys."

"What were you like?"

"A little shit," he'd answered honestly. "Picking fights for no good reason with the outside kids. Getting myself a nasty reputation by the time I was in middle school."

"Were you and Cash close?" I'd asked. Because they were close as adults. Closer even than most brothers.

"Not always. He was always tagging along. Being a pain in the ass. Cracking jokes that I didn't think were funny. Trying to be a part of my friend group."

"What changed?"

"Mom died," he'd said, his shoulder shrugging underneath my head.

"How old were you?"

"I was twelve. Cash was ten."

"I'm sorry," I'd said, being motherless myself, I understood the sting. But my mom was long gone before I could even miss her. He got twelve years to love his.

"She was too soft for Dad's life. Always worried. Always sick. She couldn't deal with the stress. One day, she got sick and never got better. Cash was a mess. Dad went off the deep end..."

"The deep end?" I had prompted.

"He might have made her life difficult with how much the chapter meant to him, how hard he worked, how often he came home bloody and bruised. But he loved our mother. And he didn't handle losing her well. Drinking all the time. Fighting. Taking off on all the runs he could go on."

"Where were you and Cash?" I'd asked, my hand running down his arm.

"Here. Some of the men were always here to make sure we were fed and went to school and shit. Vin especially."

"That's sad," I had said, my fingers brushing over his hand.

His hand moved, surprising me by grabbing mine and lacing his fingers through. "Don't feel sorry for me, babe. It wasn't that bad. I got away with shit no other kid my age would have."

"And Cash?"

The shoulder shrug again. "I took care of him."

Of course he did. Because underneath his big, bad, biker persona was a decent person. Someone who didn't just live for depravity like it seemed from the outside. He was someone who raised up his annoying little brother. He was someone who saved me. He was someone who refused to drag his men into my mess.

He might have been bad.

But he was a good man at the same time.

"Any fucking thing else or can I go to sleep?" he'd asked, but the words were softened by his hand squeezing mine.

"What's your favorite color?"

His body rolled under mine as he laughed silently. "Black, babe."

"Black isn't a color. It's the absence of color," I'd countered.

"Don't be a know-it-all," he'd chuckled, reaching up and tugging my hair playfully.

After that, we fell silent. I took a breath, breathing in his scent, snuggling closer to him, throwing my leg across his body, giving in to my need to be as close to him as possible.

"What about you?" he'd asked later. So much later that I had assumed he was asleep so the shock sent me jolting up, the top of my head slamming underneath his chin, making me yelp and him grunt.

"What about me?" I'd asked, reaching up to rub my head.

"What was your childhood like?" he'd asked, shocking me. He actually wanted to know about my past?

"Oh, um..." my past sounded silly compared to his. His was rough and sad and interesting. Mine was, well, not.

"Talk," he'd commanded and I felt myself snort at his bossiness.

But I gave in anyway.

"It was just me and my dad. He was great. Always encouraging. Always there to help me out when I needed him. Really strict about my grades, my friends, and later... who I dated. He kinda... forced me into the family businesses which I kind of resented. But, then again, I had never said anything about not liking it so he couldn't have known about that."

"What happened to your mom?" he'd asked, one of his hands moving up into my hair, slowly sliding into it and sending a shiver through my body.

"I don't really know," I had admitted, my words a little sad, a little edgy. My mother wasn't a good topic for me. There was resentment there. "My dad didn't really talk about it. He just said she was selfish and didn't want to share our lives and that it said things about her, not me, that she did that."

"Sore spot," he'd commented quietly.

"No, no it's fine. I mean I'm over..."

"Sore spot," he'd repeated, his arm around my hips squeezing me a little.

"Yeah, I guess."

"So let's stop talking about it," he'd suggested.

And we did.

**

It really kinda sucked that I was never going to get the chance to tell Reign that I finally got my answers about her. That she wasn't just a sore spot anymore. She was a giant festering wound.

At that thought, tears burned up behind my eyes.

Not because my mom was a monster.

Because Reign would have found something to say.

He would have told me to stop talking about it, to stop thinking about it.

And I would have.

And I wouldn't feel so shitty.

I tilted my head up to look at the ceiling, taking a deep breath, closing my eyes tight to keep the tears from spilling over. Because the same rules applied. I wasn't going to fucking cry. I could bury my face and I could scream. I could tell Martin and Daniel and my mother to rot in hell. But I couldn't cry.

So I sucked it up.

Eventually, sleep got the best of me.

I woke up to a hand pressing hard into my throat. "You stupid fucking bitch," Martin's whispered voice cut through my sleep fog and I was instantly alert. My eyes snapped up to his face, seeing red dried around his nose, one of his eyes blackening. "You think you can put your fucking hands on me and not get taught a lesson?"

Fuck.

Shit.

I knew it.

I knew it.

She had no control over her men.

What a pathetic fucking excuse for a crime lord.

Martin's hand meant business, his hand not pressing onto the carotid so I didn't pass out, but pressing so hard that I couldn't draw a proper breath. Or scream. Or think of anything but how bad it was hurting, how terrifying it was to feel your air cut off, and to know you could only go for so long without a good lungful of air.

"You break my fucking nose? I'm gonna break your fucking face."

Then his hand was moving from my throat and cocked back so fast, I couldn't even draw a breath before his fist landed hard next to my right eye.

The pain was like an explosion. Like fireworks. How the hit is in the center and it radiates out, spreading, consuming. My entire face felt the sting. The second the contact ended, the pain turned to a throb, deep and insistent.

"That's just a preview, you stupid cunt," he growled when a tap sounded at the door. No doubt, the buddy who was assigned to watch him.

The door opened, the light from the hall painful and I saw the outline of another guy. Not Daniel. Someone else. Someone I didn't know. Someone I had a sinking feeling I would get to know quite well in the time coming.

The door shut, plunging me back into darkness and I rested my head back against the headboard, taking a deep breath.

It was just a black eye. That was it. It was no big deal. Worst case, it was a broken eye socket. It was not fatal. It probably wouldn't be pretty, but swallowing a bullet was going to make an open casket impossible anyway so it didn't really matter.

I needed my answers.

And then I needed a permanent way out of this hell.

I choked back a weird sob as a flash of Reign came into my mind.

I pushed it away, trying not to think about him.

But that wasn't possible.

He wouldn't be happy I was dead.

I kind of liked that.

It would be a blow. Because he wanted to save me. Because he was going to make V pay for what (s)he did to me.

But it wouldn't break him.

He had lived too hard a life to be shaken by my death.

He would be okay.

—

"What the fuck?"

I forgot how alarming it was to wake up to angry male voices.

I tried to shoot up out of bed, but my wrists pulled, my shoulders screamed, and I fell back against the headboard.

"Oh, fuck. It gets worse," he sighed. I blinked slow, taking in Daniel standing in the room in a gray suit, white shirt, and gray patterned tie.

"What?" I croaked, my throat feeling like I swallowed razors.

"Mother fucker. I should have known," Daniel said, shaking his head.

"Worried Mom will be pissed?" I asked, wincing at the stinging.

At that, Daniel gave me an weird smile. "No. It's just the point," he said. "I gave you my word. Come on," he said, reaching for a key and letting one of my wrists free. "Bathroom break and then V wants to have a sit down."

"Oh joy," I drawled and I could have sworn I heard him chuckle. But that wasn't possible.

He opened the bathroom door and let me shuffle inside. I turned back to him. "I know... five minutes," I said, rolling my eyes.

He shook his head, a smirk toying at his lips like something about me amused him, then shut the door.

I took a deep breath, letting my eyes meet my reflection in the mirror.

"Shit."

No wonder he sounded pissed when he saw me.

There were defined blue finger prints to the left of my neck, a long blue band across the center from the space between his thumb and forefinger. My eye was blackened. It was a dark, awful blue and purple. But, more than that, the sclera of my eye was blood red.

It wasn't pretty.

I sighed, turning on the water like I always did before I peed so whoever was standing outside didn't hear me. It was kind of stupid to feel insecure about going to the bathroom when those men had seen me on my period, but still. It made me feel marginally less like a captive and more like a normal human being.

I washed my hands and tried to work some order into my hair. Then the door was opening and I had to give up.

"To the basement," I said in a weird, cheery tone, flinging a hand out and feeling like a total dork. But it was cool. I was going to die soon. I wouldn't have to live with the mortification for long.

I held out my wrists and was cuffed in the front. "Kitchen," he corrected.

I pursed my lips and shrugged, following him downstairs.

And, sure enough, there was my mother in the kitchen, looking well rested and gorgeous in faded bluejeans, a navy v-neck tee, and camel colored high heeled boots. Her hair was loose, falling in the same kind of wavy mass that mine did.

I felt dirty.

Once I got out of her house the last time, I showered as much as possible. Two, three times a day. Never feeling like I could scrub the dirt and sweat and disgust out of my skin.

One day back and I felt filthy all over again. It was like I had never gotten a chance to wash it all away.

"Summer," she greeted, giving me a warm smile. "I see you had a little mishap."

"Oh yeah," I said, dryly. "I somehow managed to knock myself around while cuffed to a bed. I'm so clumsy like that."

To that, she laughed. Daniel looked down at his feet.

"Well, no matter," she said, waving a hand, brushing it away like I had complained of a paper cut instead of a bloody, black eye and a crushed larynx. "Why don't you have a seat so we can have a little chat?"

Not given much of a choice, I scooted onto one of the backless stools that were pressed against the island.

"What did you want to chat about? The last twenty-four years? Seems a little heavy for coffee conversation."

Another smile. "I wanted to talk about your father."

Shit.

Reign's words whooshed through my brain: *Sore spot.*

"What about my father?"

Her head tilted to the side, watching me. "You really had no clue, did you?"

At that, I kept silent. Because, she was right, there was a lot about Richard Lyon I didn't know about. But I wasn't going to own up to my own stupidity or naïveté either.

"Did he keep you in a bubble?" she asked, shaking her head. "Last I heard you were in a good college, working at one of his legitimate businesses in the city."

There was a strange inflection on the word 'legitimate' that had my spine straightening.

"You kept tabs on me?" I asked instead.

"Your father and I made a deal when I left. He didn't mess with my business. I didn't mess with you. You were his. But a mother gets curious."

Oh, holy fuck.

They made a *deal*? She hadn't just up and left one day like the selfish bitch he made her out to be? He was in on it?

And also... her business? He knew about her business? Before the kidnapping and torture? He knew?

"I see you're confused," she said, leaning down on the island several feet away from me. "Let's start at the beginning, shall we?"

Honestly, a part of me was done. I didn't want to hear more. I was feeling freaking light headed with all the revelations. But I didn't want to appear weak. Weakness would get me nowhere.

"If you need to have your say, I'm not exactly in a position to stop you," I offered, showing her my hands.

Her lips quirked up. "I guess I didn't quite miss the rebellious stage of your upbringing after all, did I?" she asked, but went on before I could throw something snippy in. "I met Rich when I was nineteen. He wasn't the man then that he is now," she said, almost wistfully. "He came from a bad neighborhood. I came from a worse one. And he was doing pretty well for himself. He was older, charming. He offered to take care of me. I didn't know then that his brand of 'care' came with a lot of expectations, demands, and unrelenting high standards."

Well, that certainly hit home.

"But still, I was in love. Young and stupid. Not more than a year or so later, I learned I was pregnant. Rich was thrilled. I, well, not so much," she didn't say this with regret or shame like she should have seeing as I was what she was pregnant with and I was the one listening to her fucking story. "When he learned you were a girl, he was ecstatic. He always wanted a little girl to spoil and buy ponies for." She paused, looking at me. "Did he buy you ponies?"

Yes, yes he did.

"Yeah."

At that, she nodded. "By the time you were a year, his business had skyrocketed. He was very powerful. With more power, came more control issues. More expectations for me to be someone I wasn't. Endless hours at the personal trainer, with tutors, in piano lessons, and French lessons. He wanted a wife on his arm who he could be proud of, not some rough and tough chick from the streets. And I did it because I didn't see another alternative. But, when he wasn't around, which was a lot, I plotted. I planned. I got my business started. Just a barn with ten or so girls. But it was enough. I was getting a reputation. I'd drive over there with you strapped into the baby seat and handle business, then come home and cook him dinner, telling him we spent the day at the park or at baby music lessons. For a year, he believed me."

Um.

Hold the fuck up.

She used to bring *me* to her whorehouses?

"Then about a week after your third birthday, Rich got wind of what I was up to. I guess because business had quadrupled and my name was getting out there. Anyway, he was, as you can imagine, not very happy. It wasn't respectable for a wife of his to work, let alone start to build her very own empire. We went a lot of rounds. I wasn't giving in. He wasn't giving in. So then I told him I was taking you and leaving."

Oh, God.

I mean, my father was no saint, but he certainly seemed better parent material than my mother. I didn't even want to consider what life would have been like growing up with her.

"Rich saw red at that. He threatened to tear my business down. And, while I was doing well, I wasn't doing so well that his threat wasn't a viable one. So I asked what he wanted. He said you. The rest is history."

"You gave me up so you could force girls into the sex trade?" I snapped, my tone deadly.

Her eyes flashed. "Don't look down your nose at me, Summer. You grew up in a God damn criminal empire yourself. You were just too clueless to see it."

Alright.

That information was something I had started to consider myself. Back in my bedroom at my father's house, trying to figure out who the fuck he really was. It had crossed my mind.

But having validation was something else altogether.

My mother's head shook, her eyes rolling slightly as she looked to the ceiling. She looked down at me. "What did you think your father did?"

"He's an importer," I said automatically.

"Yes, but an importer of what?"

That was a good question. One I had never even thought to ask. Dad owned a chain of clothing stores. I always figured he imported clothes made in sweatshops. It was a fact I was always uncomfortable with, but never had the guts to talk to him about or even look into it when I was working in the corporate headquarters.

She shook her head at me again like I was dense. "I wanted his containers. That's why you're here. His containers that come in from South America. There's a lot of ripe, pretty girls in South America. Do you know what else there is in South America?" she asked.

I was too busy trying to not throw up over the 'ripe, pretty girls' comment to even pretend I knew. "No."

"Cocaine," she supplied and I felt her words settle like lead in my belly.

Cocaine.

My mother was a heartless skin trader.

And my father imported and sold cocaine.

What. The. Fuck?

Nothing. Literally nothing could have ever prepared me for that harsh reality. I was the child of criminals. Of God damn crime lords. And I had been blind to it my entire life. Going around sipping mimosas at brunch and getting my nails painted and thinking I had the most normal, albeit privileged, life imaginable.

Jesus Christ.

I had crime lords for parents.

And at least one of them was a fucking psychopath.

What the hell did that say about me?

TWENTY-FIVE

<u>*Reign*</u>

Three. Fucking. Days.

"You need to sleep, man," Cash said, watching me, looking just as haggard as I did.

"I'll sleep when we get her the fuck back."

It had been the same argument since I rolled in from the meeting with the Russians. After checking out the shit evidence we had. After looking in at Repo. After sitting at his bedside until he finally regained consciousness and gave us his side of the story.

"Didn't hear shit. But then I saw an outsider and he was cuffing Summer's hands behind her back. Had duct tape over her mouth. She was struggling with him. Fucking idiot I am," he said, slamming his hand onto the mattress, "I fucking called her. And she turned. And then he saw me. And then we were fighting. He clocked me to the side of the head and I was fucking out man. So fucking stupid."

"No man," I said, shaking my head. "No, you did good. You tried to protect her. You took a beating for her. You did good," I said, clamping my hand down on his shoulder.

"Prez," he said, sitting up as I made my way to the door. I turned back. "You need anything to get her back, I'm in. I know I'm not patched-in. But I'm fucking *in*," he said, his voice fierce.

And even though it was against rules, even though it would cause problems, I felt myself nodding. "Yeah, you are."

"Wolf's been gone a long time," Cash said, bringing me back to the present.

"Yeah," I agreed.

"Should have sent someone with him, man. Now we know who the fuck Richard Lyon is..."

Maybe we should have. But I didn't want to involve anyone else in my mess. It was already bad enough with Cash, Wolf, and now Repo, involved. We couldn't put anyone else at risk.

"Wolf knows what he's doing," I said, hoping it was true.

I raked a hand down my face.

Her fucking father was the biggest cocaine dealer on the East coast. How the fuck did that stay so far under our radar? Granted, we didn't deal in drugs. But we tried to keep up with the big organizations around. The MCs. The Italians. The fucking Irish. The Mexican cartels. Everything. How'd we miss a cocaine dealer? And not some little guy. He was fucking huge. Had been for the better part of twenty years.

And it had somehow escaped Summer's notice her whole life.

Not that he hadn't tried to cover his tracks. He had dozens of legitimate businesses: clothing stores, a coffee chain, a fucking luxury car dealership. He put up appearances of being a normal, everyday businessman. He went to gallery openings and held lavish charity auctions. He was in the goddamn society pages for chrissakes.

But he had an empire.

One with footmen, a mini military and dozens of dealers.

He wasn't known for being a ruthless fuck like most drug lords. He was just smart. Careful. He had his shit locked down tight so there didn't need to be a lot of blood in the streets. Which was how he kept the cops off his back and how he managed to fly under the radar of all his socialite friends and all his legitimate business partners.

The door to my room flew open, making my head jerk up.

And there was Wolf.

He was a little knocked around, his shirt torn, blood on his collar. But unharmed. As expected. He rarely ever had someone who could get the better of him.

He nodded his head at me. "Shed," he said, then was gone.

I looked at Cash who shook his head. "Who the fuck does he have in the shed?" he asked, getting up and making his way toward the door.

"Dunno," I said, my hands already curling into fists. I didn't know. I didn't fucking care. All I knew was I was going to get some fucking information. Enough dicking around not doing anything. Anything. While fuck-knew was happening to Summer.

Cash let himself into the shed where Wolf had already disappeared into. I took a deep breath, then followed in, slamming the door.

There was a man cuffed to the chair in a thousand dollar fucking suit.

My eyebrow quirked up, looking at Wolf.

Because... no fucking way. No way in hell was he that crazy.

"He took her," Wolf answered on a shrug.

"What?" I growled, rushing forward toward him.

Him being Richard Lyon.

Summer's father.

I had an international drug lord cuffed to a chair in my fucking shed.

"He took her," Wolf repeated. "V took her back."

The second of relief I had at knowing she was with her father evaporated.

"You're gonna have to fucking start from the beginning," I bit off, looking at Richard Lyon who seemed tense, but not completely freaked out like most would be cuffed in my shed.

"I don't see how it's any of your business," he started, his tone cold. "Low life gun runners. She's none of your concern."

"I made her my concern when I offered her protection from V. When I helped her work through the shit you let her go through, you sonovabitch. When I killed one of V's lackeys after watching Summer beat the shit out of him. She's. My. Fucking. Concern."

Richard's head tilted, watching me, his brows drawing low. "Summer would never beat anyone. She was raised better than that. She's not base like you."

"Watched it my damn self," Cash pitched in. "She's got a mean right hook. She also told us that when we catch the other guy who used to slice her up, that we should use knives on him."

"No, she wouldn't..."

"Then when she was done beating him," I added, enjoying his look of outrage, "she told me to have fun killing him." I watched him a beat, then laughed humorlessly. "What's the matter? Bother you that she's more like you than you planned?"

"I don't beat and kill people."

"Not personally, no. But you have it done. You've got blood on your hands just like me. Just like your daughter." That was a direct hit. His breath hissed out of his mouth.

"She only has blood on her hands because of you. You filthy little..."

He lost the rest of his sentence. Mainly because my fist collided with his mouth.

"How the fuck d'ya get him?" I asked, looking over at Wolf.

Last I'd heard, his home was like a fortress.

"V got his men," Wolf shrugged.

I turned back to Richard. "I don't give a fuck how much money you lose, but you're going to call V and you're going to tell him that you're going to give into the demands."

"Her."

"What?" I growled, my hands itching to hit him again.

"V isn't a him. V is a her," Richard clarified.

I caught Cash's surprised face, then he shook his head. "No, man. Don't fuckin' lie to us. I met V."

Richard's head turned, looking pleased that he knew more than we did. "No. You met Daniel. Daniel pretends to be V in public. But he isn't V."

"Then who the fuck is?" I exploded, getting closer to the chair.

Richard's head tilted up toward me, a look of distaste covering his features. "My wife."

Alright. Of all the things he could have said, that might have been the only one that could have made me step away from him, lose the urge to beat him into little meaty pieces. Because I needed answers.

"The fuck?" I asked, moving to lean against the wall, crossing my arms over my chest.

"V is Vanessa Lyon. She came from the ghetto and try as I might, I could never rid that street persona from her. And believe me, I tried," he said in an odd tone, a tone that made me think there was a fair amount of street underneath his suit as well. "Then I found out that she was acting as a pimp. Had herself a barn of whores. I couldn't let that be a part of my daughter's life. So I let her go."

"And she built her own criminal empire to rival yours."

"Hers is built on blood," Richard said, seeming to be insulted by being compared to her. "Rivers and rivers of blood. She's... unhinged."

"No, really?" I ground out. "How could you tell? Because she had her own fucking daughter branded, sliced up, beaten, and threatened to be raped?" At my words, Richard paled. Though I knew from Summer's own mouth that he had known she was being tortured. "Yeah. Your fucking containers of coke worth your daughter suffering like that?"

Richard's face fell to look at his lap. "You don't understand."

"Then enlighten us," Cash offered, looking like he was losing patience.

"I can't give in to her. Not even for Summer."

"Why the fuck not?" Wolf exploded. Exploded. The sound of his voice was loud enough for the walls to vibrate. Cash's body got tense, ready if needed, to try to grab Wolf and hold him back.

"There's no one to hold her back," Richard said, sounding worried. "Without me, without me standing up to her... there's no telling what she would do. She's dangerous. More than me," he looked up, staring me in the eye. "More than you."

"You have no fucking idea how dangerous I am," I countered.

"Oh, I know," he said in a tone that suggested he did. A tone that said he knew about every life my hands had taken. Every body I had broken. "But she's bigger. She's richer. And she's out of her mind."

"What the..." Cash started, but Richard went on talking.

"That's her baby. You get that, right? She carried her. She sang her to sleep as an infant. She was a good mother for those years she was with us. She loved Summer. And yet she is holding her. Beating her. Starving her. Because nothing is more important to her than power. I can't let her have that power. It would be catastrophic."

Unfortunately, that made its own kind of sick sense.

I'd been around long enough to see crime lords get too big for their britches. Get too powerful. And with power came the urge to stay in power. Which, he was right, led to rivers of blood. Often for no good reason. And it always took a bigger, badder fuck to take them down. Or the cops. But the cops weren't touching V. So she either had deep pockets or she had something else on them.

She was dangerous.

"There has to be someone who can stand up to her. Someone she's afraid of. Other than you," Cash clarified.

"Not one would get involved over one girl," Richard said, shaking his head. Like he had already maybe went through the channels. Like maybe he had been trying to get her back all along.

"Who'd you approach?" I asked.

Richard shrugged. "Everyone. O'Neils. The Grassis. Even the Changs. The Changs want to run the skin trade. But even they don't want to go to war over this."

I shook my head. "You approached the families?" I asked. The Irish. Italian. Chinese. They were old school operations. The families survived because of caution and ironclad rules. "What about the MCs or the..."

"I don't associate with the likes of motorclubs and low life criminals."

So we were back to that.

"Lo," Wolf mumbled. Low. So I ignored him.

"This is your fucking daughter we are talking about and you can't swallow your pride and approach..."

"Lo," Wolf said, louder, making me turn to him.

"Lo?" I asked, my brows drawing together.

"We'll get Lo," he added.

My eyes went to Cash and I saw a look there that mirrored what I was feeling inside.

There were criminals. Me. Cash. Wolf. We were criminals. There were crime lords. Lyon and V and the families, they were crime lords. And then there were just plain old crazy mother fuckers.

Lo was a plain old crazy mother fucker.

He was some kind of ex-military or shit like that, or that was what everyone assumed. He had a massive compound, acres up in the hills with electric fences and a dozen long, low, buildings made of shipping containers, meant to withstand any kind of natural disaster, and most bullets. He had men stationed everywhere with guns strapped across their backs. Guns that I had sold them. And then there were the dogs. Dozens of them. They were vicious breeds: Pitbulls, Rotties, Dobermans. They were dogs meant to instill fear, dogs capable of being trained for security.

He lived like he expected the government to declare a permanent Marshall Law and he wanted to be able to fight them off.

And, like I said, he was a crazy mother fucker.

I had been hearing stories about Lo for the better part of a decade. He had been slowly building up his personal army, full of ex-military and street brats who needed some way to harness their anger.

He didn't run drugs or guns or girls.

No one really knew what the fuck he did.

All anyone knew was that he took lives easily and often.

"I don't think bringing in a lunatic like that would be the best bet," Richard pitched in, as if he was part of a board meeting, not cuffed to a chair in my blood stained shed.

"Why not?" Cash asked. "You said yourself, your wife is crazy. What better way to fight crazy but with more crazy?"

"No one has even met Lo," Richard tried to reason. "We know nothing about him. If we can't control him, then we can't get Summer out."

Another not altogether stupid point.

His dedication to rationality was starting to piss me off.

"We'll go," Wolf tried, looking at me.

"Go where?" I asked.

"To meet Lo."

"That's not a bad plan," Cash offered. "Meet him. Get a feel for him and his loyalties. See if we want to get involved with him. Then go from there."

"We're wasting fucking time," I growled.

Richard's eyes found mine, and I saw the same kind of hollowness that I felt inside. He wanted his daughter back. As cold and detached as he was being about the whole affair, he wanted her back just as badly as I did.

"She's not who she was four months ago," he said, watching me.

"What are you talking about?"

"Summer," he clarified. "I raised her soft and sweet and compliant. She was a good girl. The kind of girl who never learned to fully stand on her own. She's not that girl anymore. She's stronger.

She's resilient. She survived three months under V. And we both know what happened to her there. Three months. And when I got my hands on her again, she was ready to fight. V didn't break her. Three months and she didn't even get close to breaking her. It's only been three days."

I swallowed hard. He was right. Even after what she had gone through, she was steel. "She screams," I said, the sound piercing in my ears.

"I've heard her," he agreed.

Fuck.

"Fine. Tomorrow," I declared. "We'll go to Lo's tomorrow. With or without him, I want Summer back the day after. I don't care what the fuck we have to do to make that happen."

I started toward the door when Cash's voice stopped me. "Ah, Reign..."

"What?"

"What are we supposed to do with him?" he said, motioning toward Richard.

"He looks comfortable enough," I shrugged. "Put Repo on his watch. He's dying for responsibility. Oh," I said, turning back, a smirk at my lips. "Repo is one of my men who got busted up pretty good at your hands. I'm curious to see what kind of self control he has when he learns that fact," I said, watching Richard pale.

I went into the compound, ignoring the curious eyes of the men who were hanging about and went right up to my room. I kicked off my boots and got on the bed. I needed to sleep. Even for a few hours. I needed to be sharp. I needed to get my fucking head on straight.

But as I tossed and turned, sleep didn't come.

Memories did.

**

"What is this one for?" Summer asked, lying on my chest, her fingers tracing over my tattoos, asking what they stood for, bitching at me if she found out they meant nothing, that I just liked the design. Apparently if I was going to ink something into my skin permanently, it should have some kind of personal meaning.

Her finger was running over the edge of a dark anchor.

"That one is for Cash," I supplied.

"Really?" she asked, pushing up on my chest to look down at me, her hair falling forward and I reached up to tuck it behind her ear. "An anchor?"

I nodded. "And he has the wheel." Her brows drew together, trying to make sense of that information. "It's an old sayin'," I provided. "The one with the wheel means '*be the one who guides me*', and the anchor means '*but never hold me down*'."

"Oh," she said, her eyes dropping to my mouth.

"Keep lookin' at my mouth, babe, and I'm gonna start thinkin' about what I can do with it."

She laughed, shaking her head. "I can't come again," she said, rolling her eyes. "I think four times is my max. My legs feel like jello."

I laughed. *Laughed.* I never fucking laughed. But I laughed. Then I made a grab for her, rolling her onto her back and putting my body over hers. "Care to test that theory?" I asked, running my mouth between her tits, down her stomach.

"Reign... I can't..." she objected, sounding airy.

"We'll see," I said, my face going between her legs.

We did see.

And she could.

**

"Fuck," I growled, getting up off the bed and pacing the room.

That was why I couldn't sleep. Not just the idea that she was being hurt again, that she was getting more reasons to scream at night. But the memories of the short time we got to spend together. Then I had to fucking leave her for some shitty meeting with the Russians. Which led fucking nowhere.

If I had been there, there would have been no way she would have been taken.

Mainly because we spent most of our damn time naked in bed. Or the shower.

No way would she have been outside.

Certainly not with a fucking probate like Flee.

I tore out of my room, going out into the main area, empty but for Wolf and Cash.

"What's going on?" I asked, sensing the tension in the room.

"We're both going," Cash supplied.

My head was shaking before he even stopped talking. "No. I need one of you here. You know that. And you know it's supposed to be you, Cash. But if you're hellbent on goin', it can be Wolf here."

Wolf was shaking his head. "Goin' too," he said.

"Wolf. I need you..."

"Good woman," he said, looking at me, his eyes firm.

She was a good woman. And it hadn't exactly escaped my notice that she and Wolf had gotten on. Fuck if I knew how seeing as he almost never spoke. But then again, half the time Summer didn't shut up. So I guessed it could work. He had been bringing her down to the basement little by little to get her over her fear so she could do her laundry. He was soft with her. Well, as soft as a man as hard as him could be. She brought that out. And that meant something to him.

"Fuck," I said, leaning against the bar. "Who then?" I asked, looking between them.

Cash shrugged. "Vin. For the day, Vin."

He really was the only option. Which I wasn't overly happy about. Vin was good. Stable. Level-headed. All for the brotherhood. But he tended to be too black and white. And with the gray shit we had going on...

"I guess he'll do for a day. So long as he reverts all decisions to me. Shit should be calm now. We'll keep Repo on Lyon. Tell everyone else to stay the fuck out of the shed."

"First light?" Wolf asked, looking anxious to get going.

"First light," I agreed. None of us were going to bother with sleep anyway.

So we sat, watched out the window, and waited.

—

Lo's compound was named. As in there was a huge as fuck green sign out front with white print on it, staked with steel beams into the ground like a road sign on a highway.

Hailstorm.

That was it. It was named Hailstorm.

I shared a look with Cash who shrugged, looking past the sign and behind the gates. It had been months since I had seen the property. Probably closer to a year. Lo had expanded. Red, blue, and green shipping containers were everywhere, some connected, forming a big outer hollow square building. In the center was a small brick building. There were other outer laying containers, standing alone. Each with a man or two walking the surface, looking into the distance.

The dogs were everywhere too. Alert. Sniffing. Their heads jerking when they caught an unfamiliar scent.

Beside the containers were huge white barrels for water catching. Toward the back of the property, there was a field of solar panels.

Not only was Lo some kind of psycho. He was some sort of prepper.

"Fucking hell," I said, shaking my head as we pulled up to the front gates.

"Too late now," Cash said, smiling, his thoughts aligned with mine.

Even as he said it, all eyes were turned on us, guns raised, dogs hauling ass to greet us with foaming mouths and snarls.

A few minutes later, a lone figure walked out from the door of the center shipping container. Tall. Bald head. Dark midnight skin. Strong build. The undeniable posture of ex-military. He walked casually toward us, no guns. But he didn't need one when at least ten were aimed at us.

"Henchmen?" he asked, his brows drawing down.

"We got something to discuss with Lo," I supplied.

"Got a death wish?" he asked, flashing white teeth.

"Got a situation," I said, shrugging.

"And you want Lo to be involved?" he asked as if it was the craziest thing he had ever heard.

"Maybe. That's why we're here. To feel him out."

To that, he smiled wider. "Alright," he said, shrugging. Then he walked over to a booth, hitting some buttons until the gate started to open.

"Not even gonna ask if we're packing?" Cash asked and I glared at him. We were packing. Of course we were.

"You think it'd matter?" he asked, gesturing toward the men all around, a few more coming out of the wood works to watch us.

"Got a point," Cash said, casual as ever. As if we weren't walking into a damn fortress run by a known madman.

We were led over to the shipping container the guy had first stepped out of, finding absolutely nothing inside but a bunch of boots and jackets. Then straight through a steel door to another room that was some kind of meeting area. Then we went into a living space with an open floor plan, t kitchen/dining/living in one. It was small, but comfortable. There were no windows, but more than enough overhead, standing, and table lamps to make up for it. The light was a little off and I wondered if it was UV lighting to make up for the lack of sun.

"Relax," he said, gesturing toward the kitchen. "I'll let Lo know you're here."

He left us. Alone. In the center of their weird fortress. But I had the distinct impression, though, that we weren't alone. That there were men already stationed where we had come in from. And men where our chaperon had disappeared to.

"Fuckin' weird," Wolf said, looking around.

"Got that right," Cash agreed. "They live like cave people."

"Cash, we ain't got no windows either," I reminded him with a smirk.

"Yeah, but this place is..."

"Greg says you're looking for me," a voice called, making us all jump and turn.

"No fuckin' way," Cash said, a disbelieving grin overtaking his face.

Because there standing just inside the doorway in front of Greg, was Lo.

And Lo was a fucking woman.

And not just a woman.

A good fucking looking woman.

She was tall. At least five-nine with a strong, but slim build, wide hips, and a great rack. She had long ash blond hair, a face that was all sharp edges with dark brown eyes. She had on worn jeans and a white tee. A gun was strapped to a band on her thigh, another at her hip.

"Are all the crime lords fucking women now?" Cash asked, wondering aloud what we were all thinking.

At that, Lo smiled, a tinkling laugh escaping her lips. "Can't let you men have all the fun now can we?" she asked.

"How the fuck old are you?" Cash went on, making me roll my eyes.

She turned her eyes on Cash, a smirk toying at her lips. "Almost old enough for that question to be borderline offensive."

"You're seriously Lo?" he asked, obviously not convinced. Because she was young. Not young like Summer. But somewhere along the line of our ages. Maybe more Wolf's than mine. Mid to late thirties.

"Yep, that's me. They call me Lo because I like to keep this," she said, gesturing toward her tits, "on the down low." She walked into the kitchen area, calm, casual, like it was nothing to have three hulking criminals in her personal space. Maybe it wasn't. "So," she said, pouring cups of coffee, "what brings you here?"

"V," I answered, taking the cup from her hands.

"That bitch?" she asked, rolling her eyes.

"You knew she was a bitch? How the fuck did everyone else know that but us?" Cash asked, shaking his head.

"Oh, honey," she said, giving Cash a killer smile, "I know everything. Just like I know you have a cocaine kingpin up in your shed right as we speak. Like I know that same guy had half his men taken out the day before you nabbed him. Like I know you," she said, turning to look at me, "had a woman staying at your house before taking her back to the compound. Care to fill in the missing pieces? It's been driving me nuts."

I shared a look with Cash, then Wolf. Cash shrugged.

Wolf grunted. "Gone this far," he said.

I guessed he was right.

"Alright, here's how it is. The guy in our shed is Richard Lyon who is married but estranged from his wife, Vanessa."

"V," she supplied.

"Yeah, V. The woman who was stayin' with me, she was their only kid. V wants control of Lyon's shipping containers to bring in new skin. Took the daughter to try to convince him. He wasn't giving in 'cause he thinks she needs someone to keep her in check. And that's his job. So he didn't give in no matter how much the girl got tortured. The girl got out, crashed a car. I found her. Took her to my house. Then to the compound. Lyon took her from me. V took her from him. So here we are."

"Quite the clusterfuck," she said, sipping her coffee. "You men," she said, smiling oddly. "Always making such a mess of situations."

"The fuck were we supposed to do?" Cash asked, looking like he wanted to strangle her.

"For starters," she went on, unfazed. Probably because of the sheer amount of men at Hailstorm. She was likely used to testosterone-driven outbursts. "You don't fall in love with the daughter of two of the biggest crime lords on the coast," she said, turning her gaze to me.

The fuck?

No.

What.

The.

Fuck?

Fall in love with the daughter of two of the biggest crime lords on the coast?

Summer?

I wasn't in love with Summer.

"Oh, that's precious," Lo said, laughing her tinkling laugh again. "You still haven't realized you love her yet, huh?"

Cash and Wolf's eyes turned to me.

Oh, fuck.

**

"Come on," Summer pleaded, sticking out her bottom lip in an epic fucking pout.

"No," I said for the third time.

"You know you want to," she tried, throwing her leg over my waist and straddling me, wearing one of my old t-shirts, the neck pulled wide and exposing her shoulder. My hands went out, landing on the sides of her hips as I looked up at her. Her delicate face. Her soft red hair, bed messy. Her tiny body that had taken so much abuse. Her big gray eyes that had lost so much of their fear. "Reign..." she tried, her voice dipping low because she knew it drove me wild when she said my name.

I knifed up, sending her flying onto her back, my body crashing down on hers. "I said no, Summer," I said, shaking my head.

She took a breath, looking away for a second. When she turned back, I didn't trust the look in her eyes. Then her eyes held mine as her teeth nipped into her lower lip. "For me?" she asked.

Fucking hell.

"For you?" I asked, looking down at her and she nodded.

There was a strange warm tightness in my chest as I realized that I would do it. I would probably do anything she asked.

"Fine," I sighed, shaking my head at myself.

But then her face lit up and I forgot all about why I was supposed to be mad at myself for giving into her again.

**

"Oh, fuck," I said, slamming down my coffee cup.

"You caught feelings," Cash said, beaming at me.

"Good woman," Wolf added.

Lo took a deep breath. "God, I'm a sucker for a good love story," she said, shaking her head at herself. "So what do you need from me?"

"Your reputation," I offered.

"You think that I am the big bad that can keep V in line?"

"Somethin' like that. We know your reputation."

"*What* do you do?" Cash cut in, leaning on the counter toward Lo, looking fascinated.

Jesus fucking Christ. He wanted to stick his cock in her. Typical.

Lo shrugged. "I do a little bit of a lot of things. Chasing skips. Private security. The occasional extortion deal. Some hits. Not as many as we used to do though. I have a lot of men with a lot of varied talents. I like to put them to work."

"Hits?" Cash asked.

"What? Never killed anyone?" she asked him, leaning across the island, getting close to his face. He had. Not often. But he had. "Ah, there it is," she said, nodding. "We aren't that different."

"We kill to protect our chapter. Our brothers," Cash shot back.

"So you're better than me because I kill for money?"

"Hell fucking yeah," Cash countered.

Alright. Maybe I read that wrong. He didn't want to fuck her. He wanted nothing to do with her.

"Yo, as much fun as it is to watch you two bicker like an old married couple," I broke in, watching their faces snap to mine, "I got a woman being tortured as we speak. Are you gonna fucking help us or what?"

Lo exhaled a long breath, straightening.

"Oh, what the hell. If for nothing else than to see how you look at her now that you know you love her."

And that was how we got the craziest mother fucker on the East coast in on our mission to get Summer back.

TWENTY-SIX

Summer

Four days.

Two days at my father's.

Two days at my mother's.

So far, I was pretty sure I preferred my father's. With the unlimited access to the shower and bathroom and actual decent meals. With big, hulking, silent Lee keeping watch over me. Instead of Martin. Instead of the other new guy who sat outside my door at night singing some song I had never heard about killing a man. In a sick sort of way, I almost wished Deke was still around. At least I knew what I was in for with him. The new guy, well, he had eyes like Martin.

"Five minutes," Martin growled, throwing me into the bathroom and slamming the door.

He was pissed. Probably because, for some reason, he wasn't able to get into my room the night before. Which I had a suspicion might have had something to do with Daniel intervening.

I was also uncuffed and then allowed to recuff in my front to give my shoulders a break. Again, thanks to Daniel.

I washed my hands, looking up into the mirror. If the day before was bad, this was worse. The bruises around my throat looked darker, my eye had yellow mingling with the blue and purple. And my eye was still full of blood. Apparently that didn't go away like I thought it would. It looked worse than it was though. It didn't even hurt. So at least there was that.

The door swung open.

Too soon.

I had been counting.

We were at three minutes.

Not good.

I barely had a chance to jerk my head in the direction of the door before my hips were slammed up against the sink hard enough for me to yelp and the side of my face collided with the mirror, a hand at the back of my neck holding me there. The glass cracked beneath the pressure and I felt the blood start to trickle down the side of my face. The pressure on my neck relaxed and I sucked in a deep breath, preparing. Because it wasn't over.

The hand moved up into my hair, grabbing it at the base of my neck and pulling viciously backward, and turning me until my head jerked up and I was staring into the hollows that were Martin's eyes.

"Get on your knees," he said quietly.

No.

No fucking way in hell.

No.

But the choice was taken away a few seconds later when Martin's boot swung forward and, full force, landed against my shin, sending me downward on a hiss. The hand stayed in my hair, slipping down toward the ends and pulling harder. His other hand went to the front of his jeans, popping the button and reaching for the zip.

No.

No no no no no.

That couldn't happen.

I could get over the pain. My cuts would heal. My bruises would fade. I could move on from that. But I couldn't, I knew somewhere deep down in my soul, that I wouldn't be able to recover from being forced to have his dick in my mouth.

I . Just. Couldn't.

Unbidden, an image of Reign popped into my head. Of him coming back from some kind of meeting with the rest of his men. He sat down at the foot of the bed, his back tight, his elbows resting on his thighs, facing away from me. And he just seemed so stressed out. I climbed out of bed, quietly padding across the floor and moving in front of him, sliding one of my arms around his shoulders, one slipping into his hair. And just like that, his arms went around my center, pulling me close, holding me tight. I held on for a long couple of minutes, enjoying the feel of him holding onto me like I was precious. Like I was a bright spot in his dark day. Then I slowly pulled backward until his arms loosened and lowered myself down between his legs, looking up into his eyes as I reached to unfasten his jeans. His eyes stayed on mine, mine on his, as I reached inside and started stroking him. His hand went out, his knuckles brushing down my jaw before I tilted my head and took him in my mouth.

That was the last memory I wanted to have about that particular act.

Not being forced to do it with Martin.

Happily, lovingly doing it for Reign.

I couldn't let them take anything else from me.

Martin had his pants undone and was reaching inside.

I twisted my body, bringing my boot up, and swinging my arms over to reach inside.

If ever there was a good time to do it, to grab the gun, turn it on yourself, and pull the trigger. If there was a good reason to do it, it was to keep yourself from being violated in a new and awful way.

My hands weren't even shaking as my fingers slid over the gun that was warm from being pressed against my skin.

"What's taking so long?" Daniel's voice yelled from down the stairs and I felt my heart skip in my chest.

"Mother fuck," Martin hissed, readjusting himself in his pants, dropping my hair and closing back up.

My hand slipped from my boot, my opportunity lost, and I slowly tried to get back onto my feet.

Martin quickened this by dragging me up by my hair, pulling me against his body, "This isn't over," he said in a voice full of warning and promise before I was shoved out into the hallway and made my way down the stairs.

Daniel's eyes fell on me as I got closer, a fire burning behind them. But he just clamped his jaw tight and led me into the kitchen, Martin following close behind me.

"Summer," my mother greeted, looking over my face. Showing no reaction whatsoever. "Won't you join me for a chat?"

"Like I have a choice," I countered, somewhat below my breath but she heard, her brow lifting.

Daniel moved over toward my mother, leaning against the counter, looking at his watch. Martin moved toward my side as I sat down on the stool, keeping a good four feet between us.

"We seem to have a problem," she started, watching me.

"Oh, yeah?" I asked, putting my elbows up on the island, rubbing between my eyes at the headache building. Likely from my face colliding with a mirror.

"Your father is missing."

My head snapped up, my brows drawing together. "Missing?" I asked, finding that I actually cared. Despite him lying to me my whole life. Despite him kidnapping me. I cared.

V nodded, her eyes getting hard. "I'm sure you understand that this is a rather big deal."

"Because you can't guilt him into giving you access to the containers by torturing me anymore," I guessed.

"I had men on him, watching his every move. Watching him scramble without eighty percent of his army alive to do his bidding.

No one saw anything. He was just gone. Any idea who might have wanted him?"

I knew exactly who had him.

Don't ask me how I knew. But I knew.

Reign had him.

And, again, don't ask me how I knew...

But I knew that Wolf was the one who got him.

I felt my shoulder shrug, "I imagine he has a lot of enemies, you know... being in the drug trade. Someone saw he was weak and moved in."

V's eyes went hot, like she somehow knew I was lying to her.

But before she could open her mouth, one of her men came rushing in. "V, someone is here for you."

"I have no meetings today," she countered, dismissing him.

"V..." he went on, looking uncomfortable for having to keep pressing the issue, "Says it's Lo."

V's head snapped up, her eyes going active. What they were thinking, I had no idea, but they were definitely thinking something. "Lo?"

"Yeah, and three Henchmen."

"Well, well," she said, smiling, her eyes falling to me. Like she knew. Of course she knew. "This should be fun." She turned her attention back to the man who had rushed in. "Check them for weapons and then send them in." She looked over my face with a smirk. "This could get very interesting."

I felt a cold pit settle in my belly.

No.

This was not good.

I didn't know who the hell Lo was, but I knew which Henchmen they were talking about.

The three that meant the most to me.

Wolf.

Cash.

And Reign.

At the thought of his name, a slicing feeling went across my chest and I dropped my eyes to the counter, sure they would give me away as I worked to draw up a mask of indifference.

Shit.

Whatever was about to happen, I was sure it wasn't good.

Why would they walk into V's compound, knowing they would have to lose their guns, knowing they were outnumbered?

It was stupid.

Reckless.

The door slammed closed and I heard feet coming toward us.

I whipped around on my chair, facing the hallway just as the group walked in.

My eyes went immediately to Reign.

His went to me.

And aside from a tightening of his jaw, his mask of indifference put mine to shame.

"Vanessa," a female voice said and my head snapped to find a tall blonde standing beside Cash (who was looking at me with absolute horror). Apparently he checked his mask at the door.

"Lo," my mother's voice said. Warmly.

I turned to find her smiling fondly at the woman with my Henchmen.

And then, to my absolute, complete, overwhelming horror... the women crossed the room toward one another and kissed cheeks.

My eyes went again to the Henchmen who seemed suddenly tense.

Holy fuck.

I was pretty sure things had just gone from holy shit to holyfuckingshitballs in the span of ten seconds.

Wolf's eyes went to mine and there was fire behind them.

And I knew.

I knew.

Something was wrong.

Fuck.

TWENTY-SEVEN

Reign

"She's out of her fucking mind," Cash said, close to my ear as we watched Lo walk around, tapping various men on their shoulders and telling them to meet her in 'command.'

After seeing 'command,' I was pretty fucking sure I agreed with Cash.

'Command' was the brick building in the center of all the shipping containers. And I guess I had been half-expecting it to be Lo's house. But, no. Lo live in a barracks-style room with the rest of her men. And the few other women she had in her ranks as well.

'Command' was a normal, brick home from the outside. From the inside, the brick walls were reinforced with pieces of shipping containers. The windows, I noticed after knocking on one of them as I passed, were polycarbonate. Bullet resistant. And from there, it only got worse.

Because the walls were plastered with poster boards. Poster boards that were covered with pictures, plots, plans for all their current projects.

They had two hits planned. One was a fucking senator. He was a shitbag slimelord, but a senator nonetheless.

There were three plans to surveil places. One, a government agency. One, a fortune five-hundred energy company. And one was a dog park. No fucking shit... a God damn dog park.

And then there was a collection of pictures of crime operations with small thumbnail pictures of each member of the organizations.

"That's the fucking compound," Cash said, nodding his head in the direction of the picture.

And it was. She had been keeping tabs on us.

As well as what seemed like every other organization in a two state radius.

Including V's.

And Lyon's.

I moved over toward the board, seeing a picture of Richard, in a suit, unsmiling. Beside him,there was a picture of Summer. It was a candid picture of her sitting at some outdoor cafe in a white sundress, a huge smile spread across her face.

I saw it with a kick to the gut.

Because she didn't smile like that anymore.

Open.

Unconcerned.

She smiled. Mostly with me. Different smiles. The lazy ones when she woke up and murmured something before snuggling into me. The sly ones when she was going to do something to get her way. The surprised ones when one of the men said something ridiculous and she wasn't sure if she could laugh or not.

But they were never like the one in the picture.

Because when she smiled now, it was full of the strong knowledge of how easily all the happiness could be sucked away from her. It was full of her demons.

I ran a hand down my face, staring at the picture, trying to memorize it, swearing to myself that I would do whatever was in my power to get one of those smiles out of her again. No matter how long it took.

"Dude, she's got a whole board full of government conspiracy theories. About like vaccines and the food supply and shit. She's fucking out of her mind."

I sighed, looking away from the picture.

He was right.

She was crazy.

But it was too late to back out.

"Well I guess it's good that her crazy is on our side," I said, shrugging.

"Alright," Lo said, clapping her hands once as the men (and one woman) filed inside and took seats. Cash, Wolf, and I stayed standing, legs wide, arms crossed over our chests. "We have a problem with V," she delved right in. To their credit, there wasn't even a flinch among her people. I was pretty fucking sure I would get more than a few explosions from my men if I brought that kind of information to them.

"What kind of problem?" one of the men asked.

"The kind where I need to go in with these men," she said, gesturing toward us though no one turned to look. They had all glanced at us when they walked in. "So I need six of you on the grounds. Two more from somewhere higher. And Janie, I need all the intel you have on her operation," she said, looking at the tall girl with long black hair, pale skin, and bright blue eyes. Her arms were covered in colorful tattoos. She was young. No older than early twenties and I couldn't help but wonder where the fuck Lo found her people.

"Honestly, Lo," Janie said, shrugging, "eight men seems a bit much."

"You fuckin' serious?" Cash interrupted, making the girl turn casually around and look at him. "She lives in a fucking fortress."

Janie smiled slowly, like something he said was ridiculous but she was trying to spare his feelings. "I live in a fortress. She lives in a house with a fence."

"And her own army," Cash shot back.

"Oh, please," Janie said, rolling her eyes, then turned back to Lo.

Cash turned to me, brows raised. "The fuck? They're all fucking nuts."

"Anyway," Lo went on, "The Henchmen and I will walk up to the gates at oh-nine-hundred tomorrow. You will all have already been long in place. They'll take our weapons then we will be led inside. I will try to negotiate something peaceful. If that fails, when we walk out, if my hand goes up... you go in. The only person who needs to make it out alive is Summer Lyon."

"Summer Lyon?" Janie asked again, her head snapping up. Then she turned, her eyes falling on me. Intense. Way too intense for someone so young. "Because he's fucking her?" she asked bluntly.

"Because he loves her," Lo corrected. "V is trying to gain control of Lyon's containers to bring girls in. She took their daughter as leverage. You yourself told me yesterday that The Henchmen took Lyon, Janie. V is going to start getting itchy with him gone. There's no telling what she'll do to the girl. We need to get her out. She's an innocent. You know that."

Janie sighed, nodding her head. "Alright."

"Alright," Lo agreed, nodding.

Then it was hours. Fucking *hours* of them planning and plotting.

Everyone seemed to be allowed to have their say, to contradict anything that Lo said without her so much as raising a brow. Twice, it got heated between two of the men until Janie made a weird growling noise and told them to take it outside and measure them or quit it with their 'macho testosterone bullshit.'

After that, we were led into the kitchen again. We were fed. And then we were shuffled toward the gates by Lo.

"Try to get some fucking sleep," she said, looking at me. "You'll be no good if you're tense and unfocused. She'll get out tomorrow. One way or another."

With that, the gate was opened, and we made our way to our bikes.

I looked at Cash who shook his head.

Then to Wolf who shrugged. "Gotta get her back."

I nodded.

He was right.

We had to get her back.

Even if that meant we needed to put her safety into the hands of some conspiracy theorist with her crackpot team who thought eight of them could take on three dozen of V's men.

Fuck.

I slept for about an hour and a half, waking up swearing I heard Summer screaming. But my bed was empty.

I showered and made my way toward the main room, finding an equally showered and haggard-looking Cash and Wolf chugging down coffee. I was handed one. And we sat and waited in silence until ten before nine and made our way outside.

A black van pulled up outside the gates and Lo nodded at us from the passenger seat. The other girl, Janie, was driving.

Cash's hand slapped down on my shoulder. "Let's get your girl back," he said, and we all made our way to their van

"Hop in," Lo said, gesturing toward the back of the van.

Wolf pulled the door open, revealing three rows of seats and a collection of guns all over the floor.

"Guess you guys didn't take the sleep advice," Lo said as we pulled away.

We pulled up to the gates a short while later, the air in the van noticeably thick.

"Alright," Janie said, unlocking the doors, "you guys have fun. I'll be here waiting."

With that, Lo got out. Wolf and I followed. Cash paused. "You think it's a good idea for you to stay out here alone? With V's men everywhere?"

At that, she laughed, the sound husky. "Because I'm a poor defenseless woman?" she asked, rolling her eyes. "Worry about yourself. I'm fine."

Cash hopped out, slamming the door, muttering, "Crazy fucking bitches," under his breath as Lo fearlessly walked up to one of the men standing in front of the gates and announced herself.

The man nodded, moving toward the house and going inside. He came back a few minutes later, instructing one of the other men to frisk us and confiscate weapons. Lo had come with four guns strapped on. Why, considering she knew they would be taken, I had no idea.

But then in we were walking.

The closer we got, the more tense my body got. And, I noticed, Cash's and Wolf's as well.

We were led down a hall and into an enormous kitchen. Men were there. A woman was there. All of whom I didn't even see.

Because all I could see was Summer.

Fuck.

Fuck. Fuck. Fuck.

Her face was openly bleeding, the drops slipping off her jaw and landing on her shirt. And then there was the eye. The black and blue eye. The blood filling it. And her neck. Fuck... her neck. With the imprint of someone's fucking hand.

My jaw clamped hard enough for my teeth to hurt as I tried to keep myself from flying across the room. To stroke her cheek. To beat the man behind her to a bloody fucking pulp.

Because I knew who he was. He was Martin. The man she was more afraid of than Deke. She'd told me about him, wrapping her whole body around me in bed like she was trying to disappear into my skin. "He has dead eyes," she said, shivering.

And the fuck behind her had dead eyes.

He had to die.

Slowly.

Painfully.

With knives.

I wanted to skin the mother fucker alive.

But then V's voice reached through my anger, greeting Lo like an old friend. Like she had stopped by for tea.

Then Lo was crossing the floor toward V.

And kissing her fucking cheek.

If the air was thick in the van, it was fucking lava in the kitchen.

"It's been too long," Lo said, holding V's hands and smiling.

"It has. I'm glad you came for a visit. I am less pleased about the guests you have brought to my house," V said, her face slanting toward us and landing on me.

And, fuck, she was a perfect older version of Summer. Same hair. Same face. Summer was smaller, more delicate. And while Summer had her mother's gray eyes, V's were as hollow as Martin's.

"Yes, unfortunately, this isn't a social call. We have some business here."

"Business?" V asked, her tone going glacial.

"Yes."

"I wasn't aware you were in business with The Henchmen," she said, dropping Lo's hands.

I felt Summer's gaze on me and it was taking everything in me not to look at her. But I couldn't. Because if I saw her perfect face all beat and broken again, I was going to lose the small amount of control I had over myself.

"I haven't been. Until I learned they had taken someone important to you hostage."

V's eyes cut to me again, then back to Lo. "Rich?"

Lo nodded. "Yesterday. Saw an opening. Got him."

"Trying to step in on my business?" V asked, her tone lethal, her eyes boring into mine.

"I don't deal in skin," I shot back, my tone matching hers.

"So what then? You want my daughter back? That's it, isn't it?" she asked, throwing her head back and laughing. The sound was, at once, happy and so batshit fucking crazy that I felt my blood run cold. "Oh, that's just... pathetic."

I felt my body jerk forward. But then Lo turned and her eyes pinned me. Fucking pinned me.

And it was then that I knew that everything was still under her control. It was all part of her plan. So I forced my body backward, my hands un-fisting.

"You don't think, perhaps, you wouldn't want her anymore?" she asked, looking over at Summer. And I couldn't help it, my eyes followed. "I believe Martin has been... visiting her at night," she said, her words heavy with meaning that had the bile rising in my throat, the rage turning into something else. Something stronger. Something I didn't even know existed. Something that felt like it took all the blood out of my system and replaced it with fire. "She's used goods now..."

As if on cue, Martin grinned, moving forward and pushed Summer hard. Unprepared because her eyes were glued to mine, she fell forward off the stool, landing hard on her knees.

If Wolf's hand hadn't reached out and grabbed my arm, I would have been there. I would have been beating the ever loving shit out of the mother fucker's face.

But all I could do was watch as Summer paused. Oddly. Like she was thinking. And then her cuffed hands were moving downward and into her boot.

It happened so fast I almost missed it. I had never seen her move like that. One second, she was on the floor, hand in her boot.

The next, she was on her feet, her body half-turned away from me, my gun in her hands, finger on the side, the aim right between Martin's eyes.

"Oh," Martin said, smiling, "you don't have the balls."

Summer's shoulders pulled back.
Her legs spread.
Then her finger moved to the trigger.

TWENTY-EIGHT

Summer

My mother made one mistake that morning.

It wasn't trusting a woman who, it was painfully obvious to me, absolutely loathed her.

It wasn't insulting The Henchmen.

It wasn't even showing her weakness in needing my father.

No.

Her mistake was underestimating me.

It was in overestimating how much I was willing to take, how often I was willing to be beat down, how often she could poke at me before I finally lost it.

And I fucking lost it.

My eyes had been on Reign when she delivered the blow that made me finally decide I wasn't going to be a victim again. When she insinuated that Martin had been raping me. When I saw the absolute, soul crushing fury overtake Reign. Not disgust. Not sadness. Anger.

He didn't think I was damaged.

He didn't care.

He just wanted vengeance.

Then Martin sealed his fate by knocking me onto the ground.

For the last time.

The. Mother. Fucking. Last. Time.

I was done.

My knees hit hard, the pain jolting through my system. And I knew what I had to do. For my own sanity. To take back my control.

I pulled my leg up, turned, reached into my boot.

My fingers brushed against the gun for the second time that morning.

Inside, I slipped off the safety.

Then I was flying onto my feet, the gun grasped between my two hands and turning to aim it at Martin, my finger still off the trigger.

Martin's head jerked back slightly, surprise registering on his face at the sight of the gun.

Then the idiot opened his mouth.

If he hadn't, well, things would have gone differently. Because I could feel the weight of the decision press down on me. It wasn't the rush of relief I felt when I had decided to end my own life. No, this was different. This was heavy. This was full of some feeling I wasn't familiar with that had my throat closing up, the saliva drying in my mouth.

"Oh," Martin said, giving me one of his cold, condescending smiles, "you don't have the balls."

Three month's worth of torment flew across my mind: his fists in my face, his feet in my center, his knife in my back, his hands on my throat, his hand in my hair as he reached to pull his dick out of his pants, intent on shoving it down my throat.

And my legs spread.

My finger slipped to the trigger.

"Go to hell," I growled.

And I pulled.

I pulled the trigger.

The jolt of the gun was met with the exploding sound of a bullet firing.

And I watched in fascinated horror as it tore through the center of his forehead, red splaying out in a shocking burst. His body jerked, wobbled, then fell.

He was dead.

His eyes never lost life.

Because they never had it to begin with.

"Bravo," V's voice said and I heard her start clapping. My eyes, and therefore, my gun, turned to her. Her gray eyes were bright in... what? Enjoyment. Oh, holy hell. It *was* enjoyment. She was so fucking insane. "I was wondering when you would hit your limit. I didn't think it was because he knocked you onto your knees though."

"No?" I asked, my hands starting to shake a little as I kept the aim on my mother. "Maybe it was because he had me in that very same position up in the bathroom before Daniel called me down here."

For a second, something flashed in her eyes. And I knew she knew that Martin had stopped having access to my room at night. Her taunt was meant to incite Reign.

Well, that was her second mistake.

Because, at that moment, I was a much worse threat than he was.

"I have to ask," V went on, like I wasn't holding a gun on her. A gun I had just used without flinching. My finger was even still on the trigger. "If you've had a gun this whole time, why has it taken you so long to use it?"

I couldn't tell you why. But the truth came out.

"I wasn't going to use it on any of you."

Her head cocked to the side. "No?"

"No," I answered, my mouth tight. "I was going to use it on myself."

The second the words were out of my mouth, I wished I could suck them back. Because the air in the room went sharp. It was painful. It hurt to breathe in.

"You were going to kill yourself?" V asked, her eyes squinting. "What a coward's move."

"Yes, how dare I find a way out of being beaten and starved and humiliated? How dare I try to save the people I care about from storming in here and getting themselves killed because of me?"

Okay. The second that was out, I wanted to suck it back too.

"Summer," Daniel's voice shocked me by breaking in. His hands were out, palms facing me. "Why don't you put the gun down and let V and Lo finish their meeting?"

"Fuck their meeting," I shot back.

"Summer," the other woman's voice reached me. Lo. That was her name. Her tone was firm, but soft at the same time. And for some reason, it got through. "We need to finish our meeting so we can settle things." When I didn't move to put the gun down, she added softly... "Reign?"

And then an arm was around my waist. Firm. Familiar. His other arm reached out, pressing down on the top of mine until the gun lowered to point at the floor. "Keep your finger on the trigger," he whispered into my ear and it took everything in me to not fall back against him, to melt, to finally give up fighting.

V turned back to Lo. "Well, now, what kind of offer do you have on the table for me?"

"I could turn over Richard Lyon," Lo said, shrugging.

"What? No," I found myself objecting, my body going tight again.

"Even trade. Him for the girl. She's useless to you anyway," Lo went on.

"N..."

"Sh," Reign said in my ear, effectively shutting up my objections.

V pursed her lips, taking a breath. "Can I trust you not to trick me anymore, Lo? I mean, you did bring Henchmen into my house."

"V, you know I have associates from many different organizations. I saw a chance to settle a problem for both sides before there was any bloodshed. Well," she said, glancing down at Martin's dead body (a body I was trying my best not to look at) and smiling slightly before her eyes went back to V, "any *more* bloodshed. No one needs a war around here. Things are peaceful with the cops. No one needs them involved. So let's settle this."

"I won't hand her over until I have Rich."

Shit.

If I survived that long.

Without my gun.

No way would they let me keep my gun.

Martin was gone.

But the new guy at the door might be angry about that fact.

What would that mean for me?

Reign would never allow that, would he?

"That's fair," Lo agreed and I felt my heart plummet. Sink.

"When?" V asked, sounding excited.

I couldn't even imagine the kinds of things she would do to my father if she got her hands on him. It would make the torture I endured look like summer camp.

They couldn't get him.

There had to be another way.

Lo turned to Reign, her gaze skipping over me and I saw something there. It was something I wasn't familiar with because I didn't know her, but I felt like it was something that should comfort me. "When can you have him here?"

"If Janie can pick him up, Repo will bring him to her as soon as she gets there."

Repo.

Repo was alright.

I exhaled a shaky breath and Reign's arm tightened around my belly.

V nodded at Lo and then Reign. "Make the calls."

Reign's arm slid from the gun and reached into his pocket. So did Lo's.

Then they were both speaking at once.

"Repo, I need you to get Lyon out of the front gates. A woman named Janie is going to come and pick him up. What? Yeah, I guess that's fine." There was a pause, Repo talking, and I could swear I heard something about 'weapons.' To which, Reign said tightly, "Definitely."

"Janie, get over to The Henchmen compound. A man named Repo is going to bring Lyon out and you are to bring him here. Yep. Out."

"Alright, so we wait," V said, looking satisfied. Almost giddy. "Does anyone want some coffee?" she asked, waving a hand toward the pot as if they were having a normal social call.

"Sure," Lo agreed, walking over and (no lie) going directly to the cabinet with the mugs. Like she had done so a dozen times before.

Who the hell *was* she?

"So since we have some time," V said, turning in the direction of me and Reign and I swear my belly dropped to my feet, "why don't we talk about you two?"

"No," I answered, surprised when my word came out firm.

"I think I have a right to get to know the man my only daughter is in love with."

Oh

my

God.

She did not just say that.

I felt my cheeks flame.

"I think you lost the right to ask me about my life the day you handed me over in trade for the right to be a human trafficker," I shot back. What can I say? My mother brought out the rebellious teenager in me. And I was still the only one in the room with a gun. Or with a drawn gun at least. I felt almost untouchable. Almost.

"Oh, don't be bitter. You'll get wrinkles," she said, waving a hand at my attitude. "Who you have sex with is really none of my concern. Though I'm sure your father would have an issue with a man who runs an outlaw biker gang. With the way he raised you?"

she laughed, rolling her eyes. "What was the last guy you dated? A stock broker? He was, right?"

I swallowed hard, feeling Reign's arm around me, his body tense behind me. "Yes," I answered honestly.

"And even he wasn't good enough for your father."

That was true.

I'd been lectured mercilessly about it.

"I'm only curious because if you leave here and align yourself with someone who might, at one time, be my enemy... well..."

Well, I was her enemy too.

How she thought I was going to be anything other than her enemy no matter who I dated was completely beyond me. But, I guess, you can't expect rationality from irrational people.

"So how long have you been together?"

Oh my God.

We were not having that conversation. That was a bad enough conversation to have over dinner when you finally brought your significant other over to meet your parents. It was a whole new level of uncomfortable to have that conversation over a dead body, with a gun drawn, while awaiting the delivery of a new hostage.

Like, seriously.

Who had to deal with that kind of situation?

Hell, I wasn't even sure Reign and I were together. Like *together* together. We had never had a talk about what we were. We just kinda... did our thing.

"Three weeks," Reign answered, surprising me, making my body jerk.

"Three weeks," she mused, pursing her lips. "So right when you ran away from here."

Escaped.

I escaped from there.

"Found her that night," Reign agreed.

"And you just... claimed her? Just like that?"

"Just like that," he agreed.

Were they really having that conversation? With me standing between them? It was a whole new level of weird that I didn't have a word for it.

"When she walks out of here..." V started.

"She's mine," Reign said, his tone firm.

I was his?

The words settled with a swirling in my belly.

I was his.

The thought made me so happy, I had to fight to keep a smile off my face.

V nodded. "She's not the kind of girl for your lifestyle."

To that, Reign laughed. "V, no disrespect but you don't know what the fuck you're talking about." I tensed, waiting for V to get angry, but she didn't. Her head tilted, her hand made a swirling motion that said 'go on'. "When we caught your boy and asked her to come down and just give us a nod if he was one of yours? She beat the shit out of him. Told me to have fun killing him. Then was so turned on by it that we fucked against the building."

Oh

my

God.

No.

He did not just say that.

To my mother.

Granted, she was a freaking psychopath who had me tortured for months. But she was still my mother. You don't talk about fucking someone's daughter to their face.

V laughed, looking at me. "Maybe there's more of me in you than I thought."

Oh, lordy.

I was really, really hoping that wasn't true.

If I had to choose to be more like one of my parents: the psychotic, torturing, murdering skin trader or the control freak, cold, calculating cocaine dealer. Well, I'd pick the cold, calculating, control freak every time. But even as I said it, I knew that wasn't who I was. I was hot tempered. Once out from under my father's thumb, I had a sharp tongue. I went from zero to ninety on the anger scale in two point seven seconds. I was impulsive.

Oh, God.

I was like my mother.

I was like my mother!

"Relax," Reign said in my ear, his tone bossy, not sweet.

Lo's phone buzzed and she reached for it, looking down, and shooting off a quick text.

"They'll be here in five," she announced, tucking her phone away.

"Summer dear," V said, looking at me, "I'm afraid you're going to have to hand Daniel your gun before your father gets here."

"No," I said automatically. It was the only leverage I had. I couldn't just hand it over.

But Daniel was already moving toward me, palms still out. "Take your finger off the trigger," he said, his tone softer.

"Babe, give him the gun," Reign demanded. Not soft. Again.

I sighed, sliding my hand off the trigger and turning the gun to hand to Daniel. He took it slowly, his eyes finding mine, the gaze heavy. Like he was trying to impart something silently, but I couldn't get it.

Behind me, Reign went tense, like he didn't trust Daniel looking at me. He was probably thinking that he was one of the men who tortured me.

Daniel stuck the gun in the waistband of his pants and moved to his spot, standing near the back door, facing us.

"V!" one of her men called from the front door.

"Let them in," she called back casually.

"V!" he called again. Louder. More hysterical.

And then all hell broke loose.

TWENTY-NINE

Summer

One minute, I was just standing in the kitchen in the middle of the weirdest hostage negotiation in the history of bad guys, Reign holding my belly, everyone just standing around.

The next, I was thrown onto the ground and all I heard were gunshots. And, I kid you not, explosions. Actual explosions. They were not close, but close enough that the ground shook, the world roared, glass shattered.

I twisted my head, trying to suck in a deep breath, and that's when I saw Repo walking in, a huge automatic-type gun pointed outward, my father next to him, holding a handgun, and a woman beside him with guns everywhere, walk in.

The girl, Janie, I think they called her... tossed guns around and there was yelling and gunshots and I couldn't even think clearly enough to realize I should have gotten up and found something to defend myself with.

But all I could think of was the gunfire. And Reign. Who wasn't beside me. He wasn't on top of me. And I couldn't find him.

I whirled my head around desperately, seeing Wolf engaged in some kind of battle with one of V's men. Cash had just taken off out the back door. But Reign was gone.

Then there was a hand sliding around my stomach and I felt a flood of relief. "Shut up, stay down, and don't fight me," Daniel's voice found me instead. "I'm getting you out of here alive if you do what I say," he said.

My options were to lay underneath a hail of gunfire, unarmed, or to go with Daniel and do what he said.

I nodded.

And then we were moving.

Crawling across the kitchen toward a door at the far side.

I heard my name called but couldn't register who said it.

My head twisted, seeing my father round on my mother, gun drawn.

The next moment, I was behind a closed door. The shouts and shots were muffled as I looked around to find myself in a garage. A car was in the center. There were various plastic containers of what looked like clothing on the sides. Daniel let go of me, standing and throwing some huge cabinet in front of the door, blocking it.

I pushed myself up onto my feet, feeling shaky inside as Daniel turned to look at me, pulling the gun out of his waistband.

My heart froze in my chest, my mouth falling open.

No.

He wasn't trying to get me out of there alive. He wanted to get me alone so he could kill me. Jesus Christ. How could I have been so stupid? I should have stayed in the kitchen. My father and Cash and Wolf would have protected me. I would have gotten out of there just fine. No. I had to go and be stupid and follow one of the bad guys. What the hell was wrong with me?

"Summer, relax," he said, his tone urgent, but gentle. When I looked up, the gun was pointed at me. But not the barrel. The butt. "I need you to make this look good."

"Make it look good?" I asked, my brows drawing together.

"Are you a good shot?"

Well. I mean... I had shot Martin. Right in the forehead. But he was close. I was pretty sure that didn't take much skill. "I don't know. That was the only time I've ever used a gun," I admitted.

At that, he nodded. "Okay. Take the gun, Summer," he said, moving forward and pressing it into my hand. "I need you to shoot me."

What?

No.

I was pretty sure I was at my shooting quota for the day. Or year. Or lifetime.

"No," I said, my tone almost hysterical.

"Not to kill me. I just need to be shot by you, okay? I can't explain why. We don't have time. You need to shoot me. Shoulder would be good. Close range so it goes straight through."

"What are you talking about? I can't shoot you!"

"You have to shoot me," he said, calm. He was really way too calm for someone who was asking to be shot. "You shoot me then you get in this car," he gestured. "Get in the car. The keys are inside. You hit the button on the visor. The door will open and you pull out. The windows are resistant but nothing is bulletproof so try to keep your head low. And get the fuck out of here. Do you understand me?"

He was saving me.

He was giving me a way out.

And all I had to do was shoot him. He even told me where.

"Yes," I agreed, swallowing hard.

"Okay," he said, walking close to me. "Raise the gun, Summer," he instructed and my arms went up automatically. He walked forward until the muzzle was pressed up against where he wanted it- right side of his chest, right below the collarbone.

"Daniel..." I said, looking up at his face, shaking my head. I couldn't. I just couldn't. He had been trying to help me. Granted, he had given V's orders to the men in the past. But he had also tried to defend me. He freaked out when I was bleeding and he thought Deke had raped me. He had tried to stop Martin from visiting me at night. He saved me.

"Don't think about it," he told me, his eyes watching me. "I will live through this. You will live through this. That's all you need to think about. But your finger on the trigger," he instructed and my finger slipped to follow instructions. "Pull," he said, eyes still on mine.

I heard a weird whimper escape my lips, wincing, as I did what I was told.

I pulled.

His body jerked. His eyes winced. His face contorted in pain. He stumbled back, hand on his shoulder.

"Go," he growled at me.

My heart skipping into overdrive, I let the arm with the gun drop to my side and ripped the car door open, throwing myself into the driver's seat. The gun dropped into my lap and I pulled my seatbelt, turned over the ignition, hit the garage door button, and backed out fast. Once outside, I swung the wheel, ducking down as low as I could and still see as I got the car facing the right direction and started down the driveway.

There were people everywhere. Some had guns raised. Others were going to physical blows with one another. I was praying there was no one on the driveway as I drove down.

It was then that I saw him.

Finally.

And he wasn't hurt.

Or if he was hurt, it wasn't bad.

He was just outside the blasted open gate (I guessed that was one of the explosions I heard) beside a van. And he was yelling, trying to shove past Wolf who looked like he was bleeding down the side of his thigh. Reign's arm shot out, pointing back toward the house, screaming something, moving to charge past Wolf who grabbed him and threw him into the van. He climbed in himself, slammed the door, and the van peeled off.

I swallowed hard, trying to go faster so I could keep an eye on the van.

He wanted to go back for me.

That was why he was freaking out.

He knew I was still inside.

My heart tightened in my chest.

I pushed the thought away, needing to focus. I needed to try to follow them. Because I didn't know where the hell the compound was. If that was where they were going. I needed to get to him. I needed him to know I was okay. That I got out.

There were no windows on the sides of the van so I couldn't even catch his eye as we all weaved in and out of traffic.

The compound came into view, the gates already thrown open and the van flew through. I followed, slamming the car into park, not bothering to turn off the engine, and I tore out of the car as the van door opened.

And then I threw myself against Reign, who was so surprised that he lost his footing and we went crashing.

THIRTY

Reign

It was chaos.

Lo had a plan. We knew the loose details.

But things had gone from fuckin' weird to fuckin' insane in a matter of seconds.

Repo, Richard, and Janie walked in like they hadn't just thrown together a plan in a matter of minutes on the car ride over. Like they had shit worked the fuck out. They tore in. Guns were thrown. Then bullets flew.

I could hear Lo's men close in outside as I grabbed the gun Repo handed to me, ducking behind the kitchen island and aiming out toward the men approaching from outside. Trying to get to V. Trying to protect their boss. But she was already at Lyon's mercy. And he wasn't feeling too magnanimous after she stole and tortured the only thing in his sorry fucking life that he gave a damn about.

And good fuckin' riddance. I hoped she died in agony.

Might be a lot of things, but I ain't a forgiving person. Not when someone touches what is mine. And someone had definitely been touching Summer.

My head jerked, looking over to where I had pushed Summer to the ground, tucked behind the long side of the island.

And she was gone.

Fucking. Gone.

I flew to my feet.

But she was nowhere.

Someone had her.

My eyes met Lo's and she shook her head. It wasn't one of hers. I looked over and Cash and Wolf and Repo were all accounted for. No pretty, bruised, redheads under their care.

Fuck!

But then there was no time to think, only react, as a slew of V's men came charging in.

And the next fucking thing I knew, I was being dragged toward the gate, everyone firing into the trees and grounds as we made our way to the van.

I nearly fucking killed Wolf.

I probably would have if it meant he would get out of my way.

He was a brother I had known all my life. I trusted him like I trusted Cash.

I would have taken him down to get her back.

He knew it. I knew it.

So he didn't give me the chance to make that decision.

"Holy fuck," Repo said, completely out of breath sitting beside me. He was steady as fucking ever. Not shaking. Nothing. He was steel. He was going to get patched-in as soon as possible. "That was crazy."

"Compound?" Janie asked from the driver's seat.

"Yeah," Lo answered, turning in the passenger seat to look at me. "They'll get her," she told me, her tone sure. "My men. They'll get her out."

"I want her a-fucking-live," I growled, slamming my fist into the windowless wall of the van.

"They'll get her," she repeated.

We tore into the compound, Janie warning us of a tail.

Everyone reached for guns.

Wolf threw the door open.

I jumped out.

And then I was knocked to the ground.

A tiny, gorgeous redhead was clinging to me like I was a life preserver.

"Summer," I said, my arms going tight around her.

She was alright.

She was safe.

She was back.

My hands ran up and down her body, looking for blood. Wounds. Anything. But they found nothing.

Her head lifted from my neck, a huge fucking smile on her face.

And I recognized that smile.

It was the smile from the picture on Lo's wall.

Open.

Unconcerned.

Completely and utterly happy.

My breath caught in my chest as I looked up at her.

My knuckles went to stroke the side of her face.

It didn't matter that her face was bruised and battered.

It was the fucking best sight I had ever seen in my life.

THIRTY-ONE

Summer

"I'm sure you're both happy to see each other," Cash broke into our silent moment, me smiling down at Reign, him looking up at me like I was the most beautiful thing he had ever seen, "but we kinda need to get inside where it's safe."

With that, Reign sighed, wrapping his arms around my back and knifing up, getting us both onto our feet. His arm went around my shoulders, pulling me into his side, as we all filed inside the compound, the men on the roof and around the grounds looking at us with a mix of confusion and anger.

The anger was probably at having to miss out on the obvious action.

Reign was gonna have some unhappy questions to answer.

"What the fuck..." Vin said, standing as we walked in.

"Wolf needs Doc," Reign said immediately, his voice taking on an authoritative edge.

Oh my God.

Wolf.

I pulled out of Reign's arm, turning and going right to Wolf.

"Oh my God. You're shot. They shot you!" I yelped, looking down at the side of his jeans where, while I was no doctor, it seemed like way too much blood was seeping out.

"Woman," he broke in, making my head jerk up to his face. It was bloodied. The side of his face was busted open slightly, bleeding down his cheek. "I'm fine," he said, his gruff tone somehow making the anxiety slip away.

"You're sure?" I asked, watching him.

"Sure," he nodded, his hand reaching out to touch the skin beside my eye. "You okay?"

"Oh, this," I said, making a whooshing sound, and waving a hand and giving him a smile. "You should see the other guy."

The second the words were out, my eyes went huge, my hand slapping over my mouth.

Because, yeah, the other guy was dead.

I killed him.

Holy hell.

But Wolf wasn't sharing my horror. No. He actually... threw his head back... and laughed! It was a full, throaty sound that boomed off the walls. Still laughing, he looked at me, shaking his head, and chucked me under the chin. "You're alright," he said, nodding.

"Is someone going to tell the rest of us what the fuck is going on?" Vin broke in, sounding a mix of angry and worried.

"Cash?" I asked, turning to him, my eyes worried.

"Bumps and bruises, Cherry," he said, giving me a wink, his hand ruffling my hair.

I gave him a small smile and my eyes fell to Repo. The huge, scary looking gun he had been carrying earlier was gone. His face was bruised awfully still from the night that he tried to save me. His eyes went to me, weirdly guarded.

And then my feet were moving toward him. Our toes touched. My arms went around him, squeezing him tight. There was a long pause and I could see him looking over my shoulder toward Reign, his face a mask of confusion, before one of his arms went around my lower back. "You tried to save me," I told his shirt and his arm tightened. "Thank you."

"Is everyone done putting their hands on my fuckin' woman?" Reign's voice asked, sounding exasperated.

Repo's arm fell from me and I stepped away. He gave me a small smile. "Anytime," he told me with a nod. Like he meant it. And I realized he did. He would put his life down for me in a heartbeat. Without even thinking about it. And I didn't even know him.

"Seriously, Prez," Vin's voice sounded again.

I looked over toward Vin who visibly shrank back when his eyes landed on my face. "They saved me," I said simply, walking over toward Reign and tucking myself into his side, his arm going around my shoulders.

"Reign," Lo's voice said, breaking through the tension, and everyone's eyes went to her. "It's done," she said, nodding her head, putting her phone away.

Reign nodded. "Thank fuck."

"What's done? How is it done? Where are my parents?" I pled, not able to help myself. I needed answers.

"Why don't I take you upstairs and let you get cleaned up," he started, squeezing me, "and I'll answer your questions there. And then I'll come back down here and answer yours," he said, this time to his men. "Give me an hour."

To that, they just nodded. And I was being pulled out of the room, into the hallway, toward his door.

"Reign..." I started, feeling the tension in his body.

"Just give me a minute, babe," he said, unlocking his door and shuffling me inside.

He rescued me.

I could give him a minute.

He went over to his dresser, reaching inside, pulling things out. Then he walked back to me, taking my wrist and pulling me toward the bathroom. He pulled me with him as he took a towel out of the cabinet, as he reached into the bath and turned the shower on.

"I'm gonna go get you some food. Figured you'd want a shower before we talked," he said, letting me go.

"Um, ah... yeah," I said, watching him. Worried. He seemed off. He was almost tense and distant. "Thanks," I finished with.

To that, he nodded and walked out of the room.

Alright.

I should have been freaking out.

I knew that.

I was just held hostage again. Twice.

I was beaten.

I was in the middle of a gun fight.

I had killed a man.

I had shot another man who helped me escape.

I should have been shaking and crying and beside myself.

But... well... I felt filthy.

I needed the shower. I needed to wash the last week of my life away.

So that was what I did.

I dried off, going to the counter and slipping into the soft, cozy black t-shirt (Reign's) and pink satin and lace panties (mine). Then I ran a brush through my hair. It was so clean it squeaked. There was nothing I could do about my face. It was a mess. It was going to be a mess for a while. I just had to live with that. At a loss for anything else to do, I went to the door and opened it.

I walked in to find Reign sitting on the foot of the bed next to a plate of food , changed, his hair wet. Like he had showered too.

"Why didn't you shower with me?" I asked, thinking about the slippery, sexy, up against the shower tile sex we had had in the past.

His head raised, but his gaze didn't. "Summer..." he said, his tone sad.

"What?"

"I didn't think you'd be ready for that."

"Why?" I asked, genuinely confused.

His gaze lifted, finding mine. "Because of what they did to you."

My brows drew together before I realized what he meant.

What V had suggested.

What I had kind-of insinuated as well.

He thought they finally did it. He thought that they raped me.

"Oh, Reign... no," I said, my voice small. I walked up to him, my hand slipping into his wet hair. "No. They didn't... do that. Just threatened it. It didn't happen."

"You said you were on your knees..."

"He was going to make me. Well, no. He wasn't," I clarified. At his confused face, I went on. "I had my hand on the gun. I wasn't..." I shook my head. "I couldn't let that happen."

"You were going to shoot yourself," he said, half question, half declaration. But somehow fully horrified.

"I didn't have a lot of options. I needed out. I couldn't... I couldn't live with that."

"Babe..." he said, his voice sad.

And then his arms were finally around me, pulling me close. His body went backward, mine went forward, me landing on his chest, my body touching his from chest to feet.

"You came for me," I said, looking down at him.

"Of course I did," he said, looking at me like I was crazy.

My eyes dropped for a second, then raised to settle on his hazel ones. "I killed a man today," I said, my voice quiet.

"I killed three," he said, shrugging. "Had to do what we had to do. If you didn't shoot him, babe, I would have made him suffer first."

Well, that was true.

Maybe I kept another black mark from getting etched on his soul. By etching it on mine instead. And, somehow, I was okay with that.

"He let me go," I said.

"Who let you go?"

"Daniel," I supplied, watching his face as he processed the information. "He pulled me out into the garage, got me safe. Then he told me to take the car and get out. He... he made me shoot him."

"What?" he asked, squeezing me.

"He... he gave me my gun back and told me to shoot him in the shoulder. Right here," I pointed on Reign's shoulder. "He stepped into the gun, and told me to pull the trigger. And I did."

Reign's hands started running up and down my back. "He'll live."

"How do you know?"

"Because he picked one of the safest places to get shot. He'll live."

"Why would he let me go?"

"I don't know, babe. I'm just glad he did."

"I saw you," I went on. "When you were fighting with Wolf to let you go back in. I saw you."

"Wasn't gonna fuckin' leave you there."

"I'm here now," I said, sensing his body getting tight again. He gave me a small smile. "What are you gonna do about it?" I asked, my voice dipping low and suggestive.

And then I screeched as I was being rolled and flipped onto my back. "Reign, the food..." I objected, feeling my foot hit it.

"Fuck the food," he said, his hands grabbing the hem of my t-shirt and pushing it upward, his hand closing over my breast, his fingers rolling my nipple.

My arms went between us, pulling at the waistband of his pants. "Fuck the food," I agreed, my hands reaching inside and grabbing his hard length. His hand skimmed down my belly, sliding inside my panties and rubbing over my clit. My back arched, his mouth coming down on mine, hard and urgent. His fingers kept stroking me and it wasn't enough. It wasn't what I wanted. My lips pulled from his. "Fuck foreplay too," I said and he chuckled against my cheek.

Then his hands pulled my panties down. I pulled his pants off. And he slid inside me. Slowly at first. Then full of the urgency that both of our bodies demanded. My hands dug into his back, my legs going around his waist as he pounded into me. "Harder," I demanded, wanting him to lose control. Needing it. So I could too.

"Fuck me," he growled, then thrust harder. Until I felt the tightening, my breath catching. "Come babe," he demanded, sounding close.

He thrust forward again and I came. Hard. My body clenching. Watching me, Reign's body got taut, his breath hissed out. And he came with me.

And it was fucking perfect.

His head came down on my shoulder, sucking in air. My hand went across his back, the other in his hair. "You were right," I said quietly.

His head lifted. "About what?"

I felt myself smile. "I missed you."

I saw it in his eyes first.

The warming. The crinkles by the sides. Then it spread to his lips. Slowly. A twitching. A smirk. Then a full-blown smile.

"Damn fuckin' right you did," he said, nodding.

"You missed me too," I told him.

"Yep," he agreed, then stopped what I was about to say with his lips on mine. Softer. Sweeter. Until I felt melty inside and couldn't think of anything else to say. "Alright," he said, sliding out of me, pulling away from me, his hands yanking down my tee as he stood. "Let's go order some pizza and brief the rest of the men."

I nodded, sliding my panties back on and going in search of a pair of pants. "Hey Reign..."

"Yeah babe?"

"What happened to my parents?"

He turned back to me, slipping his feet into his boots whilst pulling a black tee over his head. "Honestly, dunno," he said, shrugging, reaching for his cut and putting it on. "You ready?"

"Yeah," I said, taking the hand he was offering me and following him out into the main room.

It looked like everyone was inside, save for the probates who were outside on guard still.

This was what they called "church."

And I could tell a lot of the men weren't happy about me, Repo, Janie, and Lo being a part of it. But Reign didn't give them a chance to complain.

He just launched right into it.

"Today, with Lo and her people and Richard Lyon and his people," he started, and that was news to me. I didn't think my dad had any people left. "We went into V's territory and took Summer back. Wolf got shot," he said, nodding his head at Wolf who looked no worse for wear, holding a beer, the bleeding on his face and thigh had stopped. "But we had no casualties. Lo," he said, nodding at her.

"We had none either. Though Lyon lost three men. Your father," she said, looking toward me, "has your mother. He promised she wouldn't receive the kind of treatment you did, but that he needed to keep her from reclaiming her place and going after all of us again. That being said, we aren't safe. Down goes one skin trader, up must come another. Things are gonna get violent with the contenders. Though they won't likely come after either of our operations. They'll be too busy trying to kill one another."

Okay. So Dad had Mom. That was... well, it wasn't good. It was slightly better that he didn't plan to torture her. But, then again, for V... being under his thumb again... that was its own kind of torture.

"Yo, let's have a hero's welcome," someone said from the door.

Everyone stopped talking, turning to look at the newcomers.

And there was an older man, pushing a younger, battered one in the door. There were whoops and claps.

I looked past the bruises.

And my heart started pounding hard. My stomach twisted in a knot.

Because it was Flee.

Before I could even think it through, I reached down toward the coffee table where half a dozen guns were piled, somehow finding the one I had used earlier, slipping off the safety and pointing it.

The noise fell.

As did Flee's face when he saw me.

"Summer, the fuck you doin'?" Reign's voice found me.

I ignored him. "You don't belong here," I told Flee, my voice venomous. Traitor. He was a fucking traitor. Reign once told me that there was nothing worse to have in your organization.

"Summer..." Cash's voice pitched in.

My eyes slid to Reign. "He was the reason I got kidnapped," I told him, watching his face get tight. My eyes slid to Vin. "We were watching TV, remember?" I said to him and he nodded. "Flee came in and asked if I wanted to take a walk. I thought he had a crush. I didn't want to be a bitch. So I went. He led me out toward the side of the compound and then... and then one of my father's men got to me. Duct taped my mouth. Cuffed me. Flee ran through the hole in the fence and then Repo saw me. And then..." I shook my head, looking at Repo, my eyes sad. "I did the wrong thing. I should have ran inside for help while you fought him. I shouldn't... Well, oh well. It's done. I jumped him to get him off Repo and then I was pulled through the fence. Lee, my dad's guy, stopped the car after a while and beat up Flee so no one would suspect him."

"The fuck?" Wolf exploded, the boom of his voice enough to make everyone start.

And then I wasn't the only one with a gun.

But it wasn't Wolf who picked one up.

It was Repo.

"Look at her face, you fuck!" he exploded. "You did that. They weren't your fists, but they might as fuckin' well have been."

Flee tried to retreat, but the man behind him blocked his way, looking as angry as, suddenly, everyone around me looked.

Okay.

Not good.

I was pretty sure everyone had enough violence for the day.

I needed to fix it.

"Repo," I said, my voice soft. "Put the gun down."

"The mother fucker deserves to..."

"Put the gun down," I said, nearing a shout. His eyes slipped to me, watching me for a minute, before his hand went down.

"Babe..." Reign's voice said behind me.

"Don't 'babe' me right now. I'm trying to fix this. Okay. We're not gonna shoot you," I said to Flee and could swear I heard Reign chuckle.

"Like hell," Wolf said, his tone low and scary.

I sighed. "I think there's been enough blood today, don't you?" I asked, looking at him. I was silently begging him to let it drop. His eyes held mine, then his shoulder shrugged.

"Go back to my father," I began, and someone started to object. It was a man I wasn't familiar with. I lifted a brow at him, then turned back to Flee. "Go back to my father," I repeated. "Tell him to keep his nose out of Henchmen business. That if we find out there's another one of his men in this compound, I will shoot them myself. You got that?"

Flee's head was nodding.

"Good. Now get the hell out of here. I was promised pizza and I haven't eaten in two fucking days."

I put the safety back on and put the gun back on the table.

I turned to find Reign smirking at me, Cash out and out grinning.

"Shoot him yourself, huh?" Reign asked.

"I'm getting pretty good at shooting people," I said, shrugging.

At that, there was laughter.

And I even joined in.

I caught, out of the corner of my eye, Wolf's eyes find Reign's. And Reign did a simple badass chin lift and Wolf was storming out the door. I pretended to not know what that meant.

But I also knew Flee was going to have a few more (okay, a lot more) bruises when he finally made it back to my father.

And, somehow, I didn't really even care.

I had a few more bruises too.

Soon after, Lo and Janie left.

I was fed pizza.

Then I fell into bed with Reign. And, for the first time in months, there were no nightmares. There was no fear of being pulled back. There was just peace.

There were just the arms of the man I loved around me.

His heartbeat underneath my ear.

There was just the overpowering, comforting sensation of feeling like I finally found the place I belonged.

EPILOGUE

<u>*Summer*</u>

"You're not using a god damn AK-47, Summer," Reign said, his tone exasperated. I started to tuck my lower lip out, but he caught on. "And don't you fuckin' dare start poutin' at me."

I sucked it back in.

"I think I've proved that I am pretty good with a gun," I objected.

Cash had been bringing me to The Henchmen's target range for weeks and I was almost as good as he was.

"Yeah, babe. A gun. A handgun. You're not touchin' a fuckin' fully automatic weapon, Summer."

"Well, why the hell not?"

Okay. Reign and I fought a lot.

Not just over the big things. Like letting me use really dangerous (but really flipping cool) weapons.

We fought about everything.

Like me going back to work.

Though we usually "compromised."

And by "compromised" I meant I was browbeaten until I agreed to take a job at the compound so someone could keep an eye on me at all times as if I was constantly under the imminent threat of being targeted again.

I wasn't.

But it wasn't a huge issue. So I didn't push it.

Not like I pushed the issue of keeping me informed of what was going on with The Henchmen. Which was completely against the rules. It was an issue that led to the kind of fight that made him drag me out to the shed so we didn't wake up everyone in the compound.

He tried to keep his cool. I persisted.

He yelled. I screamed.

We reached a stalemate.

Then I used naked persuasion.

Needless to say, I got my way.

And I was going to get my way about the damn guns too.

"Look. I live here. Amongst a sea of guns and possible gunfire," I reasoned, and watched his face go hard. "Wouldn't it be... prudent for me to learn to use all of the guns around here? Just in case?"

"You think it would be *prudent* for you to learn how to use an AK-47?"

"For safety purposes," I insisted, playing to his weak spot. He wanted me safe. He didn't really like the idea that anything could ever happen to me again. Even though the nightmares had worn off almost a year ago. And no one had so much as looked my way in months. I was no one. Just Reign's old lady. I wasn't a possible bargaining chip anymore.

"Babe..."

"Oh, let the woman use the God damn gun," a voice broke in. It was distantly familiar. It was a voice I knew, but couldn't place immediately.

Reign and I both turned, him holding the AK-47 he had caught me walking around the grounds with a few minutes ago. Hence the fight. To the immense entertainment of the men on guard. And the few who wandered out just to catch the show. Apparently our fights were a source of high amusement. There were even pools in place for people to bet on when the next fight would take place. And who would win.

"The fuck?" Reign asked, not raising the gun, but his hands twitched.

"Holy crap," I muttered at the same time.

Because there approaching us, dressed in his usual brand of expensive, perfect suits (this one gray) ... was fucking Daniel.

"How'd you get in here?" Reign asked, jerking his head to look at the men at the gate who had their hands up, palms out, saying it was out of their hands.

Daniel gave me an odd smile, reaching into his pocket, pulling out a wallet fold, then flipping it open.

A badge.

An FBI badge.

"No fucking way," I found myself saying, my head jerking up to his face. "But you let them torture me. You *told* them to torture me."

At that, he winced a little. "I was undercover, sweetheart. I had no choice. I tried to keep you as safe as possible. Besides," he said, smiling a little, "you got to shoot me in the end."

"Well... that's true," I mused. "What are you doing here?"

He shrugged. "I wanted to clear the air. I felt like shit over the whole operation."

"You were working for V for years," I said, shaking my head. "I couldn't have possibly been the worst thing you saw."

"It's one thing to see things happen. It's another to be in on it."

"Your assignment over?" Reign asked, not caring the least bit that he was butting in.

"Heading to the city for a while. Lot of girls coming in that way. That's why I wanted to stop by."

"Sorry we foiled your operation," I said, knowing how disappointing it must have been to work for such slime for years and then not be able to drag her in for her crimes.

"Plenty of other scum out there to nab. Just glad V is out of commission. Your father taking good care of her?"

My father had his own mini prison built for her. It was impressive.

He went to visit her every single day.

Reminding her constantly that she was, yet again, under his thumb.

The worst kind of torture.

He was a real bastard when he wanted to be.

"Oh yeah," I agreed. "All comfy cozy."

At that, he smiled. "Glad to hear it. You take care of yourself, Summer," he said, extending his hand to me. I took it. "And as a federal agent, I am not allowed to say this," he said, then turned his face to Reign, "but let the girl use the gun."

And with that, he was gone.

I turned expectant eyes on Reign.

"Fuckin' fine," he conceded and I heard a bunch of groans from our peanut gallery. A lot of men just lost money. They were always underestimating me. "But we ain't going to your father's for Thanksgiving."

"Okay honey," I said, moving to wrap my arms around him, mostly to hide my smile. Thanksgiving had been a sore spot for weeks. "That's fine. We can all do Thanksgiving at your cabin instead."

"Summer..." he said, sounding tired.

"I love you," I tried. It was cheap and I knew it. But, hell, when you're going up against a badass outlaw biker dude, you had to play whatever you had up your sleeves.

"Love ya too, babe, but no fuckin' way."

I pulled back slightly to look up at him, giving him a smile. "For me?"

His head tilted upward, begging the sky for some kind of intervention. Getting none, he looked back down at me and sighed. His hand went up, brushing his knuckles down my cheek. "For you?"

"Mhmm," I said, letting the smile grow. I had him. I knew it. He knew it. And it was certainly something worth smiling about. Two wins in one day? It was unheard of.

"For you," he said again, shrugging, "anything."

XX

DON'T FORGET

Dear Reader,

Thank you for taking time out of your life to read this book. If you LOVED this book, I would really appreciate it if you could hop onto Goodreads or Amazon and tell me your favorite parts. You can also spread the word by recommending the book to friends or sending digital copies that can be received via kindle or kindle app on any device.

ALSO BY JESSICA GADZIALA

The Henchmen MC
Reign
Cash
Wolf
Repo
Duke
Renny
Lazarus
Pagan
Cyrus

The Savages
Monster
Killer
Savior

Stars Landing
What The Heart Needs
What The Heart Wants
What The Heart Finds

ABOUT THE AUTHOR

Jessica Gadziala is a full-time writer, parrot enthusiast, and coffee drinker from New Jersey. She enjoys short rides to the book store, sad songs, and cold weather.

She is very active on Goodreads, Facebook, as well as her personal groups on those sites. Join in. She's friendly.

STALK HER!

Connect with Jessica:

Facebook: https://www.facebook.com/JessicaGadziala/
Facebook Group:
https://www.facebook.com/groups/314540025563403/

Goodreads:
https://www.goodreads.com/author/show/13800950.Jessica_Gadziala
Goodreads Group:
https://www.goodreads.com/group/show/177944-jessica-gadziala-books-and-bullsh

Twitter: @JessicaGadziala

JessicaGadziala.com

<3/ Jessica

Made in the USA
Las Vegas, NV
13 September 2022

55222692R00156